MELOG

MELOG

MIHANGEL MORGAN

Translated from the Welsh
with an Afterword and Notes by
CHRISTOPHER MEREDITH

seren

Seren is the book imprint of
Poetry Wales Press Ltd
Nolton Street, Bridgend, CF31 AE, Wales
www.seren-books.com

Original Welsh, © Mihangel Morgan, 1997
English translation, Afterword and Notes,
© Christopher Meredith 2005

ISBN 1-85411-393-3

This book has been inscribed in the List of the UNESCO Collection of
Representative Works by the Clearing House for Literary Translation
(www.unesco.org/culture/lit)

Published with the financial support of Llenyddiaeth Cymru Dramor/Welsh
Literature Abroad

The publisher works with the financial assistance of
the Welsh Books Council.

Cover Illustration by Matt Joyce www.themeekshall.com

Printed in Plantin by Gwasg Gomer, Llandysul

TRUTH: undeceiving, true, beyond doubt, sincere, guileless, upright; correctness, uprightness; that which corresponds to the thing as it is.

The Welsh Encyclopædia

Ne sois ni fade panégyriste, ni censeur amer; dis la chose comme elle est.

Jacques le Fataliste, Denis Diderot

It is not on any map; true places never are.

Moby Dick, Herman Melville

The truth of things depends upon opinion alone... Everything in life is so various, so contrasted, so obscure, that there is no certainty in any truth.

Erasmus

Remember to tell the truth.

Rhys Lewis, Daniel Owen

MEETING

WHEN DR JONES saw him that first time, Melog was about to kill himself.

Dr Jones had come from his coldinsummer terraced house where he lived on his own without so much as a cat to welcome him home, and had walked along the high street, his head filled with the short notes he was writing for his exhaustive study of the Encyclopaedia. Dr Jones did not have a post at the university but was a full-time Welsh academic and author – that is he was out of work and living on social security. And all was well that unexceptional afternoon until he got to the Town Hall. Or at least all was as well as it could be in our pre-apocalyptic, ante-Armageddonish age. As usual, the ceaseless traffic polluted the air; adults and children wove among one another like ants or maggots and overpopulated the earth; the shops were open and selling products which are not needed, produced in factories which poison the seas and rivers and breezes with their festering waste. The sun even had a go at shining through the sick mist and the acid drizzle that drifted on the wind and birds did their best to squawk out a song above all the metallic clattering and mechanical rumbling. Naturally, Dr Jones did not notice these ordinary things at the time as they were long familiar. He was not expecting any extraordinary event which would change his unexceptional and empty daily life – he had abandoned cherishing such hopes a long time ago. Then he got to the Town Hall.

There, on the great corner, by the magnificent portal of our splendid Hall – the gates of hell, some said, as they were the way to the social security office (though they were the

gates to a school where he had briefly worked to Dr Jones) –
there was gathered an excited crowd. Not that that was in
any way unusual on a Saturday morning. Meetings or
protests of some sort took place every week in front of the
Town Hall: Parents Against Beating Children, Children
Against Nuclear Power, Nuclear Family Equals Moral
Majority, Majorities for Democracy, Democracy for Wales,
Plaid Cymru the Party of Wales, People of Wales Against
Racism, Rock Against Racism, Rock Against Fascism, Dogs
Against Fascism, People Against Dogshit on the Streets,
Keep Death off the Streets. But the crowd Dr Jones saw that
day was different. What attracted Dr Jones's attention was
the fact that they were all looking up.

At first he thought that they were either a group of people
scanning the heavens for signs of extraterrestrial visitors, or
a group of believers waiting for midday when Jesus Christ
would materialise out of the clouds and come down among
them to shake hands with those who had been so patient,
after the manner of members of the royal family.

Then he looked up and saw that a young man, thin and
stark naked, had climbed onto the roof of the Hall – the
highest building in the town – and was threatening to throw
himself to the ground. The doctor could not tell how long the
boy had been there or how he had achieved such a terrifyingly high perch, but the fact that his white skin was rapidly
turning blue (like the old advertisement for washing powder
which, it claimed, could wash shirts whiter than white to the
point where, for some reason, they turned blue) this fact
suggested that he had been standing in that condition and
place in the cold and in the 'picking' rain, as they say, for
some considerable time. And that was the first time that Dr
Jones saw Melog.

Soon after that the police and the ambulance arrived.

When the policemen started trying to persuade the young
man to come down voluntarily and by the safe route some
people among the crowd of onlookers shouted, cynically,

'Jump! Jump!' And at the time, as a confirmed cynic himself, Dr Jones saw the joke too and did not identify with the young stranger in his extremity. But when he opened his mouth to shout 'Jump!' with the others his head started to spin, and he thought that he was with the boy teetering on the precipice and then falling, hurtling down with him, hitting the pavement and his head cracking open like the shell of an egg. The feeling terrified him, and when the fragile shape moved closer – a fraction of an inch closer – to the edge of the roof, his heart came into his throat. He did not want to see him fall, not for anything in the world, and he would have given anything in the world if he could stop him and rescue him or if they could change places.

He moved to a safer position thank goodness, and allowed some of the ambulancemen to go up to him. The blood-hungry audience turned away, disappointed.

But Dr Jones could not bring himself to leave and for some reason a desire came over him to talk to the boy. Although he did not know him at the time, in fact had never seen him before, Dr Jones went to the police and told them with tears in his eyes and a lump clogging his throat – and they were notwithstanding real tears and a real lump – told them that he was a relative of the young man's and asked permission to see him. To Dr Jones's great surprise they agreed to this with alacrity. Some things are so easy, especially when you do not expect them to be easy at all. Perhaps their response was to do with the fact that he had introduced himself as Dr Jones (without saying what sort of doctor). Still he could have been someone who was after the boy's blood; might he not in fact have been the very cause, the precise reason for his contemplating doing away with himself? His pursuer, his torturer, his unheeding woegiver? On the other hand perhaps the police had reasoned that a friend or acquaintance could comfort him. But the truth was that they did not much care either way.

Shortly the old doctor was standing in an enormous room

in the Hall filled with portraits of old worthies from the town's past whom no one could remember, and luxurious wooden furniture, polished and dark. And there the strange boy sat next to a policeman. He was sipping hot tea from a thin plastic cup and he was wrapped in a coarse blanket the colour of wholemeal bread.

As he got closer the doctor saw how frighteningly thin and bony he was, rather like an insect, a grasshopper, a mantis or a prawn, or like an illustration of the human body in a medical textbook and the pictures of the 'man' in the Encyclopaedia. But what struck him most was his whiteness. His skin was white like fine, wetted paper, or like the petals of a white flower, a white rose steeped in springwater; he could see the blueness of his veins through the pale skin. His hair was white too, pure white, white as fresh snow and sparklingwhite like snowflakes falling through rays of wintry sun; utterly straight hair like threads of silver, fine, and cropped so close to his head that you could actually see the skull through it. And the eyebrows were white too and the strands of his eyelashes the same intense white. But he was no albino as his eyes were not pink but rather a pale blue, azure, a lazur chalkstone like the description in *The Mabinogi*, like rock-pools on the seashore, diamond and sapphire reflecting a cloudless sky. Their liquid blueness was truly profound though they were pale, like the far depths of the sky in midsummer.

Dr Jones's first thought was that this was a creature from another planet, an alien, a man from space.

But what to say to the stranger?

How are you? the doctor ventured. Are you feeling better now?

Eh?

It was obvious he did not recognise him and how could he be expected to when they had never seen one another before? But that is the truth of it; his first word to Dr Jones was 'Eh?'.

He's confused, the doctor said to the gigantic policeman

standing next to him – so contrastingly huge, strong and dark juxtaposed with the puny white weakling.

Sure to be, the constable agreed.

The doctor noticed that the policeman was extraordinarily fat. He rather resembled PC Plod, and Dr Jones noticed that he had no thumb or little finger on his right hand. He felt that this was rather odd. Was it not the case that policemen of all people were required to be physically complete, if not mentally?

Then suddenly without warning and unexpectedly the boy stood and the blanket slipped to the floor discovering all his nakedness, white and smooth as a marble statue. Immediately the policeman leapt into action and rewrapped the blanket round the frail body.

Of course. Now I recognise you, the youth said to the doctor (remarkably happily for someone lately intent on committing suicide). How are you nowadays? Haven't seen you in ages and ages.

He handed the empty cup to the threefingered policeman.

Thanks for the tea, he said in a strange foreign accent, though his Welsh was quite correct. I'm going home with this gentleman who is my friend.

Okay, you're welcome, another policeman said, who looked as though he was a cardboard cutout. In fact apart from him and the fat threefingered Ploddish policeman there were five other constables and they all looked like cardboard cutouts. Then this policeman added,

You can have a lend of the blanket; it's cold out – but remember to bring it back tomorrow.

It was quite obvious that the policemen were glad to get rid of their problem.

The youth linked arms with Dr Jones, the blanket over one shoulder, the other, on the side where he hung onto the doctor, bare, like an ancient Greek's – and out they went, the two of them, into the high street.

Don't look back, the thin young man whispered to Dr Jones as they turned from the cardboard policemen. They're suspicious of you. Watch it or you'll turn into a pillar of salt; if you think of turning, just remember Sodom.

Then, out in the street, still arm in arm with the doctor, he asked,

Where to now then? You know what? I fancy a bag of chips. Chipped potatoes! Could we do that? Could we have a bag of chips each?

Yes we could, Dr Jones said, as if there were any choice other than to agree. We shall go, as Saunders Lewis would put it, to a 'potato tavern'.

And what impression did the couple leave behind them as they promenaded through the town? Their appearance was, truly, very strange. The poor little doctor in his black anorak, short with fair hair (the colour of dirty hay) thinning and grizzled, a neat beard more grizzled still, in (late) middle age, the lenses of his spectacles thick over his eyes like two lychees, a red scarf around his neck as if he had the luck of Absalom; someone you would not glance at twice in a crowd. But on his arm, tall and thin and white, dressed (though half naked) in a toga, an emaciated youth. Needless to say, it was a union which drew everyone's attention. But having said that, nobody spoke to them though they craned their necks and gawped, because this was south Wales.

Everybody in the chip shop knew Dr Jones and knew everything worth knowing about him, because this was a Valleys town.

Behind the counter as usual was Jabez Ifans, the oldest fish and chip fryer in the world (official) according to a yellowing certificate he had received ten years before which hung framed on the blackened wall behind him. He was a hundred and four years old, deaf as a doorstep, and his big red nose looked just like a potato fried in its skin. Helping him was his youngest son, Melfyn, himself seventy-five and blind as a stone. Unlike those blind from birth, Melfyn (who lost his sight to a splash of hot fat from his father's fryer at the age of twenty-five) had never managed to master doing things when he was still young; it was he who wrapped the food in old newspaper – putting nourishment into words, as it were – and even after years of practice he always made a mess of it. In the end his aged father would have to help him, and that would happen with every bag of chips sold to every customer. Thus service in Ifans' and Ifans' chip shop, like waiting for selfgovernment for Wales, was interminably slow.

Chips almost ready! Melfyn would call every now and then, holding aloft a handful of paper and potatoes like a heated propitiation to the gods. Customers would then have to complain to his father, who would come to them, if he happened to hear, to rewrap the chips as best he could with his arthritic fingers. But actually the chips were worth waiting for, because as well as being the oldest, Jabez Ifans was also the best fryer in the world (unofficial).

But that day Mr Ifans glared at his two unusual customers and ordered his son into the back of the shop where they lived – as if there were some danger of his seeing the half-naked boy. There were other people in the chip shop; Dr Jones could scarcely move an inch in the town without seeing someone who knew him, and it is enough to say that their reaction on that day was not particularly tolerant. So the doctor dragged his new friend from the shop once he had soused his chips with plenty of salt and enough vinegar to drown the Salvation Army.

In the street once more, the doctor said,

The best thing to do is for you to come straight home with me so you can get some clothes on.

That is exactly what I intended to do, the boy said.

And so the unusual couple walked through the streets, which were like the houses in a toy village, until they reached the terraced house which was the home of Dr Jones.

Here is what the stranger saw when he set about examining the house. He saw a square room in which everything was neat and orderly, though it was rather bare and cheerless. He saw a white telephone which had upon it a long coiled white plastic flex; a small white and red kitchen; a small blue bathroom. In the small living-room he saw a small radio, a small sofa on which was a pattern of large orange flowers with black centres and green leaves on a background of brilliant yellow, cream-coloured cushions, cream-coloured curtains, cream wallpaper, a cream-coloured paper lampshade. When he went to look around the kitchen he saw, a coffee-making machine (black plastic), a water purifier (white plastic), two stools and a small table (white, wooden). He saw a clock upon the wall operated by battery, but what was remarkable about this clock was that its hands (red) moved backwards, widdershins as it is sometimes put – at a quarter past eleven, for instance, the clock gave the impression that it was a quarter to one – until you realised that the numbers ran the other way too – 1 was where 11 should be and 11 was where 1 should be and so on. He saw a set of teflon saucepans, knives, an assortment of cups, mugs – six of them – on a mug-tree. He saw the white microwave and the electric toaster (white plastic). And returning to the living-room he saw the compact disc player and the doctor's meagre collection of compact discs scattered across the floor – Bryn Terfel's *Caneuon Meirion Williams*, *Boom Boom* by John Lee Hooker, *Tiger Rag* by Louis Armstrong, *The All-Time Greatest Hits of Roy Orbison*.

The only pictures on the walls were a collection of photographs of Dr Jones taken at various periods in his life, every one framed in black. There was a picture of him in his academic gown, directing a spectacled smile beyond the shoulder of the photographer, cradling in his hands a scroll tied with a red ribbon. A picture of him with a beard, another of him with sideburns, a picture of him with a moustache, other pictures of him cleanshaven. There he was standing somewhere beside the sea, wearing a grey cardigan, his knuckles thrust deep in the pockets. A picture of him sitting on a doorstep stroking a grey cat which he holds against his grey cardigan – hard to see the cat. Pictures of him wearing glasses, wearing sunglasses, not wearing glasses. A picture of him in a garden standing under a tree, withered autumnal leaves around his feet. In another picture you see him striding towards the camera in the rain, his face like a fist against the wind. A photograph of him in the snow wearing a brown coat next to a snowman and both he and the snowman wear a grey scarf. Just him, alone in every picture as if no one else inhabited his world. Who took the pictures? The stranger could imagine the doctor pressing the camera on some coincidental passer-by, asking them to take the picture, and thanking them afterwards for their kindness.

He saw also the doctor's collection of books, and his desk across which a shambling heap of papers was spread like a landslide, and a complete set of the Encyclopaedia.

After this detailed inspection the youth concluded that it was quite homely, in its own way.

Dr Jones went to the wardrobe in his bedroom and selected some old clothes – a white shirt, an old pair of jeans, a green woollen jumper with a yellow diamond pattern, underpants and dark blue socks – and gave them all to the boy.

Go in the bathroom and put these on, he said.

The boy was back in a few minutes.

The shirt's a bit tight, he said, but the jeans are okay because you rolled them up instead of cutting them. A wise move if you don't mind me saying. And the jumper's okay because it's stretched. I'm taller than you but narrower.

You look rather odd, the doctor said.

So what.

What's your name?

My name's Melog.

MÊL: which is a liquid or semi-liquid substance; the materials for which are collected by various kinds of bee, but principally by the *apis mellifica*, or honey bee, and then solely by that class which is called "worker".

OG: the Amorite king of Basan, the which had governance extending over three score cities... A false book about king Og was condemned...

The Encyclopædia

THE MORNING

DR JONES was woken by his alarm clock. It took him some time to come to terms with what is called 'reality'. He rose early every morning in order to do everything in good time; he hated having to rush. He would stretch his muscleless arms and his white and hairless legs. Look through the window (not double-glazed), after hesitantly opening the curtains (floral, yellow) and see the houses opposite like children's building blocks, the bearded milkman in his silent milkfloat (the one which had run over a nine year old called Malcolm a while ago). Go to the bathroom and glance through the gap in the green and white striped curtain, at the back yard and the weedchoked garden, the backs of the houses opposite (more children's play-blocks), cats on the walls, dogs scrutting for bones in the dustbins in the lane.

He splashes his face with cold water. Now he is properly awake. It is Dr Jones's belief that we sleep in order to enjoy a little death; we practise for the grave in slumber, extinction's preliminary examination. He shaves, bleeds, has a shower. Dries himself. Combs his hair, treasuring every thread of it. Dresses. And once more after reconstructing himself, Dr Jones is ready to face the day. Each morning is a little resurrection.

He goes downstairs (the second and seventh steps, as usual, squeaking) into the kitchen. Boils a kettle and places a spoonful of instant coffee in a cup (a crack through the blue forget-me-nots on the left hand side) and pours boiling water upon it. One cup of strong black coffee, thick as liquefied coal. Another spoonful and more hot water. After his second cup, Dr Jones takes his vitamin tablets. A purple tablet containing vitamin C; an orange tablet containing codliver oil; a green one containing garlic and parsley; a blue one containing iron; a yellow one containing ginseng; a red one to finish containing a cocktail of vitamins (in case). More coffee and a slice of wholemeal bread (toasted to a mahogany plank) smeared with the slenderest suggestion of margarine. And once more Dr Jones has renewed his membership of the human race.

Normally, that is according to his until now unvarying daily routine, Dr Jones would have walked straight from the kitchen to the living-room and positioned himself at his desk (oblong, two drawers, bought for five pounds in a second hand shop) to work upon his study of the Encyclopaedia until lunch (at a quarter to one) – with a break (a quarter of an hour only) at eleven o'clock exactly – and that was what Dr Jones was about to do this morning, but as he placed his hand on the handle of the living-room door, he remembered Melog. As his guest was sleeping on the sofa in that room, Dr Jones was unable to walk in with his accustomed freedom without waking the young man. It was seven o'clock, a little early for most people these days.

What shall I do? he thinks. He considers going for a walk to town. He thinks about buying a newspaper at the shop on the corner, but there is no money left from his giro to buy a paper that day. He could go upstairs and work there, or go and sit in the back garden, but that was full of weeds and cat shit. In any case, it was raining again. Then he hit on the idea of doing a little physical exercise. He never did anything in the least energetic, so he decided to do a few press-ups.

Dr Jones lay flat upon his stomach with his face against the square black and white tiles of the kitchen. He pushed himself up from the floor on his weak, thin arms. Once, and lowered himself again. Pushed up again. And down. Up again.

In a short while he was fighting for breath and had done some injury to his back. It had been a stupid idea. What about listening to the radio? No. On the English programmes there was news about war atrocities and world catastrophes and on the 'Welsh' channel there was some nitwit like Dei Sulfryn (speaking English and playing American records).

Dr Jones sat on one of the red French tubular steel chairs in his kitchen and listened for any movement in the living-room. Numerous thoughts ran through his mind as he tried to fill the time. To exercise his memory he attempted to recall an entry from the Encyclopaedia in its entirety:

> BIRD. [A comparatively straightforward piece to remember, he thought.] By the name *Bird* are known all species of flying creature; which are called also avians, fowls, &c.; and it is their attribute that they be clad in feathers, possessed of two wings, two feet, and a beak or bill; and they all reproduce by the laying of eggs. It is a matter of some debate as to whether it was from dry land or the oceans that birds first sprang at their creation. The historian of scripture, in his account of the work of the fifth day (Gen.i.20, 21) has it that God said, "Let the waters bring forth abundantly the moving creature that hath life, and fowl that may fly above the earth in the open firmament of heaven. And God created great whales, and every living creature that moveth, which the waters brought forth abundantly, after their kind, and every winged fowl after his kind." And in the account of the work of the sixth day, the which treats of the creation of animals, reptiles, and beasts of the earth (v.23) there is no reference to avians. Yet, in the manner of a general conspectus of the entire work of creation it is said (Gen.ii.19), "And out of *the ground* the Lord God formed every beast of the field, and every fowl of the air."

But he could go no further without the printed text in front of him. In spite of that, he was pleased that he had succeeded in recovering such a substantial piece. He loved the language of the Encyclopaedia so much that the thrill of reading or remembering it like this was almost like a delicious physical pain. The archaic spellings, with their systematic application of rules that no longer held, sent a shiver down his spine. And then there were the old fashioned but still teasingly acceptable forms like 'by the laying of eggs', 'avians', 'conspectus'. But what enchanted him the most were all the refined nineteenth century turns of expression, they were so graceful and yet so economical – 'and it is their attribute that they be clad in feathers', 'has it that God said', 'the which treats of', 'Yet, in the manner of a general conspectus of the entire work' – they all cast some spell on him. But the language has changed and is still changing and will go on changing after we are gone. And then there was the attempt to be objective, scientific by the lights of the age, while at the same time accepting the word of the Bible as literal truth. Then the problem of fitting together consistently the inconsistencies of 'the historian of scripture'. It all made him swoon and he was never surprised he had decided to devote all his time to a detailed study of the Encyclopaedia in its entirety.

When Dr Jones next looked at the time it was eight o'clock (that is, it looked like four o'clock). He went to the living-room door and pressed his ear to it. Not the slightest noise. The boy must be sleeping very soundly.

Dr Jones went back into the kitchen and sat. He made himself another slice of toast, hoping that the smell of roasting bread would wake his new friend.

But who was the boy? Was he truly his friend? He behaved like a friend, and tu-toied the doctor from the start (which was a little forward of him, perhaps), but he was very strange. Where, he wondered, had he come from? That difficult-to-place foreign accent. And why on earth had a fit, handsome young man climbed onto the roof of the Town Hall to kill himself? What was troubling him at that moment? He had seemed happy enough last night, in good spirits in fact. Dr Jones did not like to question him about this for fear of exciting and upsetting him once more. But it whetted his curiosity – the emaciatedness, the white hair, the blue drills of his eyes.

And what did he intend to do next? Would he stay with Dr Jones for a while until he came to himself, or until he got back on his rocker, whatever that expression meant? Or would he want to go back to his own country, his home, wherever that was?

The doctor had taken to the boy. He was pleasant and good company, in spite of the strangeness of his appearance and behaviour. Were he to decide to stay in his home for the rest of his life, the doctor would be delighted. He would not even ask him to pay rent or expect him to go out to work. The doctor imagined them both, living together in friendship and peaceful understanding. They would talk through the night, take their meals together, stroll together every afternoon. They would run errands together into town and take a turn in the park on afternoons of mild weather.

In a way, Dr Jones saw his visitor as answering his loneliness, an answer to the prayers of an atheist who did not pray. Perhaps he was really an angel sent to him from the heaven he was convinced did not exist. He was in the sky, wasn't he, with heaped clouds as his backdrop, that first time he had seen him?

He would clear all the old boxes and cases and rubbish from the spare room and make that a home for him. He would repaint it and paper it and buy a bed and new furniture for the young man and arrange it all in his room.

At a quarter past eleven, by which time he felt that he had had rather too much coffee (seven or perhaps eight cups, he was not sure), Dr Jones decided that he would knock on the living-room door and offer Melog some breakfast.

He knocked. No answer. But he had not knocked very hard. He knocked again. No answer. He knocked again and this time called, Melog! The strange name blossomed from his mouth like a flower in a wasteland, like a song in a dungeon. He knocked again, harder this time, and asked, Melog, do you want breakfast? Toast, boiled eggs, porridge, bacon, corn flakes, kippers, croissants? No answer. Melog? Are you there? No answer.

What if he had killed himself in the night while Dr Jones slept? Perhaps hanged himself, slashed his wrists, put a plastic bag over his head, swallowed a bottle of pills? For anyone determined enough, there were many ways to commit suicide.

Or perhaps he was still just asleep after all. Dr Jones had no choice but to go in. And what if he was naked? What if he were to get angry for being woken? What if he was used to sleeping in until midday, or two or three in the afternoon?

Dr Jones nerved himself and inched open the door.

The chief ambition of the dog is to serve its master and to earn his approbation... In a palace it is full of high ambition; and in a hovel, serfly. In all places it is heedless of all save its master and his companions. It recognises the beggar by his garb or by his demeanour; and does its uttermost to occasion him to keep away. At night, when upon its vigil, it appears to take pride in its office; and if a stranger come near at this time, it puts on the mask of cruelty and vanquishes him itself, or makes such a din as is likely to raise someone to its assistance.

The Encyclopædia

THE DOGS

NO ONE slept on the gaudy sofa; there was no one in the room at all. Neither was there any sign that anyone had been there. On the floor next to the sofa in a neat pile were the pillow, the clean white bedlinen, the woollen blanket, folded like envelopes exactly where Dr Jones had left them for the young man last night before retiring. And no one had touched them. There was no note saying goodbye. No thank you either. He had gone, vanished.

So there was nothing to be done but to set to work on the Encyclopaedia. Dr Jones sat at his desk and tried to start straight away.

Adamant. The meaning of the word is *unvanquished.* The adamant is the hardest and most brilliant of the precious stones... It is in general devoid of colour.

But the doctor could not go on with the work. He felt that there was something comic, something unintentionally funny about the entries and their formal language. Usually he had nothing but huge reverence for all the conscientious labour of the Encyclopaedia, but occasionally, and this was one of those occasions, the whole thing seemed like some enormous mistake, a wrongheaded waste of time.

In any case, it was time for him to go to town to sign on at the social security office if he was to get money for his food and keep for the week. He hated the process, but there was no alternative. How else was he to finance his work as full-time academic and author?

He walked into town along the toylike streets, past row upon row of houses. He would turn a corner and walk along another row of houses. It is not possible to describe the towns of south Wales without using the words 'brown' and 'grey'. The houses are brown, the roofs are grey. The people are grey, their clothes are brown. The mountains are brown, the sky is grey. The streets and the pavements are grey, the cars are brown. The cats are brown, the dogs are grey (or occasionally the other way round). The birds are brown. The rain is grey, the puddles are brown.

Dr Jones went to the Department of Social Security and sat on one of the grey benches in the brown room to wait his turn. In front of him sat another row of grey people waiting to sign a piece of paper granting them permission to survive another week at the state's expense. At the end of the row, a large hairy man frowned at the floor. His overcoat was hairy too, so that he resembled a bear. Beside him sat a thin young man; thin hair, thin nose, thin coat, thin moustache, thin glasses. He held the hand of a thin boy. Were these people real? Dr Jones felt as if he were looking at illustrations in a children's book; cartoons, caricatures. But on the other hand he could not dispute the green snot streaming from the child's nose or the fact that the father next to him had released a quiet but extraordinarily noisome fart, or the air of menace that emanated from the hairy man's every look and gesture. The doctor (whom everyone suspected of being the fartcracker) could not observe the others without turning deliberately to look at them, which, as it might anger people, would be a foolish and dangerous thing to do. Therefore, Dr Jones frowned at the brown floor like the rest of them. As a consistent and long-term visitor to the office, he was perfectly familiar with the routine. The bear approached the man behind the glass partition. Only his hand and blurred shape were visible through the dirty water of the smirched pane.

The thin man and his child slid along the bench. He was next. Dr Jones moved. He pressed closer to the man next to him and someone moved to fill the space on the other side. The rest bunched together after him until the gap left by the bear had vanished.

Shortly, the bear left the office and the thin man and his son went to the glass partition. The rest compressed against one another again like bench sardines.

The thin man talked to the milky glass. He raised his whining, nasal voice to a shout. He beat the glass with his fists wildly, ferocious with anger. The child started a screeching bawl. Then, the disembodied hand slid a piece of paper through the narrow slot between the glass and the counter. The thin man took the sheet and, propitiated, he turned away, dragging his son from the office.

Later on it was Dr Jones's turn to go to the partition. Before he could get to his feet a voice shouted from behind the glass, DR JONES. This would happen without fail every week. No one else was called forward by name and title. Every time, it caused Dr Jones embarrassment. He would blush, imagining all eyes on him, their owners trying to work out what a doctor was doing in the centre, assuming, of course, that he was a medical doctor and jumping to the conclusion that he had done unspeakable things to his patients, and that that was why he was unemployed.

Ah, Dr Jones. How are we this week?

Fine.

The doctor could not see the person behind the glass, only a brown shape in a grey mist. But the voice was the same every week. Patronising and complacent, without the least concern for the state of Dr Jones's health or anything else about him in spite of the question. The doctor looked through the glass trying to see the owner of the voice, but it was just like when he went out without his glasses and saw the world through a veil of smoke.

Very good. Now have you been looking for work?

Yes.

You've really been looking?

Yes.

Truthfully making every effort to find work?

The doctor nodded.

You've been unemployed for quite a while now. Let's see… Yes, six years. Well look harder, Dr Jones, search conscientiously. Sign this, please.

Thank you.

Thank you, Dr Jones. And if you happen not to get a job by next week, please don't be late again. You're late too often. Good afternoon.

Dr Jones was always relieved to get out of that dreadful place. It was torture. Colditz. After he had come out of there, for a few minutes the air would feel pure and healthy, until he recovered fully when he saw that it was merely as grey and as brown as usual.

Instead of going straight home the doctor went for a walk. He walked along the path of the old railway line where there were bushes and blackbirds and weeds and thorns, where there had never been greatness. It was one of the few parts of the town, apart from the park, that had something of the countryside about it, and the doctor did not expect to see many people there that day.

He walked a mile or two along the iron track. A perfectly straight path, and at last he came to the rag and bone yard. As he approached he heard a din of voices and barking. The rag and bone man, Jaco Saunders, hairyarmed, squarefingered, bluechinned, was yelling at his pair of murderous Rottweilers.

Satan! Satan! Stop it! Fang, don't! Come 'ere!

It was obvious that the dogs were not listening. Dr Jones was about to turn and run away, but he caught a glimpse through the yard gates (two sheets of rusted brown corrugated iron) and saw what the hounds were baying at.

Standing in a corner (bits of bicycles, engines, bedframes and assorted scrap metal), in fact cornered by the dogs, and whiter than usual, white as proverbial chalk, was Melog.

The dogs' jaws were snapping at the air like steel traps on the legs of foxes. Their eyes were red and savage. Their teeth were hard as diamond and their flews demonically ruddied. The young man could not escape without being torn into small pieces by the dogs.

FFUGLITH [ffug-llith; L. Legenda]. One of the meanings of the word *llith* is enticement, or that which entices; it also signifies a lesson, lecture. *Ffug* signifies magic, enchantment; deceit, deception &c. In the composite word ffuglith, ffug is an adjectival prefix: thus the word signifies an enticing or enchanting lesson, a lesson founded upon magic or invention or riddling, rather than upon fact or truth. The meaning of the Latin word *legenda* is that which may be read.

The Encyclopædia

MAPS

MELOG'S DRILLING BLUE EYES stared straight into the red eyes of the two hideously ugly mastiffs. And quite suddenly, they both stopped howling and padded to the boy, obedient and tame as puppies, and started licking his hands and squeaking playfully about his feet and waggling their cropped tails for joy. It was an astonishing transformation.

What the hell have you done to 'em? Jaco Saunders asked, amazed, as if he had read Dr Jones's thoughts.

Now that he could see that it was safe, the doctor went into the yard.

By this time Melog was crouching with his arms round the necks of the exmonsters, who were licking his ears and his strawberries-and-cream cheeks and his icing sugar forehead, as if he had reared them both himself on spoonfuls of milk.

Jaco Saunders insisted that Melog and Dr Jones go into the house for a drop o somethin nice after the terrible shock. The modern bungalow did not fit the stereotype of a home for a rag and bone man; it was not at all like Steptoe and Son, stuffed with second hand nick-nacks, but orderly and colour-ful, with a colour television, a CD player and a huge collection of Royal Doulton. That was his treasure, the apple of his eye – his real reason for inviting the two into the house was to have them admire the porcelain models of slimlegged horses, the sheepdogs, the bluetit chicks in a nest (perfect in every feather) the endless Toby jugs (Ronald Reagan, Churchill, Dr Johnson, among others). Every piece fragile and intricate. Who would have thought that such a rough looking man would keep such a pretty house and have a taste for such fine things?

This is my life, Jaco said. I hate junk. I canna bear shabby old things with no grain on 'em.

He was a rag and bone man who hated rags and bones. After drinking their drop and expressing sufficient wonder at the collection (Isn't that beautiful! Lovely! So realistic!) Dr Jones and Melog made their excuses to leave. Melog went to say goodbye to the two dogs. Even though the young man had pacified the exwolves, Dr Jones was unwilling to go near them, and so he urged Melog to come back to his house for tea.

At home, Dr Jones ventured to ask him more questions, hoping to get to know him better and learn more of his history.

Where are you from? You aren't from Wales, although your Welsh is excellent if I may say so without sounding patronising.

It's the accent that gives me away isn't it? I can speak several languages: Laxarian, Sacrian, English.

Apart from English I don't believe I've heard of any of those languages.

Laxarian is the language of Laxaria, my fathertongue, Melog said, stretching out on the hangover-coloured sofa, but not many people speak it any more. Laxaria's been conquered by Sacria and the language is prohibited in its own country. I had to learn Sacrian in school.

Where are Laxaria and Sacria?

Who knows? Who knows where anywhere is? Melog said, sitting up on the sofa now, his long arms extended wide like wings across the backrest.

So, Sacria and Laxaria are remote places? The doctor said. Remote?

Far off. Out of the way.

Everywhere is far away from somewhere, Melog said impatiently, reclining once more à la Chatterton. Everywhere is out of somewhere's way! Britain isn't the centre of the world, for sure, or Wales either, or London, or New York, or Tokyo, or Paris, or Berlin, or Hong Kong...

Okay, okay. I take your point, Dr Jones said patiently. Well, Wales is where we are now. I'd like to know something about your roots.

Roots? Melog said, resting his chin on his fist, his elbow on a cushion. I don't like that image. Instead of going on about roots I'd prefer to talk about strides or steps. This is the step in life I've now arrived at. He thumped the arm of the sofa and a dustcloud puffed from the sick-coloured upholstery.

Yes, Wales, the doctor said again.

So Wales is this room?

No, you know perfectly well that this house is in a street in a town in Wales.

I don't know that at all, though I'm prepared to accept your word for it. But the truth is I don't know where this house is or where Wales is, or what it's for, for that matter.

I'll show you. The doctor got up and took his copy of the Welsh atlas from the desk drawer. He opened the atlas to page forty-two. He took the book to the sofa and placed it on Melog's bony knees.

That's where Wales is, where we live, where this house is and the street and the town.

Bit little isn't it? Melog said. Hard to believe you keep it in a book like that and keep the book in a drawer. Convenient though.

Of course *this* isn't Wales, Dr Jones said uncertainly. He was not sure if the young man was pulling his leg. The doctor gave a little laugh as if to join in the joke. On the other hand perhaps the young man, who had been on the verge of flinging himself from the roof of a high building to the hard ground, was simply bewildered. Perhaps he was, as they say, unhinged, after standing all that time in the cold, utterly naked and thin and vulnerable.

This is a map, Dr Jones said. A map of Wales.

Not Wales itself?

No. A map which describes Wales.

But that map describes Wales as a little flat green thing. Something you can keep in a drawer.

No no. You misunderstand. The map is a little picture of Wales, which is much larger. Not Wales itself. A description of it.

I don't get it. To be a description I could understand properly the map would have to be the same size as Wales showing everything in or on it, like this house and the street and the town and us in the house and all the stuff in the house too.

But then there'd be no room for us and the map.

So where is Wales?

Around us. It's too big to show.

So Wales is the world.

Well Wales is a small piece of the world. It's a very little country to tell you the truth.

But it's too big to show me. Melog chewed a fingernail. (He had only stumps of fingernails.) His interest was beginning to wane.

Yes, but that's where we are now.

Can I see Wales now?

Well, a part of it. This room.

So this room represents Wales? The young man lay on the sofa staring at the ceiling, his head hanging over the armrest, his neck arched.

No no. The map represents Wales – or that is, that's the only way that I could show you Wales at the moment.

And yet, Wales isn't everything. He shrugged in the Gallic manner.

Well, it's everything to us here, now.

But I don't think I can grasp this. I could be in Laxaria for all I know.

And where is Laxaria? Dr Jones asked, scratching his crown. Laxaria, he thought. It sounds like the sort of medicine that first eases your motions and then gives you diarrhoea.

In Sacria, like I said.

Well, I've never heard of the country, or the Sacrian language either, ever, the doctor said.

Look in your book. Perhaps there's a map of it. The young man relaxed back on the sofa – the joints of his emaciated body were so flexible and smooth.

The doctor looked in the index.

Sacramento, Sacriston, Sádaba, no Sacria. Laxey (Laksa), Laxford Bridge (Camas Bhradan). No, no Laxaria either, I'm afraid.

That doesn't mean they don't exist. You can't prove the existence of Wales to me, any more than I can prove the existence of Sacria and Laxaria to you.

But you maintain that you come from these countries and somehow or other you've come to Wales. Perhaps you're a Welshman after all. I don't know what to believe. You've talked about other countries, and Berlin, Paris, New York. You know more than you pretend. All right, suit yourself.

I don't know where I come from, that's what I said. And I don't maintain that I came from Laxaria or Wales either. I speak Welsh, but I speak Sacrian and English too, but I don't claim to come from England.

No, Dr Jones said, losing patience a little, you maintain you come from another planet in outer space.

I didn't say that either. I said that's how I feel sometimes, that's all.

There was silence. Dr Jones felt uncertain again. Who was this man? He looked at him. His appearance was strange. He had, by means of a sort of perverse rise-taking, succeeded in confusing the doctor about so many things of which he had felt certain. Where was Wales, after all? Who could prove that the earth was round? He remembered Prince Metternich's remark: 'Italy is a geographical expression.' (His head was full of decontextualized fragments because he liked to browse through dictionaries of quotations before he went to sleep.) Perhaps those photographs from space were all tricks. This young man appeared to be a stranger to everything. It seemed that maps were new to him, he'd never seen one before, yet he knew the word *map*, he knew the word for everything, and so didn't this indicate that he was familiar with everything he knew the word for? And yet he behaved as if everything in the world around was strange to him. Perhaps he was a sort of Kasper Hauser.

What's the meaning of your name, Melog?

My father gave me my name. He'd been reading the epic poem, the Canipalaat, from our great national treasure, the Imalic (which has been lost). It was composed in Laxaria but now the Sacrians are trying to claim it as their own national literature. The Sacrians tried to get hold of all the old manuscripts in Laxarian and burn them and put fake Sacrian manuscripts in their place. But by trickery some of our scholars managed to save a few of the most valuable texts. One of these heroes was Professor Lalula, who's exiled in this country now. But coming back to my name: in the Canipalaat, there's a pantheon of heroes and monsters and marvellous creatures that can speak that have various adventures. One of the animals in the story is the winged unicorn and his name is Melog. He was white and he could fly out of trouble and escape his enemies and several heroes in the epic use his services to get out of the clutches of hideous giants or the oneeyed demons. In one part of the story, for instance, it's Melog the unicorn who's responsible for carrying a message for one of the heroes, who's imprisoned in a cave by a cruel magician, to the hero's father on another island. Unfortunately this happens towards the end of the manuscript and the very end hasn't survived in any of the versions, not in any of the fake versions in Sacrian or in the unique Laxarian original, which I'm looking for. But my father liked the idea of Melog the winged unicorn helping father and son.

Can I ask you a question? the young man asked suddenly. His voice was warm, as if Dr Jones were an old, close friend.

Yes of course.

You speak very formal Welsh, don't you; you have a trace of foreign accent, don't you?

You're very observant, Dr Jones said. My compatriots tell me I talk like a book. What does a book talk like?

That's strange, Melog said. The Sacrians accuse me of speaking Sacrian like a book too.

Well so be it, the doctor said bookily. Therefore let us be books. I love books – some of them – having devoted so much time to reading and studying them. I'm making a study of the Encyclopaedia at the moment. I'm perfectly happy to be a book.

So am I, Melog said. When I was a child and people asked me what I wanted to be I always said 'I want to be a book'. Let us be volume one and volume two.

A limited edition with a run of two.

Two texts, each a direct translation of the other.

Or better still, two printed books from the same manuscript.

That suits me perfectly, Melog said. I've come to Wales a refugee and like an old style scholar – without a scholarship or money or a patron – without a course, even, without a subject, just the need to learn. I've escaped from Sacria and at the moment I see Wales as quite like Laxaria before the Sacrians turned against her and banned the language and our books completely on the grounds they were 'racist'.

You're a student without a university and I'm an academic without a university, the doctor said.

They both laughed. After that afternoon, the doctor would spend less time on the Encyclopaedia.

LANGUAGE... Men of exceptional learning had grown quite mad upon this subject, which is to say the question of which was the original language; until at length there grew up systems of the utmost idiocy. Van Gorp asserted that the language of Paradise was Lowlandish or Dutch: Andre Kempe, in his work upon the language of Paradise, asserted that the ELOHIM spoke with Adam in Swedish; that Adam responded in Danish; and that the Serpent discoursed in the French tongue... It appears that Grotius stumbled upon the truth when he said, with reference to the original language, that "it did not exist in any one place, but that the remnants and traces of the ORIGINAL LANGUAGE were to be found in every language uttered or spoken throughout the world".

The Encyclopædia

LANGUAGE

I CAN'T UNDERSTAND how you speak such fluent Welsh, the doctor said.

Well, it's a long story. When I was boy, a young man came to our village to teach English to a group of us children. Nobody in the area could speak English, of course. In fact hardly anyone had ever heard the language. The teacher's name was Mr Cadwaladr. After a few weeks us children were saying good morning, good night and good afternoon, asking the time and discussing the weather. Our parents were keen for us to learn 'the world's greatest language' and we were willing enough. On top of that, Mr Cadwaladr was an exceptionally gifted teacher as well as being extremely keen. Every lesson turned into playtime. We stuck name tags in English on everything we could – the doors, the chairs, the windows, even grass and stones and the trees. In a few months we could string conversations together in a new language, a bit jerkily, and Mr Cadwaladr would hold spelling and recitation competitions and run clubs to distribute copies of story books and encourage us to write for our own little newspaper in a foreign language. The teacher's energy was infectious and he was endlessly inventive in lessons. He'd write plays with huge casts of characters so we'd all have parts and the chance to use the language in public. So it wasn't really surprising that some of us were more or less fluent in about a year.

And then – Melog continued – an important man arrived from one of the Sacrian cities. He was Laxarian actually, but he'd gone to live in Sacria and got an education and a good job and changed the spelling of his name from Laxarian to Sacrian and he'd married a well-to-do Sacrian, and he'd Sacricized to the point where he *was* Sacrian, virtually. But to be fair, he didn't forget his aged mother and still came to visit her in her old hovel in the village. All credit to him, he came to see her regularly. Every five years, to check if she was dead. Well when the gentleman called that year us children all ran up to him to welcome him in our best English. But he didn't understand us. Nobody was much bothered by this because you didn't hear much English even in Sacria. A bit later, an inspector came to the school and tested our English and that's when they found out that Mr Cadwaladr had been teaching us a different language altogether – not English but Welsh. Mr Cadwaladr vanished that night, although he gave us some drill in the subjunctive mood first, and relative clauses and the spirant mutation. Some of the locals were pretty annoyed – hopping mad to tell you the truth – that a foreigner, for reasons nobody could understand, had taken advantage of the innocence and ignorance of our people, and a few of them set about organising proper English lessons straight away. But some of us were quite happy to go on working on our Welsh and learning about Mr Cadwaladr's country.

What happened to Mr Cadwaladr after that? Dr Jones asked.

I don't know, Melog said. It's a bit of a mystery.

Why on earth did he do a thing like that, do you suppose?

I'm not sure. But personally I was happy enough try to retain my Welsh – after I got to know that that was the language I and some of my friends had been enjoying so much – and although I learnt English with the rest later on, my grasp of it's not so good as my understanding of Welsh. The English teachers we got instead of Mr Cadwaladr weren't half as good. So Mr Cadwaladr's strange experiment to disseminate the Welsh language worked in one case, at least. When I got to Wales I was disappointed so few people speak the language, till I got to this town of course.

Yes, Dr Jones said, this town's exceptional. Everybody speaks Welsh here. An unusual thing in the Valleys.

Lucky I came here then, wasn't it?

Melog stretched to his full length on the sofa like a cat luxuriating in the elasticity of his own muscles. The inevitable cigarette smouldered in the iciclelike fingers of his right hand. Its cloud was swollen around him as if he were a magician materialising or vanishing under his own spell.

And what do you intend doing here in Wales? Dr Jones asked, feeling as if he were falling into a trance.

I'm looking for a book, he said. An old manuscript.

Then he got up from the sofa and walked slowly round the room, picking something up every now and then – a rubber, an ashtray, a paper clip, the phone book – and examining it absently, as if he had never seen such a thing before, and after examining it, putting it back carefully in the same place. And as he moved around like this, he told the doctor his story.

It's a unique book, indescribably priceless to Laxarians because its contents are our country's ancient myths. Its name is – and I say *name* rather than *title* because we consider this book which contains such a huge body of stories as a person – its name is the Imalic, which means something like 'wet snow falling'. At the turn of every page of this book, stories unfold like doves' wings and fan out like the tails of peacocks. Characters are set like jewels in a golden crown and poems appear like flowers and like many-coloured butterflies. There is only one copy in existence – if it does still exist – and that dates from the tenth century.

Melog paused while he stared at the doctor's spectacles case, turning it over in his hands, and then as if satisfied, he replaced it in its own silhouette in the dust on a bookshelf (where it had lain for months) and he continued.

Until about a half a century ago, he said, the Imalic was kept securely in the National Library in Tiorry, the capital of Laxaria. Then the Sacrians came and conquered the country and banned the language. Our libraries were closed down. Most of the books and manuscripts in Laxarian were burned. But luckily, a great uncle of mine, a man called Benig, escaped with the Imalic and got to this country. He went back to Laxaria about thirty years ago – and didn't have the Imalic with him. The Sacrians knew he'd hidden the manuscript somewhere and in trying to get the truth out of him, they tortured him to death.

Melog became silent again, a sad, distant look in his intense blue eyes. He picked up a small wooden bowl and stroked it.

I inherited my great uncle's papers, Melog went on, and shortly before I fled from Laxaria and Sacria, I came across a note in one of his books. Well, to cut it short, I have reason to believe he came here, to this town, and that the Imalic is still hidden here. I've started searching for it already, of course, but I don't have much to go on. I'm stumbling round in the dark.

I'm ready to help, if I can, Dr Jones said.

I should be most grateful for any assistance, Melog said, and he went to lie down on the sofa once more.

PILGRIM: the name given to one who journeys to visit the relics
and graves of divers departed saints. The action itself is called
pilgrimage.

The Encyclopædia

ACCOMMODATION

MELOG DECIDED that he was going to look for accommodation and that he would find a place to live quite easily.
This would be a considerable achievement in a town where
there was no industry and no work, and which was not at the
centre of anything at all. The provision for lodgers was very
scarce, because in such an unremarkable place the call for
accommodation was very small.

Melog's first lodgings were quite depressing. They were a
narrow room with a narrow window, a narrow bed, a narrow
chair, and a narrow space to cook in. He had to share the
toilet and the bathroom with the other lodgers, who were
cross-grained and anti-social. Melog was thankful that he did
not have to encounter them often, except on his way to or
from the bathroom, or while he waited his turn in the dark,
narrow corridor.

On his visits to see Melog, Dr Jones was unlucky enough
to meet some of these neighbours. One of them was a short
man with the nose of a prizefighter, a square head, and bris-
tling unshaven chops, who, when you passed him in the
corridor, growled like one of Jaco Saunders' dogs. He was in
his early twenties and had a chain linking one nostril to his left
ear. Dr Jones thought of Gogol's story; perhaps his nose was
yearning for travel. This man, who was called Jonathan, had
so many silver rings studding the edges of his ears that Dr
Jones imagined it was possible to peel the rims away easily,
like tearing stamps off along the perforations. As well as the
piercings in his nose and ears he had rings through his lips

and eyebrows. Melog said he had them in other parts of his body too – though the doctor was not sure how he knew this – and that he had all but run out of places to punch holes in.

I did suggest to him, Melog said, that he ought put a hole for a ring through his brain, but he didn't seem to think much of that.

He had other puncture-marks too, without the rings, in his arms, and once again he had used up almost all the space. Jonathan invariably dressed in black to match the blackness around his eyes and his spiked hair. It seemed to Dr Jones that Melog and Jonathan should have made very good friends but for some reason that never happened.

I greet him every time I see him in the corridor, Melog said. I say good morning, good afternoon and ask how are you – I get nothing, just some animal sound in his throat.

Part of the problem, Dr Jones said, is that he's always playing music through his earphones; he can't hear anybody speaking to him.

No he can't. He spends all his time listening to loud music and watching television. But he doesn't want to talk. He's happy enough in his own little world as far as I can see.

There was another neighbour whom Melog and Dr Jones called the Saint. He was insuperably cheerful and all too serene. Or at least he smiled at all times, displaying a row of teeth which had rotted to black stumps. He invariably carried a Bible under his arm. God, he said, spoke to him every day. ('My boy,' said The Lord, 'it's time you changed those socks – they simply reek.')

Are you worried about the future of the earth? was his usual greeting. Do you see more famine and war and killing and violence in the world?

This was of course his artless ploy to start a discussion about religion and the Bible which would conclude in convincing you of his vision of peace on earth and the eternal life to come with the Saint and his like in heaven. It was all, he said, in the Bible.

39

Do you believe in the Bible? Melog asked him once.

Yes, every word, the Saint answered, flashing teeth as black as the boards of his Book.

Every word?

Every word. I believe that every word of His Word is the truth.

There's a unicorn in the Bible, isn't there, in the Book of Job. Do you believe in unicorns?

If it says it in the Bible, then it's true.

What about hell? Does hell await evil people in the next world?

Oh yes. It says so in the Bible. And to prove it, people who've had near death experiences have seen beautiful sights, some of them, and others have seen horrific, hellish things, truly.

People like that scare me, Dr Jones said.

He's harmless enough, Melog said. There's no bad in him at all.

I don't know about that, Dr Jones said. People like that will swallow any old rubbish if it's in the Bible, but if he went to the trouble of reading a novel he'd expect it all to be completely realistic.

You're being too critical, Melog said. In Laxaria we were always very forbearing with people suffering from religion; we'd let them do what they liked. But the Sacrians tried to prohibit it. Quite a stupid thing to do, like trying to ban alcoholism or kleptomania or insanity. Needless to say, religion is flourishing underground so to speak, in spite of all the stern laws ordering it not to.

Each day it was Melog's custom to visit Dr Jones or for Dr Jones to visit Melog. They would go to town and take tea in a café and stroll in the park, or go to the library, or they would spend hours talking in one another's home. To all appearances they had become great friends. In other words Dr Jones's life had changed. But he did not yet know to what extent.

THE EXHIBITION

ONE DAY Dr Jones and Melog went to the private view for an exhibition at the Gallery on the Hill. Melog scarcely bothered looking at the landscapes, the studies of still life (green apples in a yellow bowl), the lumpen sculptures, the indifferent ceramics, the overblown, stupid, garish embroideries. His chief pleasure was the cheap wine, the salted nuts, the crisps, and the little cubes of cheese mounted on toothpicks. Dr Jones felt as if he were leading a mule around the hall.

Someone came up to Dr Jones to talk to him. He was a selfimportant man, so important that it was he who had opened the exhibition. He had a square head and a square body (six feet by six feet), glass of wine in one hand, cigar in the other, the finger and thumb of that hand trying to hold onto one of those toothpicks with a baby pickled onion on it. Once more there was something flat and cartoonish about this individual.

Dr Jones, and how are you? he asked (a blend of nicotine and vinegar on his exhaled breath) but without waiting for an answer went on excitedly, his breath short, his face red as a copper kettle overheated on the flame to the point of exploding:

It's quite a skill to keep one's grip on all these things – you need to be an octopus – and while trying to look at the output of our country's most gifted artists at the same time – isn't it so difficult? And how is your work coming along? I myself am in the midst of writing a paper for the *Studia Panceltica* which is entitled 'Prolegomena to an Undiscovered

Manx Fragment of the Eighth Century'. I'm very deep among the footnotes at the moment, ninety-nine of them, so far. It is rather a long piece, you know, painstaking, wearisome toil, if truth be told. And who is this gentleman, if I may make so bold?

Oh, I beg your pardon, Dr Jones said. This is Melog; Melog, this is Professor Berwyn Boyle Hopkin… Melog?

But Melog was not listening. He was standing in the middle of the gallery, his jaw hanging open as if he were thunderstruck or petrified into white marble on the spot. In fact some of the guests mistook him for a piece of modern art, a super-realist sculpture or a wax effigy à la Madame Tussaud. Other guests thought he was giving a performance, and they stood and looked, marvelling at the artist's detail – the fine hairs of the eyelashes, the pitting of the skin, the precisely placed pimple on the jaw. But the general opinion was that the eyes were unconvincingly blue and the hair was unconvincingly white. Then he moved, making the onlookers jump.

Melog, what's the matter? Are you all right?

Well, I must apologise, but I really should mingle, the Professor said, shimmying away and melting into the crowd, leaving Dr Jones to take care of his exceptionally strange friend.

What's the matter? the doctor asked again. What would happen if Melog were in a faint or having a fit? The doctor would not be able to say 'Stand back, it's all right, I'm a doctor' like they did in films – although he had been tempted when he had seen people keel over in parties or collapse in the street. Then he saw that Melog was staring *at* something. The doctor looked in the direction of the blue gaze.

His first impression was of a conical arrangement of flowers, or a gigantic cake, a sort of upside-down knickerbocker glory, the three in one – the broad shape was of a pyramid, intricate with details like flowers, and as colourful and edible-looking as confectionery – pinks and red and purple and white and blue and mauve and violet. But this ceramic sculpture was composed of six monstrous, demonic creatures; creatures out of Bosch or Richard Dadd; facing one another and gripping one another and clambering over one another. What were they? Shellfish? Insects? Birds? Their long legs were insectlike, their bodies were lobsterlike, and their wings were somewhere between a bird's and a beetle's. But their heads were human – to Dr Jones's mind, that was what made the figures obscene. And these heads were bent back, the faces and necks straining out and upwards as the devils clawed at one another for the highest place in the heap like rats or like ants, and their jaws were stretched wide. Candles were stuck into the mouths, because the piece was in fact an extraordinarily intricate candelabrum.

That turns my stomach, Dr Jones said.

It's wonderful. It's a masterpiece, Melog said, starting to come to himself. It seemed it was this sculpture that had transfixed and taken possession of him.

It's fantastic and I've got to have it.

Dr Jones went closer to the table to look at the price-tag: 'Untitled by Gwynfryn Sween, price £4,599'. It was the doctor's turn to stare. When he told his friend the price, Melog's comment was,

I haven't got a penny in the world.

So you can't have it then, can you?

But I've got to have it. I can't live without it. Have you got any money? I could borrow it from you.

Me? I haven't got that sort of money. I haven't worked in years – I'm in debt as it is, Dr Jones said.

Therefore we have only one alternative.

What alternative's that, Melog?

We'll have to steal it.

Steal it?

Don't shout, Melog said.

We'll have to steal it will we? We?

Well you are going to help me, aren't you?

No I'm not. Not at all.

But you've got to, Melog said.

Got to? Why?

Because you're my friend. You're my only friend in the world.

Your best friend would advise you to chuck this mad idea straight away.

But I must have that sculpture. I can't live otherwise.

Why don't you get in touch with the artist, this Gwynfryn Sween, and ask him to make you a smaller one, something similar but a lot cheaper, and try to arrange to pay him in installments – over a very long time?

No. I must have that one. I don't want something similar but a lot cheaper, I want that one and stuff Gwynfryn Sween, whoever he is. That is a creation of my own invention and I'm going to get it tonight – and you're going to help me get it. Right?

Melog's blue eyes drilled into Dr Jones, and the doctor could refuse him nothing.

I'm going to the toilet, Melog said, and I'm going to hide there. Don't bother waiting till the end of the evening. You can go home.

And that was what Dr Jones did.

At half past one in the morning a knock came at the door and when the doctor opened it there stood Melog with the sculpture under his arm.

Melog. You haven't really stolen it?

Well isn't that rather obvious? I waited in the toilet till everybody went. Came out, grabbed the sculpture, climbed out through the toilet window. The alarm went off but nobody saw me and I got away all right. And now this wonderful new sculpture belongs to me and to Laxaria.

Melog placed the masterwork on the living-room table on top of Dr Jones's notes for the Encyclopaedia and stepped back to gaze at it, and he was radiant with pride.

GOING FOR A WALK

WHEN DR JONES walked through the town, although he had lived there all his life and though many of the local people and passers-by knew him – by sight if not personally – he was as it were an invisible man, like the invisible Ysgolan. Sometimes he would greet his acquaintances and he was invariably answered – 'Hello, Dr Jones', 'Dr Jones, how are you?', 'Good morning, Dr Jones', 'Good afternoon, Dr Jones', 'Good evening, Dr James' (that was someone who did not know him very well). But, unless he greeted them first, no one would say a word and more often than not, because he was shy, he greeted no one. Then it was possible for Dr Jones to walk through the town without uttering one word, and at those times he felt himself to be as grey as the pavements and the sky, as brown as the house sparrows, as contemptuously familiar as the statue in the centre of the square which was a memorial to nobody knew who because everybody had forgotten who he was. As unremarkable as the litter underfoot, monochrome as rain. Sometimes he asked himself why nobody looked at him, why he failed to attract anyone's attention at all. Was it perhaps because he was in a prematurely withered late middle-age, or because he was short? Or was it because of the myopia that meant he always wore spectacles? Or because he was slight, with narrow shoulders permanently hunched from his years of study? Or perhaps because his face was partly hidden by his beard? Or because he always wore dark clothes? But after ruminating on this matter for a long time he concluded that none of these considerations was relevant, ultimately, because no one ever looked at him for long enough to be aware of them. No one was aware of how old he looked, or his size, or whether he wore glasses or not, or what the colour of his hair was or whether he was losing or had lost his hair, whether he was bearded or moustachioed or cleanshaven. And certainly no one ever noticed his clothes – which was a pity, as Dr Jones spent hours each morning considering what to wear – a complete waste of time as almost all his clothes were grey or brown.

Dr Jones knew that he truly was invisible and that he could move through the busy streets like something less than a shadow, something less substantial than the wind, that he had vanished and was emptier than space. He tried to comfort himself with the thought that there was more flesh and blood on his notes for the Encyclopaedia than there was on his own body, but knew as he thought it that this was false consolation – no one would read his study, and even if someone somewhere did, he would not be able to sense their eyes on his words. Every morning he would ask himself what was the point of getting up and having breakfast and going out and sitting at his desk and writing. If he were to lie in his bed until he starved to death nobody would miss him; life would continue and it would be months, years, perhaps whole ages, before someone happened on his unspeaking bones.

But when Dr Jones walked through the streets with Melog, everything was different. Melog was as exceptionally visible as the doctor was invisible. People could not help but see and hear Melog. Everything about him attracted the eye and the ear. There was his whiteness to start with – his frost-white hair and his ivorysmooth skin, and next there were the glittering, deep, penetrating, thrilling, gimletting – no, no one adjective would do – eyes, eyes that nailed the eyes of others, lapis lazuli eyes, eyes more blue than anything in the world except for the blueness of the watery things of the sea. And then there was the exceptional tallness; he was literally head and shoulders above everyone. And the energy and magnetism of his youthfulness. And as well as all that his skeletal emaciation. A horrific, Belsenish thinness, the romantic thinness of a consumptive. Thinness that made you wince when you saw the young man and think, 'Don't move in case you hurt yourself. Don't move in case you break'.

When Dr Jones walked through the town with Melog people would stare at him openmouthed, unable to conceal their amazement. Some people would stumble over dogs and litter bins, others would walk into telegraph poles and yet others would collide with one another while both parties stared at Melog. He was the cause of a number of accidents. When Melog walked past cafés and restaurants people would freeze where they sat and gape. One time, a huge blubbery man was gobbling blancmange when he saw Melog; he sat unmoving, his laden spoon hanging in mid-air between the bowl and his waiting mouth.

And Melog seemed to be oblivious to his effect on the world around him.

To Melog, meeting people, talking with people, making friends, were all as natural as was swimming to a dolphin. Of that Dr Jones was just a little jealous. Melog *was* in the extreme. Dr Jones *was* not at all.

WASH-ING-INGS-ERY: to cleanse, to purify; purification; baptisms; a place in which to wash, a bath. Washing the body with or in water has been a common ritual in every country, and especially in oriental lands, since the earliest times; this conforms to the consideration that it is beneficial to health and to comfort.

The Encyclopædia

SHYNESS

MELOG WAS LYING in the bath (white with brown dents and scratches), soap bubbles foaming around him and hiding all of his gleaming white body except for his head, the bony shoulders and the extraordinarily long thin legs. Every now and then he would turn the taps on and off with his long, flexible toes – Dr Jones had never seen such long feet, like a hare's hind legs. A drop of cold water, a squirt of hot, steam rising from it and filling the bathroom, a layer of condensation speckling the mirrors and the window panes and the bare lightbulb. The hair on Melog's legs caught the light – fine, whitepure, platinum hairs. Dr Jones could not prevent himself from wondering if the hair in other, hidden places could be as white as that. (The myopic glimpse at the Town Hall had been fleeting.) But this was an immodest thought and immediately he pushed it to the back of his mind. In any case, the answer soon became clear. As you might have expected, bathing for Melog was a protracted process of luxuriation to savour and stretch to its limits. This was why he came to Dr Jones's house to bathe rather than using the bathroom at his lodgings – where the room was cold, the water merely tepid, and where the other tenants constantly knocked on the door and asked him to get a move on. That was why, too, he enjoyed Dr Jones's assistance – a cup of tea (the pink teapot, sugar in a glass bowl, milk in an Ewenny pottery jug), a Milky Bar, ice cream (vanilla and strawberry flavour – the colours of the young man's cheeks), magazines

– someone had to serve these things up before him.

Dr Jones, would you be so kind as to change this music? What about a spot of jazz; Joe Williams, Duke Ellington, or Count Basie, perhaps?

And then there were the essential, ubiquitous cigarettes, indispensable to the feast. But because the young man's long white fingers were wet it was necessary for the doctor, himself a confirmed nonsmoker, to take the tobacco from its tin, stretch the fine strands along the thin paper, then roll the paper, and, as he had seen Melog do dozens of times every day, draw his wet tongue along one edge of it. Having placed the freshly rolled cigarette between the young man's redwhite lips, the doctor would have to reach him the lighter (plastic, electricblue) and spark the flame. Whereupon Melog would dry the slender fingers of his right hand so that he could hold the cigarette himself.

Would you pass me that loofah, Dr Jones, Melog said, bending forward in the water so that his chin rested on his knees, and would you scrub my back with it? Not too hard if you don't mind.

Does everybody in your country wash like this? Dr Jones asked.

Yes we do. We always do this kind of thing. Bathhouses and the bathroom are very important places in our culture. It's a new thing, or a comparatively recent thing, as you know, to have a bathtub in the home. The private bath came into houses in about the year 1800, that is about the same time it started in the West, but instead of being a luxury confined to the homes of the wealthy in Sacria and Laxaria, the bathroom was welcomed from the start by everybody and they were in homes at every level of society from early in the nineteenth century, partly because we had plenty of water with our rainy climate.

What, rainier than it is in Wales, even?

It rains quite a lot and everyone carries an umbrella – or brolly, rainshield, parapluie, gamp – hard to choose a name, isn't it? Whatever you call them the people of Laxaria and Sacria carry them all the time. In fact if you have several names for them in Welsh, there's more than thirty words for umbrella in Laxarian, hundreds of terms connected with the various kinds of rainshield and more idioms than there are grains of sand, or maybe I should say raindrops. The term *niwtaag*, for instance, means something like 'thesecondbestumbrellawhichIcarrywithmeinordertogofora strollintheparkonSundayeveningsinthespringincaseoflight showerssimilartotheshowerinthebathroomthatisshowers ofunnaturalappearance'. Thus we have a word for umbrella that contains a reference to washing too. And there you have it, a brief history of ablutionary habits in Laxaria and Sacria and something about the language – and I'm not going to say any more; I don't like talking about my father-land. Could you reach me those towels, please, Dr Jones? I'm ready to get out now. I hope they're dry and warm.

I've dried them carefully.

Thank you. You can turn your back now.

He handed Melog the towels and modestly turned his back. Dr Jones could hear his friend rising from the waters, which slithered and rilled from his sleeksmooth flesh with sounds of musical, oceanic wetness. He could hear the flannel material energetically buffing his petalsoft skin to dryness. He caught glimpses of him in the cracked mirror of the medicine cabinet above the sink – Melog had forgotten about that – or perhaps he was conscious of it too, because it was impossible to see anything clearly in the misted glass. And then a layer of steam formed on Dr Jones's glasses too. Melog's nudity and privacy were safe.

Why, he wondered, had a brazen young man, who a little while ago was shameless enough to walk the streets dressed in nothing but a slippery blanket, why had he suddenly become so shy? And yet he remained sufficiently extrovert to ask – in fact to demand – Dr Jones's assistance while he bathed. He was a strange mixture of shy innocence and fearless confidence.

MOROCCO

ON A FOGGY MORNING, Dr Jones went to call on Melog. He went straight to his lodgings where Melog would be waiting for him, as usual. But when he knocked on the door of his room (a stipplework of drawing pin holes and the rusted heads of drawing pins), there was no answer. There was nothing out of the ordinary in this, as the old doctor always had to knock the door until the boy got out of bed. But though he knocked and knocked that morning, no answer came. The doctor was about to give up and go to town on his own, hoping he would come across Melog there, when the Saint appeared and gave him a jet-toothed smile.

Good morning, Dr Jones, and blessings upon you, the Saint said. You won't get any answer this morning, of course.

What do you mean 'of course'?

Well, he said, hiding his mouth behind the dirty fingernails of one hand, Melog's gone away. Didn't you know? He went last night.

Where to? Back to Laxaria? Dr Jones asked, holding his head to one side, leaning to the other like a parrot.

Laxaria? Where's Laxaria? No, Melog's gone to Morocco.

Morocco! The doctor's pallid, scanty eyebrows disappeared into the fold across his forehead.

That's right. There's clearly nothing wrong with your hearing.

But why Morocco?

Now how would you expect me to know that? the Saint stood close to the doctor, smiling a noisome smile. He was your friend, wasn't he?

51

But he didn't say anything. Not one word, and I was talking with him just last night.

Oh, he did leave you a message, the Saint said with the complacency of one who is in communion with God.

Why didn't you say? If you don't mind my asking, where is it? The doctor asked impatiently but with just enough self-control to stop himself from stamping his foot.

There's no need for you to be nasty, is there? the Saint said. 'But let patience have her perfect…' and so forth. Now then, where did I put that envelope? Don't tell me I've gone and lost it. Is it in this pocket? No. What about this one then? No, not there either. Well what about this pocket then?

Have you got this message or not? This time he lost control and stamped.

My goodness my goodness, Dr Jones. I am looking for it. Why so hasty, anyway? Your friend left hours ago, and you don't have a job to go to, do you? You're just the same as everyone else here, even if you are a 'doctor'. No work. Nothing waits for you, does it? Except for eternity.

Quite true, Dr Jones said, but in the meantime I would like to have that message Melog left for me, please.

Ah, here's the envelope, hiding in my cardigan pocket all the time. Cheerio, Dr Jones. I shall remember you in my prayers.

Dr Jones tore open the envelope with his name on it and read the typed words:

> Dear Dr Jones,
> Going to Morocco for a bit.
> Yours truly,
> Melog

Black with anger, Dr Jones left the house where, until a few hours ago, Melog had lodged.

Hadn't he devoted hours on end to the young man? Wasted his time on him instead of working on the Encyclopaedia?

And this was the treatment he got. This was his thank you. He had an urge to rush straight to the police and tell them about the sculpture Melog had stolen from the exhibition.

But Melog was gone and the doctor did not expect to see him ever again. He was a free spirit who travelled round the world in that way, tricking innocents like the doctor into taking pity on him, taking advantage of the kindness of fools and anyone stupid enough to believe him. Well, all that was left was to try to forget about him.

But the doctor could not forget. His house was empty and even his notes for the Encyclopaedia depressed him. It seemed to Dr Jones that he was as trapped as Melog was free. He felt himself, as it were, circling inside the little town and circling inside the lonely rooms of his house like a moth in a lampshade. Dr Jones's ability to change his world was no greater than the influence of a goldfish on its bowl. The hours dragged, though they were the same length they had always been; which is to say there were still sixty minutes in each of them and sixty seconds in every minute, and therefore three thousand six hundred seconds in every hour, and thus thousands upon thousands of seconds in every day, though there were still only twenty-four hours. He spent some of these hours trying to sleep but his mind could not slacken its grip on consciousness and drop into the delicious nothing that prepares us for death. And when he did achieve the wished-for state, the doctor had difficulty every morning shaking free of it, and he could not throw off the warm comfort of his bed without arguing with himself, his eyes shut: 'Time to get up. *What for?* You've got to get up. *Why?* There's a new day in front of you. *So what?*'

But he would get up and make himself go to the desk and look at the Encyclopaedia. To start with he would look for a subject, considering and rejecting as he went along – Academies, Atheism, Ark, Arthur, King Arthur. But after thinking about Arthur he turned to Myth-s, Mythology, Mythography, and decided on that. But the index and the text of the volume did not match, as far as Dr Jones could see at the time – which happened quite frequently in his experience working on the Encyclopaedia, which was a labyrinth of mysteries and inconsistencies. In the end for the sake of convenience, he chose this entry:

ARTISTIC, ART-S: skillful, decorative, craft, decorativeness, mystery [Dr Jones was startled to see that word in the definition]; knowledge.

'Let art hide its purposes.'

Prov.
'The expert let him conceal his design.'

'The three pillars of the arts,
Marcwlf and Gadw, the mighty senses,
And Solomon the great observer.'
Ll.P. Moch, to D. ab Owain.

'Unhappy is he who would behold many arts, and manners, and learn of them nothing.'
Prov.

[Dr Jones liked these unexpected quotations at the head of the entry]) Art has been described by Bacon as the appropriate representation of things in nature by the mind and experience of man, such that it answers the manifold requirements of mankind. In this sense, art stands in contradistinction with *nature*. [He read over that sentence again.] In this sense, art stands in contradistinction with *nature*. By art is understood a system which serves to expedite the completion of some acts; such as building, printing, &c.: and in this sense it stands in contradistinction with *science*, or a system of theoretical principles. The arts are subdiv [he was beginning to grow tired of copying] subdivided into handicrafts and the fine arts.

He was sick of the ancient book, with its foxed pages and its grey smell. He went for a lie down on the sofa. In a dream, Dr Jones saw the pages of the Encyclopaedia unhitching themselves from their black binding and flapping away from him like gulls winging towards an horizon of words, paragraph clouds.

Strange things were happening to Dr Jones. To begin with – and who is to say that this was not the starting point? – he had read an article – he could not remember what it was about – by Borges, in which he mentions Zeno of Elea, and that was the first time Dr Jones had ever heard of Zeno's paradox. The same day, in the afternoon, he read an article by R.S. Thomas – again he could not remember exactly what article – in which he refers to Zeno, and that was the second time in his life that Dr Jones had heard about him; that night – still on the same day – Dr Jones was listening to (or hearing without listening to) the radio when the speaker, whatever the programme was, mentioned Zeno. Three times in the space of twenty-four hours. It seemed to the doctor that this strange coincidence was a sign of some sort.

The same week, though not the same day, Dr Jones went into the garden to clear leaves from the path (it was autumn) in case he should slip (not that he went into the garden often, but just in case) when, to his great surprise, he found a tortoise under a heap of withered leaves. He inquired among his neighbours and put an advertisement on a card in the newsagent's window, 'Tortoise found', but failed in his attempt to trace the owner of the creature. So he kept the tortoise and called him Zeno (what else?) and fed him on only lettuce leaves and a little meat on the advice of the vet (who told him that the animal was worth about three hundred pounds because there had been a ban on importing them into this country for several years which had made them exceptionally rare and valuable).

Quite soon after he had discovered Zeno (both the philosopher with his paradox and the tortoise) Dr Jones remembered that some other Greek philosopher or dramatist – he could not remember which – was killed by a tortoise which fell on his head out of the sky. Because Zeno (the tortoise) had appeared as it were out of nowhere, perhaps he too had dropped from above, Dr Jones reasoned, and therefore when he went out into the garden, Dr Jones would take great care to look up every now and then in case there was another tortoise in the clouds. On one of these occasions Dr Jones saw a light aircraft trailing smoke which spelt out the word 'congratulations'. The aeroplane flew away, leaving the wordcloud as the only blotch on the immaculate blue. The smokescript took a little time to swell, the letters to lose their shape, to blur into a fog, then a dark smudge, then vanish leaving only blue. But Dr Jones knew that the blueness of the sky was not truly there, that the colour was an illusion, a deceiving of the eye. Even so, the fakeblueness was extraordinarily pleasing and flawless now, after the disappearance of the message – to whom? Congratulations on what?

Tired of gazing at the firmament – *firmament*, one of his favourite words, a very encyclopaedish word – Dr Jones went back to the house, rather dazzled, probably, by the mockblueness, and he trod with his full weight on Zeno who had crawled slowly and quietly off the lawn and onto the path. He was killed on the spot.

There was nothing for it but for the doctor to dig a little oblong grave and lay his old friend to rest in earth. While he was digging the hole for the old shoebox that was to be Zeno's coffin, Dr Jones came across something made of metal. He dug a little deeper into the small stones and weeds and worms and whitened roots and pulled out a tin box about six inches long by five wide and three or four inches deep. On the tin there were pictures of birds: blue tits, great tits, chaffinches and bullfinches. He straightened his back and tried to lift the lid (a goldfinch with its wings outstretched) but it was rusted solid. He would have to take it indoors and use some tool or other to prise the top loose.

Before he did this Dr Jones dropped Zeno's coffin into the hole and spread earth over it. He did not pray; there was no need to turn the occasion into a big production; a tortoise is a tortoise after all.

On his way to the house Dr Jones shook the tin. Something rattled. Just stones perhaps, he thought, preparing himself for disappointment. But then again the contents could be valuable – gold or silver or some other treasure.

In his kitchen, Dr Jones used a variety of instruments in his attempts to lever the box open. Knives, pennies, forks, spoons, keys, a spanner. At last he succeeded using the little screwdriver with the red handle.

Inside the tin (which had probably originally contained biscuits or chocolates) there lay a pretty model of an angel; he was dressed in a silver gown, had yellow hair, a halo round his head, the hands pressed together in a gesture of prayer, red lips and pink cheeks, and wings – the prettiest part of the angel – made of pale blue feathers, measuring exactly five inches from one side of the tin to the other.

Who had buried the angel and why? Some child – one of the children of the former owners of Dr Jones's house perhaps. But why bury him?

In bed that night Dr Jones dreamt about an angel. The angel's face was not clear. In fact you could not make out the face at all, only the golden body, the rows of hard muscles across the stomach, the arm muscles and the chest muscles, and the wings like a swan's wings stretching from one wall to the other of Dr Jones's cramped bedroom. But when he opened his eyes there was no angel there, only his bedroom, narrow and empty.

But that day, straight after the dream, when he was walking into town to do some shopping, his string bag dangling from his right arm, he saw a gang of labourers working on the road, and because the autumnal sun was still warm they had stripped to the waist. Dr Jones saw the body he had seen in his dream, the rows of muscles across the stomach, the swell of the arms and the breasts. This was the body of the angel, there could be no doubt about it, the same one, without the wings of course. Or a body like it. A similar body. Not the same body at all.

After that he forgot his errands and did not go to the shops.

He went back to his room and lay in a pit of silence. It was not late but Dr Jones waited on his bed until it got dark. That night he had another dream. This time he saw himself in a tree standing in the garden, his arms in the air forming branches. He had no feet; his feet were roots pushed into the earth. Then at the base of his trunk an ivy leaf appeared, then another and another. The ivy spread upwards over his body, or the tree trunk, and over his face (he did still have a face) until the whole tree was hidden, until it was impossible to tell the difference between the leaves of the tree and the leaves of ivy.

Dr Jones had to get up the following morning because it was his day for signing on. He dragged himself out of bed, washed and dressed, took the tablets which were good for his health, and was about to go out through the door, and when he opened it, there standing tall and thin and white and staring at him with sapphire eyes was Melog.

Good morning, Dr Jones. Are you going into town? I'll come along with you. I've got to find new lodgings now I've come back.

How was Morocco? Dr Jones asked, trying to hide his shock and sound lighthearted.

Well, Dr Jones, as you can tell, I didn't manage to get a tan.

THE CAR

AFTER MELOG CAME BACK from Morocco – that is if he had truly ever been there – the doctor had room to doubt the story, and in fact he did not even feel certain that this Melog was the same person – he went to see Dr Jones and the two went for a walk in the town. They went to Jabez Ifans's potato tavern.

Everybody in this town eats chips, Melog observed, lifting a particularly long one from his plate using his index finger and his elongated thumb and pushing it into his mouth.

True. Everybody in south Wales eats chips all the time and smokes and worries about not having a job and not being able to make ends meet because they've been out of work for years and votes for a Labour government every time and gets a Tory government every time and that's why they have heart attacks before they get to fifty. That is if they don't get cancer first. This area has the highest rate of heart disease in the world.

Imagine all that fat pouring into our veins, Melog said, eating another golden chip, furring up on the vein walls until the blood can't squeeze through them. Ych-a-fi. We eat chips and swallow the fat at the same time, then we swallow down some tea and the fat turns to solid lumps inside our bodies. Ych-a-fi.

The young man swallowed some of the tea, to which he had added six spoons of sugar, in spite of Dr Jones's comment that sugar was meant to sweeten tea rather than thicken it.

Don't take it too seriously, Dr Jones said. Anyway, fat's not a problem for you. You could do with a bit of meat on your bones. You've got quite starved since you went away, and you were thin in the first place. There's a touch of the valley of the shadow of death about you nowadays.

The valley of the shadow of death, Melog said, a furrow appearing between his silver eyebrows. What a cheerless expression. It sends a shiver down my spine.

It's a Biblical expression, Dr Jones said, as he carefully cut his food with his knife and fork like a surgeon working on someone's heart.

Oh well then, no wonder it do give me the willies, Melog said. He was keen to acquire a little of the local dialect.

Dr Jones watched the young man as he flooded the chips with a layer of tomato sauce so that his plate looked like a road accident.

Once, Melog said, two friends of mine were eating in the same place in Laxaria, but not together: one was with one group of people and the other with another group of people. They were both friends of mine but not friends to one another, if you understand. Didn't even know one another. That's the story as I heard it.

Anyway. The two of them were eating in the same restaurant, the one, Steffan, celebrating passing some exam or other with his party, and the other, Iago, celebrating with his friends because one of them had a fortieth birthday. Towards the end of the evening, Steffan realised that he couldn't finish the chicken on his plate, even though he was enjoying it; the meat was tender, the sauce was delicious. It broke his heart to leave it. So one of his friends suggested that he should ask the waiter to put the food in a bag so he could take it with him. When the waiter came he was an old man with poor eyesight and Steffan asked him if he could have what was left of the chicken wrapped up and the waiter went off with the plate and the bit of meat on it. Well, the meal went on, dessert, coffee, cheese and biscuits, fruit, a smoke, chocolates, mints, the bill. And off Steffan went with his friends out of the restaurant and forgot all about the chicken. Then when Iago and his friends were just about to leave, the old waiter came up to one of them, Charles, the one whose birthday it was, and presented him with a package, a small box with the name of the restaurant on it in gold letters and a silver ribbon done up in an arty bow, and the waiter said, 'With the compliments of the chef, sir'. Well, Charles was convinced that he'd got a cake or some special chocolate because the restaurant staff had noticed that he was celebrating his birthday. He didn't open the parcel till he got home, and of course he wasn't expecting to see a lump of cold meat with a bone sticking out of it and it gave him a terrible shock and he had a heart attack and dropped dead that night, the night of his fortieth birthday, because of the confused waiter's mistake. Iago was convinced that Charles thought that somebody had put something disgusting in the bag, a body part or something, an animal maybe, and that this was a signal that somebody was going to come and kill him.

That's a terrible story, Dr Jones said. He pushed his plate away, the food unfinished.

After Melog had eaten his chips the two friends went out into the street. Melog's appearance caused a slight stir, as usual. They had not walked far when he stopped next to a gleaming, blue, brand new car. Then he opened the passenger door.

Would you like to go for a spin? He asked.

I didn't know you had a car.

Melog went round to the driver's door, got in, and sat at the steering wheel.

Have you fastened your seatbelt, Dr Jones?

Yes, thanks.

The car lurched forward and Melog almost ran over some people walking in the street.

Melog. You see the pavement?

What about it?

Well you aren't supposed to drive on it.

I'll be all right when I get out of the town centre. All these cars and pedestrians make me nervous. Where would you like to go? The north? South? Somewhere in England?

I don't mind. I'll be happy to get out of this town; it's like a goldfish bowl. You go round and round in the same circle seeing the same places and faces. The home patch isn't enough.

Well, Melog said, flaying some gears, I'm going to go north for a start.

The car continued to lurch and bounce, and when they came to a corner Melog would throw the car into it.

You're going to go through the red light! Watch the people on the crossing, Melog!

If you're going to criticise everything I do you may as well get out now.

Sorry. I won't say another word.

But it was not easy for Dr Jones to keep this promise, so wild was Melog's driving. He hurtled through the streets at incredible speeds and in no time the car was in open coun- tryside screaming along narrow mountain roads – the faces of steep slopes on the driver's side and the brinks of abysmal cliffs on the other side, the passenger's side – Dr Jones's side.

What about putting the CD on?

Dr Jones pressed a little black button like a round sweet and the car flooded with lovely music. Unfortunately, because he was worried that he might soon be dead, Dr Jones could not relax into the luxurious leather seat or gaze at the landscape or listen to the entrancing songs. Trying to settle his nerves, he said –

I didn't know that you like the songs of Schumann.

Is that what this stuff is? Melog said.

Well it's your compact disc.

It isn't actually, Melog said, looking in the rear-view mirror to preen his hair.

What do you mean? Dr Jones said. He felt the sweat on his forehead grow cold.

I haven't heard this music before, Melog said, overtaking a lorry at terrifying speed.

So what's the disc doing in your car? Dr Jones asked. He sneaked a look at the speedometer and saw the needle touching one hundred and ten miles an hour.

It's not my car, Melog said.

Melog. Whose car is it?

I don't know.

What? You've stolen this car?

I don't look on it as theft, Melog said, slowing to 90 miles an hour to take a corner, I look on it as a loan. (The wheels went over a hedgehog.) All property is theft, as they say.

In his extreme terror Dr Jones gripped the soft deep sides of his seat with all his strength.

Pity I didn't pick an automatic though, isn't it? Melog said. Bet it's a lot easier than having to change gears.

When did you pass your test?

Oh, I haven't taken the test.

Melog, Dr Jones said, his face as white as Melog's hair, how many driving lessons have you had?

One. In Morocco. That's where I learnt the simple way to open car doors too. Easy isn't it? Opening doors I mean, not driving. You've probably noticed I still find driving a bit tricky. But I'm improving all the time aren't I? It's a matter of common sense, really.

The car flew over a bump in the road, leaving Dr Jones's stomach some way behind, hanging in the air about three feet above the road in another county.

Melog! Stop! Please!

Don't be such a chicken, Dr Jones.

I don't want to die, Melog.

Think of death not so much as an end but a change.

I'm not ready to change.

But don't you think this is fun? I like speed. Look, I've got her up to a hundred and twenty miles per hour. Now, you can't see with your hands over your eyes, Dr Jones.

Thank you for that information, Melog. What if we have an accident? What if the police are after us?

We aren't going to have an accident. I've got my lucky pebble in my pocket. It looks after me on all journeys. Anyway that's what the woman in the market told me when she sold it to me. It must be true because I paid a pound for it.

Melog, I beg you, stop the car. Stop the car. Where are we going?

That's a stupid question, Melog said, killing a second sheep. If I stopped the car we wouldn't be going anywhere, would we? In any case, I'm not really exactly sure how to stop. That's the snag.

What'll we do?

Keep going till we run out of petrol.

Don't pull out – there's cars on the other side!

Lucky this car's so powerful, ey? Accelerating out of trouble like that. There was no need for him to do all that light-flashing. I was far too fast to have hit him.

Although he was not religious, Dr Jones put his face in his hands and prayed for deliverance.

Open your eyes, Dr Jones. Here we are. Mid Wales.

But we've only just left the south.

Yeah, I have been hammering it a bit, remember, Melog said.

At that moment Dr Jones heard a screeching of brakes and smelt burning rubber and saw smoke around the car.

You're stopping! At last! Oh, thank you, Melog, thank you.

Yes. I've stopped to give these two fellers a lift.

Melog stretched over to the back of the car and opened the door for the hitchhikers. While he was welcoming the boys Dr Jones tried to open his own door so that he could escape, but his legs and hands were rather weak as a consequence of shock, and then it was too late; Melog had shut all the doors using central locking, and they were away again lurching at first like a jumping frog, and then hurtling like a rocket.

Now, then, what are your names? Melog asked.

Buzz, one boy said. He wore a leather jacket decorated with skulls and had black hair and long straggling whiskers.

Zog, the other one said. He had red hair, shaved off at the back and sides with a pony tail at the crown, an orange beard, and on his nose and forehead were pink and mauve pimples.

Dr Jones observed that the hitchhikers were rather smelly.

Where are you off to? Melog asked.

Who cares, aye?

Dr Jones felt uncomfortable with this terse answer. He had no faith in the surly boys, any more than he had in Melog's driving.

Well that suits us perfectly, doesn't it, Dr Jones? Because we don't know for sure where we're going either.

Silence from the back. Silence with menaces. Dr Jones had heard all sorts of stories about picking up hitchhikers. Although drivers frequently attacked passengers, there were plenty of stories of passengers threatening drivers and stealing all their money and leaving them helpless in a pool of blood in a ditch by the side of the road. Dr Jones felt unwell. In an attempt to soothe his nervousness concerning the strangers in the back seat, the apparently bottomless declivity at his side, and Melog's rather uncertain skills at the wheel, the doctor attempted to strike up a conversation.

There's a rather amusing short essay by R.T. Jenkins in which he searches for a place called Llandeloy. Every time he sees a signpost for the place, an odd thing happens. To start with it says Llandeloy 1 mile, then the next sign says Llandeloy 2 miles, then 4 miles, then the next one says 3, but then the next one goes back to 4 miles. And he never gets to Llandeloy.

Dr Jones fell silent as it was obvious that no one was listening or taking any interest in his story. Anyway, he was starting to feel very ill.

I don't feel well, he said.

Don't throw up now – it's too awkward to stop here.

It was then that Dr Jones felt something cold and hard and sharp against his throat and a hand grabbing his thinning back hair. And judging by the way the car was zig-zagging across the road, something similar was happening to Melog at the same time. Dr Jones was unable to turn his head to see his ex-friend, the driver.

Now, one of the voices said from the back, Zog or Buzz, Dr Jones could not tell them apart by the sound. Now you're going to give us your money, aye?

Are we? Melog asked. There was no quavering or any sign of fear in his voice.

Not the wisest time for a joke, Dr Jones thought. Two villains threatening to kill us and he tries to be funny.

Yes, aye? one of the voices said.

Well, Melog said, how can we do that? Dr Jones can't move because you're holding his head and I can't move for the same reason and also I'm trying to drive the car. Apart from which, we haven't got any money, have we, Dr Jones?

Dr Jones did not answer. He hated Melog. He hated cars. He was praying again, promising to be good for the rest of his life, to go to chapel three times a day every day, to do good work for the elderly, to give money for starving children, if only he could get out of this with his skin intact.

Don't joke with us. Big flash car like this and you say you haven't got any dosh, aye? Pull the other one.

Yeah, come on, aye? Get the cash out now or we'll kill the two of you and get it anyway.

Oh, I wouldn't do that, Melog said, with the composure of the speaking clock. If you harm Dr Jones I'll drive over the edge, and if you harm me, I'm bound to drive over the edge. Anyway, I'm bound to drive over the edge sooner or later because I stole this car and I don't know how to drive, as you can see.

You're lying, aye.

Yeah, aye.

But as if to prove his point, Melog swerved heartstoppingly close to the edge of the drop, exactly as if he could control it. He went terrifyingly fast after that, a hundred and ten, a hundred and twenty miles an hour.

The boys relaxed their grip with a sudden shout as the car screeched to a stop with a front wheel teetering over the rocks.

Out! Melog said. The boys leapt out and ran for it, even though they were in the middle of nowhere.

Dr Jones said nothing. He was unconscious.

East, west, home's best, Melog said.

DREAM: a vision during sleep; those images which are composed
in the mind when the senses are locked in slumber; a piece of
vanity or baseness, a counterfeit, a baseless invention. It is likely
that there are few things which have engendered greater differences
of opinion than the philosophy of dreams.

The Encyclopædia

A DREAM

WHEN MELOG SAID that he wished to have his picture
taken in the photograph booth at the back of the post office
in town, Dr Jones went along to keep him company.

Why do you want a picture? You aren't going away are
you? A passport photo?

No. I want a record of how I feel and how I look at the
moment.

He combed his hair and looked at his reflection in the
mirror on the side of the kiosk. Dr Jones looked at the two
Melogs staring into one another's large blue eyes; four blue
eyes, two straight noses, two sleek foreheads.

I don't know how these boxes work, Melog said. There's
nothing like them in Laxaria or in Sacria either.

He disappeared into the cabin, drawing the curtain that
hid only the upper part of the opening. Dr Jones could see
Melog's feet and legs and his backside sitting on the seat, and
then saw his right hand spinning the screw-stool to adjust the
height. Melog sat quietly for a little while and then Dr Jones
heard the coins dropping into the photograph machine. A
moment later there was a flash and he heard the boy exclaim-
ing with surprise; another flash, and another.

You can come out now, Melog, Dr Jones said.

The young man looked startled, half dazzled by the
quickfire lights.

Where are the pictures?

We have to wait for five minutes and then they come out of that slot. We can go for a stroll and come back and collect them.

We'd better wait, Melog said. I don't want some hairy fist swiping them.

It's boring waiting here, Dr Jones said, leaning his left shoulder against the kiosk.

Yes. Nothing to do. Nothing to see here except for people collecting their giros.

Last night, Dr Jones said, I had a dream, a very literary dream. In my sleep, I saw the Argentinian writer, Jorge Luis Borges, in a maze, a labyrinth made of evergreen hedges, like the ones that were common in the gardens of big houses at one time. Dense, high hedges, skilfully trimmed, like green walls, almost. Well, the blind old man was walking slowly between these neat hedges, tapping his white stick on the gravel of the geometrical paths. When he came towards one of the corners he would touch the hedge in front with his stick before he bumped into it, and sometimes he would have some difficulty, like a wild bird that flies into a house, or a bluebottle or a bee trapped in a window, but on the whole he managed to make his way around the maze quite easily. Of course, he had no idea how often he came along the same path or how often he turned the same corner. He doesn't know how far he's travelled from the start either, or how far he's got to go to the end and the way out. In spite of this he remains patient and persistent, in his element trying to solve the puzzle. But suddenly and quite unexpectedly, he hears a tiger roaring for blood, not far off – somewhere in the maze, in fact. But Borges thinks: I am certain that this is merely one of my imaginary tigers. And he carries on walking. Then he hears the tiger roaring again, and this time, Borges knows that the animal has heard his white stick tapping on the gravel, and he's traced his scent on the breeze, and he's looking for him. I will fear not, says Borges to himself, again. If I remember Zeno's theory, the tiger can never catch me.

The distance between him and me will be halved, and then halved again and then halved again ad infinitum, and the tiger will never reach me. But then the old writer thinks: if Zeno's theory is true for the tiger, then it is true for me too, and I will never reach the door out of the maze, because the distance between me and the way out will be halved ad infinitum, and I will spend eternity wandering here in my darkness among the hedge walls. As he thought this, the tiger leapt over the hedge and ate the world-famous author, leaving nothing behind except for his white stick. What do you think of that strange dream, Melog?

There's pretty often no sense at all to dreams, there's no head or tail to them, is there? They aren't worth remembering, are they?

I usually don't remember my dreams at all, Dr Jones said.

Then the pictures spewed out of the slot in the photo booth. Melog could hardly wait for them to dry before looking at them. But he was very disappointed when he saw them.

What's the matter? Dr Jones asked.

That's not me. There's been a mistake. These pictures are of somebody else.

No, Dr Jones said, that's you.

No, Melog said. Either somebody has stolen my pictures or somebody else is in the box shoving fake pictures out.

But there's your hair, your eyes, your nose, Melog. It's not a particularly good likeness, but that's how it is with these booths.

But he's got red eyes, Melog said, pointing at the second picture on the strip.

The flash causes that effect sometimes, Dr Jones said.

But look at the expression on him, Melog said, still referring to the pictures as though they were of somebody else.

You weren't ready for the first picture, Dr Jones said, weren't ready for the flash, and after that you moved, then looked round, and obviously in the last you've been startled.

No. That's not me in these ugly pictures. They're similar, but different. He's too bony for one thing, like a skeleton, those sunken cheeks, the way he's scowling. And the hair. Ych-a-fi. I combed my hair before I went in, didn't I? You saw me, Dr Jones. There's a counterfeit Melog about the place. Mimicking me, taking me off, getting there before me, like that man Goliadkin in the Dostoyevsky novel.

I'm afraid that that is you in these pictures, Melog. But the best thing to do is to keep them in a drawer and forget about them and look at them again in ten years' time. Pictures improve with age, Dr Jones said, except for the one of Dorian Gray.

INVENTION… The word can also sometimes denote fakery and deception…

The Encyclopædia

THE BODY

ONE MORNING, Dr Jones woke up betimes, got up, and looked at the birds feeding on the nuts which he had hung from the post of the clothesline: chaffinches, house sparrows, great tits, blue tits, coal tits. Afterwards he soaked in a hot leisurely bath – he was spending a great deal of time in the bath recently, and never rushed. He massaged coconut oil into his thinning hair, and afterwards shaved himself closely and carefully. Then breakfast: orange juice, All Bran with prunes and banana, toast, marmalade, and tea. Then he dressed: white pants, a white vest, red socks, grey trousers, an orange shirt, a variegated tie, a yellow cardigan. After this he made a pot of tea and took it with a cup and saucer – all of this carried upon a tray – into his cell and sat at his desk by ten o'clock and was ready to begin work on the Encyclopaedia when the phone rang.

Hello?

Dr Jones?

Speaking.

It's Melog here.

Dr Jones was rather surprised as he had not heard from Melog for a while. The last time he had seen him, Melog was dancing on a little board on the pavement in the town, having taken tap dancing lessons at an evening class in the College of Further Education (and having abandoned them after two lessons because he believed he was a better dancer than the teacher even without lessons). He was giving his all to this dance and grinning like a cat throughout, but he did not collect much money. People stood and watched, but in a

Valleys town those willing to throw money away are rare. When he saw Dr Jones throw fifty pence into his tin on the pavement, he stopped for a cigarette. He still had a look of the valley of the shadow of death about him and he was thin and white as a strand of toothpaste.

Melog, how are you, where have you been? Dr Jones asked down the phone, perhaps a little too eagerly.

I haven't been anywhere, but I'm all right. Well, I'm not all right at all.

What's the matter? Dr Jones asked, expecting to hear that he was in hospital having had surgery to remove at least three quarters of his intestines.

I saw a terrible thing last night. But I can't speak on the phone, in case. Can you come and see me?

Yes. Where are you?

Where I live of course.

So where are you living now?

Oh sorry, you don't know do you?

Melog gave him his new address and in less than an hour Dr Jones was standing in another of his friend's appalling rooms. To the doctor, these places where Melog lived had no identity – no numbers, no location, no names on the houses or streets, even. Once again he was living on the top floor, in an attic this time, which meant scaling a Snowdonia of stair-cases. It was impossible to stand upright in the room as it was set into the low triangular shape of the roof. Even in the centre, Dr Jones's head touched the ceiling, and he was much shorter than Melog, who had to crawl on all fours whenever he wanted to move around.

As was his custom, Melog did his best to decorate the walls with labyrinthine patterns in the traditional manner of Laxaria. The doctor could barely see the designs because the air was thick with the blue smoke of cigarettes. In the corner stood the sculpture Melog had stolen from the exhibition.

Why don't you open the window? Dr Jones said, staring at the glass like a prisoner.

In case the cats climb out and fall and kill themselves. It's okay for me to do that, but I wouldn't like to see the cats having a tragic accident.

Cats plural? How many cats exactly? The doctor asked, shaking his head and turning down the corners of his mouth.

Three. Not counting the kittens of course; I've got to find good homes for them. Don't want a cat, do you?

No thanks.

Will you sign this, by the way, while I make a cup of tea – sorry, coffee, there's no tea. And there's no milk or sugar either, sorry.

What is it?

The visitors' book.

Dr Jones opened the book, which had a floral cover with four black cats; Melog had decorated its edges with a Laxarian labyrinth pattern. There were no names inside.

Oh, the doctor said. I'm the first.

People have been here, Melog said, rolling a cigarette while he waited for the kettle to boil, but I forget to give them the book till they've gone and then I remember and then of course it's too late. Apart from that, I don't get many visitors. Not proper visitors, not friends and all that, just social security people, the electricity man, neighbours complaining about the cats.

Dr Jones wrote his name in the book and added a quotation to enliven the contribution. He considered some of the proverbs he had come across in the Encyclopaedia. Two about whiteness came into his mind: 'White all that's new, grey all that's old' and 'To the mother crow her chicks are white'. But neither of these was appropriate for Melog. In any case, he was concerned that referring to his hair and skin like that could be misinterpreted and might offend the young man. So in the end he wrote: 'Both work and play pass time away'.

Melog took the book from him to see what the doctor had written.

That's an old Laxarian saying; how on earth did you know it? Melog said, his hand hovering over the words like a white butterfly over a flower.

I didn't know that it was originally Laxarian. I heard it on the radio, or read it in an old magazine in a waiting room – the doctor's or the dentist's.

Well, that proves that culture seeps from anywhere to everywhere doesn't it? Even from Laxaria and Sacria.

You sounded as though you were in quite a state on the phone. What's happened?

The doctor was beginning to lose patience and wanted to get to the point.

Well, Melog said in a conspiratorial voice, pouring the coffee and settling on a cushion on the floor in front of the doctor (there were no chairs) with his cigarette and his cup; well. Late last night, at half past two in the morning to be exact, I was standing on tiptoe looking through the high window there, that's the only way you can get a good view is on tiptoe, looking at the moon and listening to Fats Waller singing 'I'm gonna sit right down and write myself a letter', it's one of his own songs, as you probably know. I love Fats Waller. Think of the way he sings 'Ain't Misbehavin'. When Joe Williams sings 'I'm gonna sit right down' the letter's never going to arrive; when Louis Armstrong sings it the letter's never existed; when Bing Crosby sings it the letter's already gone; but when Fats sings it the letter's there on the spot and he's writing it.

Melog, what happened last night? the doctor said, sitting cross-legged like a tailor.

Well, like I said, I was looking out of the window. Then suddenly I see something moving. If you look out of the window and across the road you'll see a patch of empty waste ground that's all weeds and rubbish. Well, I noticed this man dragging a black plastic bag. Whatever was in the bag it was terribly heavy. Well he left the sack after he'd hidden it and then he got away. But I've been keeping an eye on the spot all night. And I know exactly where that sack is and nobody's been anywhere near it.

Well? What do you expect me to say?

What should I do? Phone the police, do you think? I almost rang them last night.

Why?

Oh come on, Dr Jones. Nobody drags black bags around in the dead of night and then sneaks off from bush to bush unless there's something very nasty in the air.

Like what, for instance?

Like a body, for instance.

Are you sure?

We Laxarians, Doctor, we can sense these things, Melog said, tapping the side of his nose with a finger that was six inches long.

So what'll we do?

Will you come down to that yard with me and have a look at what's in that sack?

Oh, very well then. The doctor sighed through his nose like a tired, discontented, hesitant horse.

So the pair went down the narrow staircases and crossed the street. It was difficult to do even something so innocent as this as people turned to look at Melog or followed him with their eyes because of his extraordinary appearance.

Well here we are, and I'm sure everybody in the street is watching us from behind their net curtains.

Who cares? Melog said. We aren't doing anything wrong; we're innocent. We're investigating suspicious circumstances.

Dr Jones imagined finding the body of a child in the bag and the police accusing him and Melog of murder.

There's the bag!

What do you expect me to do? the doctor said, hands on hips in a stubborn gesture.

Well open it and look, of course.

Why don't you look? Dr Jones said, ready to turn his back.

I can't. I'd be sick, he said, and his eyes became sad, like a sheepdog's listening to Trebor Edwards singing.

What about me?

You're a doctor aren't you?

Yes, but I'm not a medical doctor and you know it. The doctor crossed his arms.

Oh go on. You're braver than I am.

Oh yes?

Oh come on, Doctor. The curiosity's driving me mad.

All right then. For goodness' sake, to get it over with, the doctor said, moving to the sack and trying to peer through a hole in the side.

Well…? What's in it?

READERHOOD. Man is endowed with the capacity to convey to others not only his thoughts, but also, in the same instant, his feelings, which is to say by means of either utterance, writing, or the printed word; and the art of reading well comprises both of these elements, which are the bringing forth of the sense of that which is read, together with the temper which is appropriate to it. It is an aspiration worthy of every Welshman that he should be a good reader…

The Encyclopædia

A DIALOGUE OF DR JONES AND MELOG

WELL…? What's in it? Melog asked, taken over by his own echo.

Nothing.

But there is something in it, Melog said.

So there is. Rubbish.

Rubbish? The young man had become an echo chamber.

Yes, rubbish, waste, trash, litter, spoil. Anyway, Melog, what do you expect on a rubbish tip? Take a look around and that's what this is. You live opposite a rubbish tip.

The two went back to Melog's room without exchanging one word until after they had had a cup of coffee and sat on the floor to pet the cats and relaxed, looked at magazines and listened to the radio. Melog lay at full length on the floor with a cushion under his head, a cigarette between the fingers of his right hand, and read.

What's the book? Dr Jones asked.

A Week in Future Wales, Melog answered.

What do you think of it?

It's all right, except…

Except what? Dr Jones asked. The cat on his lap purred like a dishwasher and spiked him with needle claws.

Except that I don't like titles in fiction that include the

names of real places, like *Dubliners*, *War in Syria*, *A Time of Weeping* – *Senghennydd 1913*, *Tiorry Tilng Puttag*. To tell you the truth I don't like novels that talk about real places. For instance, I'd never write a novel about Laxaria, and I certainly wouldn't put a title like *Journey Through Tiorry* or something like that on it. By the way, Tiorry was the capital of Laxaria until the Sacrians said we couldn't have a capital city and they renamed it. Tiorry's still there, of course, only the name's changed – and the language, and some of the buildings and most of the people and all of the culture. I don't like specific places in novels. Fiction is fiction. The novelist's task is to make his own world, a new world, a different world; that's what his novel is.

But, Dr Jones said pressing his back (which was beginning to hurt from his having sat for so long on the floor) against the wall, all novelists base their stories on things in the real world, things and places they're familiar with, usually. And the naming of real things and places adds to the feeling of reality. Every novelist reflects reality, in the end.

And what, Melog said as he blew from his mouth bluredged smoke rings, what is reality?

The world around us.

This book, the teapot over there, the carpet, that armchair, the sculpture, this pillow? Do you mean this sort of thing?

And other things too, of course.

There's the problem. The other things are without end, and we can't agree on what they are. Laxaria is more real to me than your Wales, even though I'm in Wales at the moment and Laxaria's just a far away place in my head.

One of the cats jumped onto his chest and lay down as the young man had settled back on the floor.

Well you've changed your tune, Dr Jones said victoriously. When I showed you the map of Wales you weren't ready to take my word at all. At least now you accept Wales exists.

I accept that Wales exists, that's why I came here. But I'm not sure what Wales is, Melog said, pushing the cat away.

79

And I'd like to know more about Laxaria, Dr Jones said.

But more than novels with placenames in the titles, Melog said, ignoring the doctor and changing the direction of the argument, what I really hate is novels where the characters discuss the business of writing novels or what is reality and boring stuff like that.

I hate things like that too, Dr Jones said, looking at the patterns of smoke in the air (horses, feathers, scarves, flowers, castles, the sea, a mushroom), tricksy, pretentious things. Do you know, that's the worst thing you can be in Wales. You can kill children and beat elderly people and bury their bodies in the garden if you like, so long as you're unpretentious and 'of the people' – which means putting the word *rabbit* in at least once in every sentence you say – so long as you're of the people you'll be forgiven everything and canonised.

But, said the young man (who had not listened to the doctor's meditations while he reconsidered his own contention), now I come to think of it there are novels I like with real places in the titles. *Amerika* by Kafka, and *The Squire of Havilah* by T. Hughes Jones. But I like those because the real places get turned into brand new worlds in the authors' imaginations. Kafka isn't portraying America but a place in his mind called America. Anyway, it was Max Brod gave it that title after the author died. The title Kafka gave it was something like 'The Man Who Vanished'. And it's imagining, inventing Havilah with it bdellium and onyx that preoccupies Daniel Jones.

And drives him to insanity, Dr Jones said.

If I'm out of my mind that's fine by me, Melog said.

He drew on his cigarette and took it from his mouth again and let a stream of smoke (lilac tinted) escape from his nostrils, like a reclining dragon. Weren't the wreaths of smoke near the ceiling, which twined into intricate Laxarian patterns and rapidly vanished, just as real as the fossil of a leaf in a shard of coal? It was Dr Jones who thought this, but he said nothing to Melog, who, as it happened, was thinking the same thing exactly.

EXECUTIONER: hangman, avenger, soultaker, deathsman. "And immediately the king sent an executioner"; Mark vi.27… The word executioner denotes one who is such as part of his office. In those times there was no such specific officer.

The Encyclopædia

THE PUBLIC EXECUTIONS

I DON'T UNDERSTAND why you buy all these newspapers every day, Melog said, his long arm describing a broad, open arc to indicate the journalism scattered across Dr Jones's living-room floor. You get the news on television and on the radio.

The newspapers offer a more thorough analysis of affairs, Dr Jones said from behind an enormous spread of newsprint.

In Laxaria and Sacria, and even in Mocatria for that matter, Melog said, nobody pays any attention to the news on the media and nobody buys newspapers. They're full of lies and gossip.

Then they're just like the newspapers here.

Exactly. That's why I don't understand why you have such an appetite for following the news – you buy three papers every day, you listen to the news on the radio all morning and all afternoon and then you watch it all again on television in the evening. The news isn't new any more by the evening anyway, Melog said, lying on the sofa with his knees crooked in two pyramids, his left hand under his head and the other holding a cigarette.

I like to know what's going on in the world, Dr Jones said, folding back a closely printed page. I don't want to remain ignorant like so many of the people in this country.

But how do you know what's going on? The boy shook his fists at the doctor, who could not see him from behind the *Times*. You just said it's full of lies.

I'm sure that a little truth percolates down through it all, especially if you take the trouble to get your news from several sources, which is what I do by buying three papers and following several programmes. And to be fair the BBC has a good reputation throughout the world for objectivity and thoroughness.

Dr Jones lowered the paper to look at Melog over the owlish spectacles on the end of his nose.

The BBC! Melog shouted. So you believe the BBC's propaganda? How often does the BBC mention my country? He crushed his cigarette in the saucer of his coffee cup as if he were extinguishing his anger. Does the BBC ever do a piece on the conflict between the Sacrians, the Laxarians and the Mocatrians? Does the BBC ever report the traditional public executions they hold all the time in Laxaria?

Executions? Dr Jones asked. His self-confidence crumbled and with it his voice grew small and childlike.

There you go, Melog said, starting to roll another cigarette. You haven't even heard of them in this country, have you?

No, we haven't, Dr Jones said, feeling as if he were personally responsible for Great Britain's remissness in this.

You and your BBC and your objectivity. The young man, his eyes shut, licked the edge of the cigarette paper as if it had a bitter taste.

Melog, tell me something about these executions, Dr Jones said, letting his newspaper slip from his hand to the floor and leaning forward in his chair.

I don't like talking about them, Melog said, the cigarette unlit between his lips.

I won't press you, the doctor said. I understand perfectly well if you don't wish to discuss these painful matters.

On the other hand, Melog said, swinging his feet to the floor and sitting up in one smooth movement, perhaps I have a duty to educate the people of this country about the atrocities which happen so frequently in my own land.

You must decide whether you want to discuss the matter or no, Melog. It's your choice.

My choice? Melog said, his right arm extended across the backrest of the sofa. Have I truly got a choice? Not really. No more choice than those wretches had getting hanged and shot in front of an audience every month in Laxaria. No more choice than many of the people in the crowds that had to watch. I didn't want to go and see people getting killed but I didn't have any choice, I was forced to be with the others. After all it wasn't only criminals, not just murderers or terrorists who were getting executed, it was ordinary innocent Laxarians.

Melog stood up and looked out through the window, past Dr Jones's rubber plant at the street and the dustbins outside, as if he could see his homeland and not the rusting cars parked along both sides of the street, the dog pausing to lift its leg, the children screaming and swearing and playing with toy guns.

Every month, he continued, the cigarette trembling between his fingers as he spoke, every month envelopes would go out to every house in Laxaria. Grey envelopes. Everybody was scared of them. All the inhabitants, everybody of whatever age, babies and adults and old people, would get an individual envelope. It was against the law to ignore the envelope or refuse to open it. The letter inside the envelope would tell you if you were one of the Ten Winners, as they called them, the ones who'd get executed in public that month. Needless to say, most people considered themselves lucky if they were among the thousands of the officially Unlucky. But for the unlucky officially victorious individuals it was the end of their world, literally. They couldn't escape. Any family that tried to escape the Conductors, the ones who came to fetch the winners, was killed. If one of the winners was a child or a baby, even, there was no mercy. No family dared hide a child; the whole lot would be executed. So every month the execution of the winners was staged in front of a crowd of people in the capital city. Everybody was expected to travel from all parts of the countries to see these horrible ceremonies – or get killed for not conforming. Execution days were big events in the capital of Sacria; everybody wore their best clothes, the shops were full, makeshift stalls sprang up in the streets selling anything and everything: beads, sweets, furniture, toys, clothes, ornaments, fish, puppies and kittens, cards, umbrellas, matchsticks and meatstuffs, great stacks of meat; brown meat and red meat, but especially red, bloodfilled meat – the Sacrians really liked their meat. It was like a fair, a carnival for the Sacrians; after all, they weren't going to see their own relatives getting killed; only Laxarians and Mocatrians would be the winners. Then, about mid-day, the crowd would gather around the gallows in the square, or behind the marksmen – sometimes winners were hanged, sometimes they were shot – arrangements were completely arbitrary. Silence would fall on the audience like a shroud – even the Sacrians were quiet – until the winners were led onto that appalling stage by the Conductors. When the first one of them appeared the crowds would cry out with one joy-filled voice.

Joy? Dr Jones gasped.

Yes. Enormous joy. Then the first would come to the gallows or the shooting-wall to be killed, then the second and the third and so on until they got to the last one and they were all finished. But after every one of the deaths, the audience would stand and applaud and show its exultation. It was an occasion of celebration and pleasure.

What on earth were they celebrating?

The Sacrians were celebrating the fact that Laxarians and Mocatrians were getting killed, and we, the Unlucky ones, were celebrating the fact that we weren't one of the winners. Everybody was thinking about his own life. Afterwards, there was dancing and singing and eating and drinking and general carousing round the city till the early hours of the morning. Execution day was a Feast Day.

Who organised this?

The Government of Sacria.

But what was it for?

Well, like I said, only we and the Mocatrians were in the running to be among the winners. But nobody in Laxaria opposed the system because they were scared. But having said that, our people had become a collection of selfish individuals and everybody was just trying to save his own skin. Many Laxarians enjoyed the holiday and the celebrations and the theatre of the executions – or at least they pretended to. After all it was dangerous to show any opposition, and making out that it was fun was self-defence. But sometimes I'd feel that plenty of my countrymen weren't faking enjoyment but really were enjoying themselves. Nobody opposed it till they were chosen as one of the winners. But the majority deluded themselves that the envelope would never come to them. I saw literally hundreds of these events. But unlike many of my friends and relatives I never got brutalised by it or fell into thinking that I'd never be chosen. Every time, when the grey envelope arrived, I'd say, 'This one's mine.' Even when I saw that I was Unlucky I wouldn't go giving out a sigh of relief. I knew that other people were suffering and that this was just a postponement.

This is horrific, Dr Jones said. He jumped from his chair and started to pace the room, troubled. It's hardly surprising that you fled that awful country. Those bloody Sacrians are worse than the Nazis, worse than the Inquisition. They make a show of it. Turn death into entertainment.

Yes, true. But it's not that long ago that they hanged people in public in this country.

But they weren't chosen at random and for no reason at all. Anyway, we've managed to get a bit more civilised than that, I hope.

What are you doing, Dr Jones? Melog asked, when he saw his friend stooping over the telephone directory.

I'm going to phone the papers, I'm going to phone my

MP. I'm going to tell them what's going on in Laxaria. I'm sorry, Melog, I didn't realise, I'd never heard anything about all this. Nobody in this country knows anything about these iniquitous goings-on in your country.

Dr Jones, don't, Melog said, quietly but firmly.

I have to, Melog, the doctor said, fanning through the pages of the directory.

I must beg you not to.

But I have to try to put a stop to this wickedness.

The executions finished last year. Last year we had the very last of them, thank goodness. The new President of Sacria doesn't like them. That's one change for the better in our part of the world recently. Although, things are still bad enough.

I'm sorry, Melog, but I got the impression that these things were still a regular occurrence. That's the impression you gave me.

Well, it seems to me as though they have never stopped.

INVENTION… The next meaning of the word invention is riddle.

MOVING

MELOG had moved again. He moved frequently, from nameless streets to unnumbered houses to rooms in which there was no cat-swinging space (in spite of the young man's growing number of cats). But Melog's latest rooms gave Dr Jones a fright when he went to visit him in his new home for the first time. The window- and doorframes of the house in the middle of the town were badged with the remains of aged yellow paint like some disease. Melog's rooms, inevitably, were on the top floor, and Dr Jones had to go through a long, dark, narrow, intestinal corridor and up nightmare staircases, past numerous suspicious doors where more of the faceless lived, in order to reach Melog's sanctuary. There was no door dividing his part of the building from the others' territory; that is, there were no doors in the jambs. He had a kitchen, and inside that was a toilet and shower and a small room (again with no door in the frame) where he had his bed and small possessions, his Laxarian patterns and the sculpture from the exhibition.

What an awful place, was the doctor's first comment.

What's wrong with it? It's somewhere to live.

An awful place.

It's not that bad, it's a roof over my head. What else does a man want? I've got somewhere to sleep, somewhere to wash and have a shit, somewhere to do my food. What else do I need?

Solace, comfort?

I'm comfortable enough, thank you.

At that, they heard noises from one of the rooms below

Melog's. The sound of shouting and doors slamming loud enough to rock the building. As if trying to drown the uproar, loud music started up in another room.

Neighbours, Melog said. 'Love thy Neighbour' and so on.

This place is unbearable, Melog. How are you going to put up with it?

I've lived in worse places.

Where? In Laxaria?

Yes, and in Wales too.

It would break my spirit and my heart.

It is not that which surrounds a man, that which is external to him, that is important, Melog said, but that which is within him. I possess a kernel of inner calm which is as armour about me, proof against the raucous noises which beset me.

Then Melog rose from his chair, leapt up and down with all his weight, and shouted: Quiet! SHUT BLOODY UP!

After that the young man quietened and regained his composure. His outburst unfortunately had no effect on his co-lodgers; exactly as before, the hellish music continued in competition with the door-slamming and arguing.

Care for a cup of coffee? Melog asked, with a smile like an advertisement.

Tea, the doctor said, though he felt a yearning for hot chocolate.

I haven't got any tea, only coffee.

Coffee, then; milk with two spoonfuls of sugar, the doctor said, still dreaming of sweet, frothy hot chocolate – or something stronger, even.

I haven't got any milk or sugar.

Black, then, the doctor conceded.

Let's go into the kitchen, Melog said, leading the way to a cupboard on the stairhead where there were shelves, an electric ring and saucepans and a sink.

Melog filled the kettle with water. While he waited for this to boil, he drew his cigarette-rolling gear from his cardigan pocket; the packet of rice papers, tobacco, matches. He took one of the papers and placed it on the corner of the table, took a pinch of tobacco (a golden blade of grass) and unravelled it in a long strand on the paper, half rolled the paper into a parcel, licked the edge, rolled the rest, and the cigarette was made. Strike the match. Suck cigarette until it brightens and begins to smoke. In this ritual which the young man performed many times a day there were no variations. When Melog sucked on his cigarettes he drew deep, as if he were taking salving waters. He would hold the smoke in for a long time – where? In his lungs? – and then let it go and with a sigh release the blue clouds through his mouth and nostrils. It was such a slow process – slow and difficult and painstaking. Sometimes he would tug a hair of tobacco from the tip of his tongue with his thumb and little finger while holding the cigarette between the index and middle fingers. Dr Jones considered this quite a feat. Melog lived on coffee and cigarettes. The coffee kept him going and quenched his thirst while the cigarettes killed his hunger.

You know that thousands of people die every year of lung cancer, the doctor said, sipping his coffee (and regretting it because the inky goo was quite undrinkable). People who've never smoked in their lives, like me. They call it passive smoking. They die of smoke from other people, people like you.

Stupid little so and sos, Melog said.

You don't care, do you? Smoking is going to kill you.

When you first met me, Dr Jones, what was it that I was doing? If you remember, I was about to throw myself off the top of the Town Hall, that's what I was doing. So I'm not likely to be that worried about my health, am I?

No, but I worry about my health when I'm with you sometimes.

Don't worry, since I smoke so much I'm not likely to be with you for all that long clouding up your life, am I?

You aren't bothered by the thought of dying, are you?

I've told you before, Doctor, death's not an end, it's a change, a transformation.

Transformation into what? Ashes, food for worms.

The two sat once more in Melog's living-room-bedroom. Melog sat on the bed and the doctor sat on the only chair, after he had pushed the cats from it. The sculpture stood on a small round table against the wall as a focal point for the room, and though it was ugly in Dr Jones's opinion, its intricacy and its unearthly colours, as well as the fantastical figures, almost made the wretched place seem beautiful. The room was neither bare nor uninteresting because of the complex and colourful patterns Melog had designed and attached to the walls around the flat.

I'm sure these must remind you of your home, Dr Jones said, pointing a stubby finger at one of the designs in a black frame above the bed.

They do. But do you know what I miss the most?

What?

Cows.

Cows? Well there are plenty of cows in Wales.

Yes there are, but not in this town. When I was feeling low in Laxaria I used to go out into the fields and talk to the cows. I'd pour out my troubles to them. Cows are silent creatures – different to the neighbours here – quiet in their spirit. Their eyes are full of sympathy. I miss the cows, but there aren't any in this area, which is a great pity because I feel in dire need of the company of cattle.

Why? Are you feeling sad at the moment?

Of course I am, the boy said, lounging back on the bed. I always feel sad and I suffer from depression. I've searched for the Imalic in the library, in junk shops, in second-hand book shops. No luck. I'm starting to give up hope. I've only been happy three times in my life. But I can see that you're able to sympathise with that, Dr Jones.

Dr Jones looked at his friend with calf-like eyes. 'This,' he thought, 'is a very pretentious young man.'

WIZARD: This is a general term which denotes all classes of swaggerers who take it upon themselves to explain obscure matters, and to foretell future events. A proof of this is that the names applied to the various classes are quite frequently employed in the Bible as if of equivalent meaning; such as astrologers, charmers, conjurors, enchanters, magi, magicians, necromancers, seers, soothsayers, sorcerers, those that have familiar spirits, and the term in question – wizards – all are of the same class, but practise different stratagems and rites in order to accomplish their vainglorious work.

The Encyclopædia

THE MAGICIAN

HERE'S AN INTERESTING advertisement, Melog said. He was visiting Dr Jones and was leafing through a stack of backnumbers of the Welsh-language community newspaper, *Clecdwr*. An advert for a fortune-teller, in this town. A medium in the media. He reads palms, tealeaves, tarot cards, the runes, the crystal ball, does personal astrological charts, the I Ching, and he holds séances.

I know him. Well, I half know him, Dr Jones said from amid his notes for the Encyclopaedia on his desk. He's a very strange man.

I'd like to go and see him and see what he's got to say about my future.

A silly thing to do, Melog. He gets everything wrong. He's a charlatan anyway, from what I've heard about him.

But aren't you interested in the future? Wouldn't you like to know what's going to happen? Then you'd be ready and you wouldn't have to worry.

Or perhaps you'd worry all the more. Sometimes it's just as well that the future's a mystery to us, the doctor said, scribbling another exceptionally important note on a rectangular card.

But I'm really curious. I want to know. I want to see

what's on the next page of my life.

But Melog, it's obvious that nobody can read the future, the doctor said – once more his young friend had succeeded in drawing him from his research. If somebody could tell what's going to happen to you perhaps you wouldn't like it and you'd do something different trying to avoid it and change the future, and then the prediction wouldn't be true and the future would be different.

Oh, who cares? Let's go and see this man for a bit of fun. We don't have to take it seriously, do we? Anyway, there's nothing else to do in this town. That's all this local paper is is a list of deaths.

After they had had coffee (black coffee with a roll-up in Melog's case) Dr Jones phoned the fortune-teller and arranged to visit him that afternoon. The two went to Jabez Ifans's chip shop, where Dr Jones dined on egg and chips and Melog had chips and mushy peas.

The street where the fortune-teller lived was not far from the street where Dr Jones lived, a street between Dr Jones's house and Melog's lodgings at the time (wherever they were). Dr Jones rang the door bell and it was answered by a small, thin man. Emaciated like Melog, and dressed entirely in clothes of cherry red: red shoes, red socks, red trousers, red sweater, red shirt, and even his tie was red. He extended a hand to Dr Jones and then to Melog and they shook. His small hand was cold and floppy and felt to Melog like raw liver.

I am Tudno, your local wise man. You may enter.

The two friends followed the sorcerer up narrow stairs (are all the terraced houses in the Valleys built by the same mad architect?) to a small bedroom. The bed was on a sort of platform and under this there was a low circular table surrounded by red cushions, in the centre of which stood a crystal ball, which gave to the space the exotic air of a gypsy's booth. The atmosphere was added to by many small items: bones hanging from red ribbons, the bones of small animals such as birds and mice and snakes; flasks containing poisonous-looking fluids – mauve, blue, yellow, green and even black; candles, pictures of wizards.

Please be seated, Tudno said, indicating the cushions on the floor to his customer-visitors while he went and squat-sat on the far side of the round table.

Now then, gentlemen, which service may I offer you? Tealeaves, tarot cards, runes, crystal ball, horoscope?

I know about my star sign, Melog said, sounding extremely knowledgeable. I was born on the first of December so I'm Sagittarius, the Archer, and a friend of mine in Laxaria did my chart…

You are not an Archer, Tudno said, interrupting him. If you celebrate your birthday between the twenty-seventh of November and the seventh of December then you come under a different sign, which is Ophiucus, The Serpent Holder.

Melog looked dashed and a desire to laugh overtook Dr Jones but he tried to smother it by biting hard on his own hand until the pain stopped him.

All right, so what about reading my hand? Melog said, stretching out his hands (palms up) towards the little man like two branches.

The fortune-teller grasped the elongated, bony hands and gazed myopically at the palms, his nose almost touching the skin.

Thus will I, Tudno said in archaic Welsh of a tantalizing formality, thus will I deliver before you the chronicle of your future life, as if it were a history that had already come to pass. I see before me yourself and your companion, the Dr Jones, journeying to a far island. And I see also rich pastures, aeroplanes, and castles in your future. For you shall gain eminence and wisdom. And I see that you shall remove you to a glorious dwelling. I see elephants and tigers, peacocks and serpents. I behold a thorny forest closing about, but you shall fear not. I behold you in a burning desert, but you will thirst not. Further on in the course of your time on this earth

I see things that will come to imperil your life, but you will not be conquered. I see a large, dark figure, a man who is dark of skin, who enters your life and goes from it, but he does not tarry long. I see two and I see two, and the first two are not the same two as the second two, and the second two are not the same two as the first two. I see letters and research for a book but I see no ending to the path. Again, in this vision of your life which even now is revealed to me, I see tigers and lions all about you, but you will worry not, for when these things befall you, there will be no fear in your heart. And then I behold a blaze of light, I behold a fiery furnace in a dwelling-place... but of this dread happening I cannot speak more. And after that I see carousal and merriment, and I behold there not yourselves alone, but myself also – a thing which I do not as yet understand, for it is a mystery. But this is passing, and as to that which is to happen afterwards, thereof I cannot further treat or speak.

The wizard fell silent and Melog looked at him, surprised.

Is that it? he asked.

That, Tudno said, is it. And having let go of Melog's palms he put out his own hand in a you-can-pay-me-now gesture.

The doctor paid in silent disgruntlement with two fifty pence pieces.

On their way back to Dr Jones's house the two friends held a post mortem on their visit to the fortune-teller.

So, 'thereof I cannot further treat or speak'. What was the meaning of that?

The meaning of that, Dr Jones said, his eyes glittering, was that the wise man wasn't wise to the answer.

Could he see something or not? Melog's forehead was seamed with puzzlement.

I don't know. All that talk was nonsense. Blather. Hot air. A load of shit. Twaddle. Tripe.

And Dr Jones slipped for some time into a flow of vituperative rhetoric.

INVENTION… The invention, or the riddle, while it was unfair from the point of view of those who had accepted the challenge of elucidating it, since they were ignorant of the specific action the knowledge of which alone would enable that elucidation; yet it answered to a laudable aim of the riddle or invention in that it comprised an artful and intricate attempt, in obscure, ambiguous and contrarily worded terms, in order to give practice to the skil-fulness of others in extracting its meaning.

The Encyclopædia

— *Riddle demands some work from reader*

PAPERS

I DON'T UNDERSTAND, Melog said. He was standing looking over Dr Jones's shoulder while he worked (some-thing Melog did frequently, to the doctor's irritation). What are all these bits of paper on your desk and all these little cards with handwriting like fleas' footprints on them?

Dr Jones had been working on a note on illustration 367 in the Encyclopaedia, The Bay Tree. Under the heading he had been copying:

> GREEN BAY TREE. This name occurs only once in the Scriptures, namely in Psalm xxxvii.35; "I have seen the wicked in great power, And spreading himself like a green bay tree" (*ezrach*). Translators and commentators differ in their opinions as to the meaning of this term.

They're my notes on the Encyclopaedia, the doctor answered, his heart sinking, because he knew he would get no work done while Melog was there. And by the way, Melog, the idiom you want is 'spidery handwriting' not 'fleas' footprints'.

I think I'm right for a change this time, doctor. Fleas have got smaller feet than spiders and your handwriting is incred-ibly tiny. But what do you do all this work for? Who's this old Encyclopaedia relevant to?

Well, nobody, that's the point. The Encyclopaedia contains everything – everything educated men knew in those days, anyway. My work is to try to make it relevant for people. To demonstrate its value. The Encyclopaedia was the most ambitious publishing project in the Welsh language. Imagine all the work John Parry did on these huge volumes (Dr Jones tested the weight of a stack of the encyclopaedias in his hands). John Parry was Wales's answer to Diderot.

Melog took a sheaf of pages from the table and sat on the sofa for a quarter of an hour, frowning sniffily at the lines, a fleshy cross in his forehead between his silver eyebrows.

Tripe, he said at last, tossing the papers on the floor.

Don't do that! Dr Jones shouted. I've done a lot of work on those pieces.

Well, they're miserable, boring, dull. Why don't you write something worthwhile, a novel or something?

There are too many writers in Wales already, the doctor said.

There are too many writers in the world and too many books too, Melog said, flinging himself back on the vomit-coloured sofa and laying himself out like a vampire in a coffin, but that doesn't stop other people from adding to the word mountain, the literary midden.

Help me pick these papers up. You've messed them up completely, the doctor said angrily, on all fours on the floor.

But Melog lay at full stretch on the sofa, his long legs hanging over the armrest.

Oh, what difference does it make? Leave them on the floor. Chuck them in the dustbin.

The dustbin? Is that what you think of all my hard labour?

Hard labour? And for what? Let it be. Give it up. What's the point? You won't get another job in any college, you won't get another degree. The social security are trying to get you out of this house.

Melog, you've been reading my letters. The corners of the doctor's mouth turned down like a horseshoe.

Nobody appreciates the work you do already so why bother? Even if you finished this work, who'd read it?

Melog looked at the kneeling, doubled figure of the doctor and saw that his shoulders were shaking. Could he be crying? He could not see his face, only the nape of his neck and his head which was bent forward and almost touching the carpet. Melog stared, quietly studying his friend for a few moments.

You try my patience sometimes, Melog said. (He was in a provocative mood). You make me want to grow up.

Throw up! the doctor shouted. Throw up!

Okay, throw. So what? The point is, all this scribbling's a waste of time. You're wasting your life on this Encyclopaedia.

Everything is a waste of time, Dr Jones said, raising his head and gathering papers from the floor. His face was red where blood had drained to his head.

He put the pages neatly in their place on his desk and organised them once more.

Everything, he repeated, is a waste of time. All work. We are all wasters of time and this is my own special, individualistic method of wasting the time allotted to me.

Well then, Melog said, I'm off out for a bit of fun.

Go then, the doctor said, sulking.

Melog put on his coat and wound his long scarf around his neck so that it hung on his back like a flaccid snake. Before he went through the door, he turned to look at his friend.

Why do you do this insipid, monotonous work? It's like you're doing a penance. You don't have to do these notes like a child doing lines, being punished for being naughty in class.

Perhaps the truth is that the work is a penance, a punishment. I don't know.

I'm off out, then.

Goodbye, Melog, Dr Jones said from his desk.

Cheers.

After Melog had gone, his voice echoed in the emptiness.

INVENTION... The delight of the creator is engendered by the puzzlement he occasions for his listeners, and their own delight at their ability to overcome that difficulty, the which is generally renewed by their offering up a new invention.

The Encyclopædia

THE ISLAND

BUT MELOG CAME BACK later and went to lie on the sofa to read once more. Dr Jones was still trying to put his papers in order like a conjuror with a pack of cards on the table before him practising his tricks.

Suddenly Melog raised his head from the pages and shook a hank of white hair from his sapphire eyes.

A book, he said, sitting bolt upright, is an image of life.

What on earth do you mean? the scholar asked.

Well, like a life, a book exists between two nothingnesses.

I don't understand.

'One brief thrill twixt two long nights', Melog quoted. He had steeped himself in Welsh literature in a short time. That's what life is. Nothing before we're born and nothing after we stop being. Well, don't you see how much a book is like that?

No, Dr Jones said, his nose touching the card which commanded his attention just then.

Well, before the front cover there's nothing, then there's the book, full of words, full of life, then the back cover, and then – nothing again.

But both sides of the book, the doctor said (it was too late – he had taken the bait), there is something. There's nothing apart from everything. The world surrounds the book.

But that world's not the same as the world of the book. The world of the book is different from and independent of that other world you're referring to. It's a slice of the ideal implanted in the realm of reality – whatever reality is.

Anyway, that world exists both sides of the 'brief thrill' of the individual too. Not the book, maybe, but the reading.

But I can reread a book, but life is 'one brief thrill twixt too long nights' with the emphasis on the 'one'.

You have to spoil everything don't you? Melog said, turning back sulkily to his book. I'm sure there's an answer; I just can't think what it is at the moment.

Dr Jones wrote three lines of notes on the card in pencil in his flealike italic handwriting. He was beginning to tire of his friend's naïve philosophical arguments. He considered the note:

> The extent of knowledge in the world is now so great, and contains such a multipicitie [sic] and variety of subjects, that it is entirely hopeless for one man to

He picked up the rubber and erased the words. He looked at the emptiness of the page:

He took his pencil again and wrote the three lines again – exactly the same words as the ones he had just erased, in the same places on the same lines of the card:

> The extent of knowledge in the world is now so great, and contains such a multipicitie [sic] and variety of subjects, that it is entirely hopeless for one man to

He was about to add to them when Melog interrupted him enthusiastically once more.

Every reading is an image of life, he said, because every reading is unique, like every individual. It's true that you can reread a book as you do in cases of sections of the Encyclopaedia, but every reading will be different from the one before. Readings change not only from individual to individual but from reading to reading even inside the experience of one individual.

That, the doctor said, is about as interesting as the pencil point that just snapped as I was writing and rolled off the table onto the floor to join the many hundreds of other pencil snappings in the carpet.

Your jokes are so rare, it's worth waiting even for one as longwinded as that. I'll probably burst out laughing after I get home.

Thank you very much.

You're still sulking because I said there's no point to working on the Encyclopaedia.

There's no point to my pencil.

Do you fancy a walk in the park?

What about my work on the Encyclopaedia?

Come on. Don't waste your one brief thrill. The book'll be there when we get back.

If we get back.

So you're coming, then?

Yes, the doctor said, as he had lost the battle to concentrate on his work.

And so the two went to the park. It was getting late and the air was clouded with thousands of midges. There was that lovely mournful light – greypink and cooling – so typical of summer evenings, redolent of childhood and romance and appalling murders in the hedgerows, and that was the quality they felt in the park as the two friends walked side by side; the time of the year and the moment of the day conjured in words like twilight, dusk, gloaming.

Perhaps we'll see a bat, Melog said. Bat. *Stlum*. One of my favourite words in the Welsh language. *Stlumod*. Bats.

Some people say *sglum*, the doctor said, and other people say *slumyn*.

What a beautiful selection of words, Melog said. *Stlum, sglum, slumyn*. It's the 'u' I like. So open and liquid next to the 'm' and after the 'l' – *lum*. It conjures up a pool in a cave; just the habitat for *stlumod* or *sglumod*, when you think about it.

They had arrived at the lake. People were still rowing

boats around the circular island in the middle. Old people were sitting on benches at the water's edge. Others walking with dogs. The voices of children and lovers in the distance.

Isn't that island interesting? Melog said.

Dr Jones looked at it afresh, with the eye of childhood. Yes, he had seen the island in that way once, an interesting place, a place to go to, a place of adventure. But he had not thought of it like that since he was about nine years old. He had grown up and, like all the grown-ups, he had taken it for granted in the familiar middle landscape of the park. A fake island in an unnatural pond. Or, now, perhaps, for the very first time he saw the island as a mystery, as magic, a place that drew the imagination. But it was a myth, wasn't it, the notion that children were so imaginative? A nostalgia for youth. It was adults, wasn't it, with all their experience and memories and associations, who were the inventive ones, not children?

Can we go and get on it?

What? Onto the island? No, Melog, we can't.

Why not?

Those are the rules. The island is a garden and no one is allowed to walk on it. That's why the lawn and the flowers are in perfect condition.

But I want to go there. Let's get one of those boats for an hour and go to the island.

Melog, we can't. The park keeper would go crazy and we'd get fined. Anyway, the park is shutting before long and they're already calling the last boats in.

I've got an idea.

No, Melog. I don't want to hear.

Why don't we wait till the park's shut? Get locked in. Then take one of the boats in the dark and row over to the island and spend the night under the stars? How about it?

It's illegal. It's getting cold. There are too many insects around and they're biting. Anyway, it's a stupid thing to do. It's childish.

Well what's that stupid island for, then? It's there to tempt people onto it. That's what it's there for.

You're talking about a little artificial island in the middle of the public gardens in the town park, Melog. You're thinking about it like a child, as if it were some far away land.

At least I've got some imagination, Dr Jones. And I'm certain a lot of people would like to do exactly the same thing except that they're too unadventurous and craven and – bourgeois.

And you know there's a rule, so you've got to break it.

What's the point of having rules if you can't break them? And what's the point of having islands if you can't walk on them and explore them?

Explore? It'd take about a minute to explore that island. And you won't find any treasure or wild animals or savage tribes or Man Fridays.

Yeah, pity, that, ey? Melog said. Still maybe we'd see things from a new perspective, and we'd definitely be experiencing something only some privileged gardener gets to experience once in a while. Anyway, it reminds me of Laxaria. It makes me homesick.

For some reason, it had not occurred to Dr Jones that Melog's home might be an island. And so he had to give way to the young man once again.

So, what are we going to do then?

A snip, Melog said. We've got to hide in the trees till nightfall. After it gets dark I want to stand on the big rock in the middle of the stone circle like the Archdruid in the Eisteddfod and call out 'Is there peace?'. Then we can go and pick a boat for the lake-voyage.

Feeling miserable, his hands deep in his anorak pockets, Dr Jones followed Melog into a stand of trees.

Here we are, Melog said. Isn't this exciting?

I hope no one sees us skulking about here acting suspiciously.

Don't worry, it's plenty dark already. Nobody'll see us.

The two listened to the sounds of the park falling asleep.

A bell rang to warn the townspeople that the gates would soon be locked. Dr Jones and Melog stood under the branches, absorbing the darkness and listening to silence. They were aware of natural life busy about them; birds, squirrels, insects, rats, mice, ants, moths, *stlumod* too; sleeping, waking, hunting and biting and eating and shitting and shagging and killing to survive, and dying. Blood and dirt, claws and teeth – there was continuous war.

A little later, the two walked to the stone circle set up at the end of the park. Melog went straight to the centre, mounted the two steps, and stood on the great stone.

Is there peace? he whispered. Dr Jones could scarcely hear him.

Melog had no need of white robes; even in the dark, Dr Jones could see him clearly because of his whiteness, his incandescence.

Is there peace? he whispered again, as quietly as before.

Peace.

The young man leapt down from the rock.

It's a strange response, isn't it? Not 'There is' or 'There isn't', just 'Peace'. The question's pretty strange itself of course. I suppose there is some sort of peace somewhere or other in the world all the time. Though there are wars somewhere or other in the world all the time too.

Yes, it is a strange question, Dr Jones said. I never thought of it before. And you're right that it's a strange answer too. It's like saying 'Eggs' if somebody asks 'Are there any eggs?'

The two laughed quietly. The night was colder than they expected and their breath formed from their mouths and nostrils as though they were dragons at rest.

Then they were standing at the edge of the lake. Melog stooped and began to unravel the painter of one of the boats with his dextrous fingers.

Come along, Dr Jones. All aboard.

The young man was standing in the boat, offering his long slim hand to the doctor, who felt unsure in the dark. But he gripped his friend's hand, trusting him completely. One foot in – the boat wobbled in the black water – and then the other. The boat wobbled again. Dr Jones sat on the bench in the stern where he felt a little safer. Melog took the oars and pushed off from the lake shore. Inwardly, the doctor said goodbye to solid land. In open water he felt certain that he was going to drown, or get caught.

The moon's reflection floated on the dark waters, along with old cans, papers, cigarette ends, assorted litter.

Well, Doctor. Isn't this a bit of fun?

Yes, the doctor said, not succeeding in concealing the nervousness in his voice.

Suddenly the boat collided with the shore of the island; it was not very far. Melog tied the painter to a rock and clambered ashore. Dr Jones found it more difficult than the young man, but once again Melog helped him.

So here we are, Melog said.

The two looked about them and saw a circle of water like ink, the far shore of the lake, and the familiar benches around it. Beyond that they could see nothing in the darkness except the silhouetted trees against a blueblack sky and the jaundiced moon.

Everything looks strange, Dr Jones said. I've been coming to this park regularly all my life, but this is the first time I've seen it like this. It's like a new country.

You're looking at the familiar from a different angle, that's all, Melog said. Some of us have to look at everything, even our own homeland, from a different position to everybody else.

Then he ran around the island flapping his arms as if they were wings. He followed the edge of the island.

I've been on this island for forty years, he said in a stage whisper. I haven't talked to a soul for forty years, I'm going off me head, I'm a lunatic, me only pals are the beetles and the birds, and I'm losing me language 'cause there's nobody to talk to!

During this performance Dr Jones retreated to the middle of the island where there was a bush and stood until Melog's outburst had spent itself. He did not have to wait long. The boy came and sat at his feet, out of breath. Dr Jones sat beside him.

It's wonderful here, Melog said.

He looked across the water into the distance. Dr Jones looked at his friend's face in the moonlight. His skin was like sleeked ivory. Suddenly, the doctor felt happy in the young man's company. There was no one near. No one could get to them. And in that instant of intense closeness, the doctor was possessed by a need to speak, to put his feelings into an envelope of words, to let it all out, to say something. But the something was as vaporous as the midges in the air or as Laxaria, far-off and locationless, and the words were as hard to voice as the blackness in the water, and the abyss between him and the boy, for all his closeness, as unbridgeable as the island and the far shore of the lake.

Come on, Melog said. I'm cold; I want to go back. We'll have to climb over the wall.

It is scarcely necessary to mention that the use of written letters signals a high degree of culture and civilization. Where letters would be practised, it is necessary that a consistent system of characters, either phonetic or ideographic, be acknowledged; it is necessary that men should be taught to write, and it is necessary that they be possessed of the instruments with which to write.

The Encyclopædia

THE LETTER

DR JONES HAD NOT SEEN Melog for some days, perhaps a week or two, and this time he was sure that he was dead. He imagined that he had fallen under a bus or had electrocuted himself changing a light bulb in the damp bathroom of some hovel of a flat, or that he had been drugged and abducted into slavery, or sent back to Laxaria, or that he had become a drug addict, or that he had been taken ill and had lost his memory and died in some hospital where no one recognised him, or that he had finally got cancer and had a heart attack after living on nothing but all those cigarettes and all that strong coffee, just coffee and cigarettes and nothing nutritious. All sorts of scenarios whirled through the doctor's head as he worried about his friend while he was working on the Encyclopaedia.

But every one of these pessimistic guesses was wrong. As was his habit, the young man appeared once more, and in fact called in to see Dr Jones.

I've done something terrible again, he said in a low, conspiratorial voice, a little out of breath.

What have you done this time? the doctor asked, his patience starting to wear thin already although Melog had been back in his life for scarcely five minutes. Stolen another sculpture? Or a car?

Absolutely not. I don't steal things.

Well, Dr Jones said, ignoring the counterfeitinnocence, so what have you done now?

You know where I'm living now, the big old house? (The doctor did not know.) Well I've been there for weeks and I've never had a single letter. Nobody writes to me. The letters that come to the house are put on a little shelf on the wall behind the door. A lot of people live in the house, as you know, of course. (The doctor did not know of course.) Every room's let out to somebody, a temporary home. In the home there is a country, as one of your poets says. And every day a new pile of letters arrives. And not a single one for me. Nobody in Sacria knows my address. You never write to me.

I didn't know where you were living. You move all the time. And you never give me the new address. My address book is full of your temporary homes. I'll have to get a new address book just to keep track of your wanderings.

Yeah, whatever, Melog said, not letting the complaint bother him for a second. I noticed that there was one pile of letters that had grown without anybody ever opening one of them. The landlord never clears them out. These were the ones sent to people who used to live in the house; people who've moved on without giving their new address to the people who send them the letters. Friends and family who've lost contact. They're letters that have died. Missing missives, lost in the no-man's-land between the sender and the receiver.

I know what you've done before you say it. You've opened the letters haven't you?

Only one.

You've got no right to open even one of them.

But it'd been behind the door for weeks, maybe months.

It doesn't matter, Dr Jones said, trying to sound disciplined and strong. It's possible that someone will eventually come to claim the letter. You can't tell.

Anyway, Melog said, unaffected by Dr Jones's severity, there was this sad little envelope behind the door, day after day, gathering dust, going yellow in the sun, grey in the damp, spiders weaving webs on it, nobody wanting it, completely ignored, and there I was dying for a letter and I never got even a single one. The name of the person who sent the letter wasn't very clear on the envelope anyway. In the end I had to take the letter and open it and read what was in it. I was going to seal it up again after and put it back in its place behind the door to stay in the mail cemetery with all the other letter-bodies and wait till resurrection day or till they got cast down into epistolary hellfire. But after I'd read what was in it I couldn't do that. Here's the letter. You'd better read it.

Dr Jones read:

> Dear…[the name was not legible, and the doctor had some difficulty in interpreting the handwriting.]
>
> Great to see you the other day. Although I left early I didn't get back till nearly midnight, believe it or not. Trains terrible. The train stopped not long after we left your town. No explanation. Middle of nowhere. Got to Manchester late after that and missed the connection. The result was that I had to wait in the city's boring, dirty, ugly station for an hour and a half. I tried to imagine Lloyd George waiting for a train there in his day. Couldn't. When the next train came it was hot and heaving and I had to go in a smoking compartment. Yuck. I felt ill straight away. Sneezy. Itchy eyes. I had to change again in Crewe. The arsehole of all the railway stations of the world. Half an hour there with nothing to do. I wasn't going to buy anything in the café and pay through the nose for a bag of crisps and a coffee in a polystyrene cup. On the train from Crewe to Shrewsbury later I had the company of two spotty youths, one next to me and the other opposite, talking loudly about soccer. And then two hours in Shrewsbury. Station like the Mary Celeste. Unbearable. I walked to the town. Everything shut by that time of night – what do you expect, especially on a Sunday night? My train wasn't till five to ten. Walked around with my heavy cases looking in dark, closed shops, feeling like a tramp. Later, on the train home there was a person with one of those gadgets that play music through earpieces. But though he was sitting six rows of seats behind me and even with his earphones I could still hear the music –

Phantom of the Bloody Opera. I cursed Andrew Lloyd Webber (not for the first time) and Michael Crawford. But instead of just sitting there feeling jealous of the deaf, I wrote this poem which I'm sending you now.

Ivy

may the ivy grow upon everything
and beautify each ugly building,
leach to concrete walls and crawl over floors. O!
Ivy! fine of leaf and green evermore, O!
cordial benefactor of our unsightly environment.

Okay, it isn't what you'd call beautiful, I admit, but you have to take into account the difficult circumstances in which I composed it. In any case, as you can see, I got here healthy and in one piece in the end. Hope you get somewhere to stay that's to your liking before long.

All the best [Completely illegible signature]

What a boring, miserable letter, Dr Jones said.

What are you saying, Dr Jones? Have you read the letter carefully? Do you realise what it means?

Yes, it's a straightforward letter complaining about a normal, uncomfortable train journey from somewhere in England to somewhere in Wales.

You are so clichéd and lacking in imagination, Dr Jones. Isn't it obvious to you that this is a coded letter that hints at where the manuscript of the Imalic has been hidden?

No, Melog, it isn't obvious at all. Not to an idiot like me, anyway. But I'm sure you're going to explain the code to me.

Well to start with have a look at the poem. Don't you see something significant?

All I see, Melog, is a short, inspirationless, abysmally bad poem.

Look at the poem again, Melog said.

Dr Jones subjected it to a histrionic glare to keep Melog happy, and to take a rise out of him.

You aren't really taking this seriously, are you, Dr Jones? Melog said, shaking with impatience. The first letter of every line spells 'The Imalic'.

Dr Jones studied the prosaic piece of verse once more.

No it does not spell The Imalic, Melog. It spells Malic, that's all.

But if you include the title, 'Ivy', you get Imalic, don't you?

The doctor was forced to concede that this was true yet again.

Now then, what do you make of that? Melog asked, blowing victorious cigarette smoke into the doctor's face.

I think that it's some sort of coincidence, a sort of accident, that's all.

Dr Jones, Melog said as if he were a teacher speaking to an irritating child, there are no coincidences, no accidents. Everything has been organised in advance and preordained by the great Author in the Sky. This letter is a secret message to me which is going to lead me to where the Imalic is hidden. I think I can detect hidden references in this letter to Laxaria, Sacria and Mocatria, and to the Imalic and Benig and other things intended as clues for me. For instance – Melog snatched the yellowing old letter out of Dr Jones's hands – take this line: 'What do you expect, especially on a Sunday night?' It's obvious to me that this is a cryptic reference to Benig.

The doctor covered his mouth with his hand to hide a smile.

But Melog, my boy, the letter wasn't even addressed to you. Who could know that you'd be staying there? If he knew you were looking for the Imalic, wouldn't he have addressed the letter to you rather than somebody else? Did he just hope that some time or other you'd steal the letter and open it? He was taking a big chance, wasn't he?

That's what I like about you, Melog said, your ability to analyse every situation coldly and cynically, your sceptical nature. You doubt everyone and everything, don't you, Dr Jones?

Sad faced, Melog folded the letter and put it back in its envelope.

It's probable that you're right this time, Dr Jones, but I'm going to keep the letter in case there's something in it after all, in case my Laxarian intuition is correct and the poem truly is a secret message.

The working of iron and the manufacture of musical instruments are recorded in Gen.iv. 21,22; while no reference at all is made, either before or after that period, to the origin or discovery of writing or to the origin of language itself. Given that, is it too much for us to believe that God, through direct revelation, has given the art of writing to mankind?

The Encyclopædia

GRAFFITI

DR JONES had received a nasty letter from the social security department concerning his house, so he went to see Melog, not to ask his advice (a waste of breath) but rather to distract himself from his worries. The two went for a walk in the town and a spiteful rain started to fall. Looking for shelter, the friends went into the museum.

Well here we are in the smallest and least interesting museum in Wales, the doctor said.

The two went slowly and carefully from object to object, the doctor following the pale young man whose eyes drank in every sight. The fossil of a leaf that had fallen to earth from some prelapsarian tree in the world's small hours; the fossil footprint of some creature that scurried in the dirt under such a tree.

I'm sure the techniques for dating these things are incorrect, Dr Jones said. Some of them are older than I am.

Hieroglyphs on a fragment of Egyptian papyrus – words as pictures and pictures as words; a Celtic cross, solid and round, a symbol of stubbornness; a Goya engraving depicting the tortures of the Inquisition.

It's a plush place considering how small it is, Melog said. Look at the chairs and the carpets and the velvet curtains; they're lovely. And all these treasures: a gold torc from some druidic priest, Merlin maybe, or Gwydion; Arthur's silver armlets; Caractacus's nose stud.

Let's have a sit down for a bit, Melog. My feet are starting to hurt.

Come on, Dr Jones, look at this lot. This is what I like, misshapen creatures, freaks, freaks of nature.

Melog went to a corner where there was a collection of jars and stuffed animals. There stood the skeleton of a cockerel with four legs. A stuffed monkey with two tails. A twoheaded cat in a jar. A toad with four eyes. But then Melog stopped before a white blackbird in a glass case, a piece of branch in its claws, its wings unfolding as if it were on the point of flying away, and behind it in the case, a landscape portraying fake woodland, in the middle of the woods the roofs of a village and in the distance the steepled belfry of a church.

Melog studied the white bird for a long time as if he were communing with it.

The doctor had seen his friend standing and staring like this once before when he had seen the sculpture in the exhibition. The boy could identify with other freaks too, of course, but this was his own image. Dr Jones contemplated the paradox of seeing two unique things – uniquenesses that were identical.

Isn't this a wonderful place? I love it! Melog said. Let's go into the next room. There are pictures in there.

The collection was surprisingly respectable, if conventional. The inevitable Richard Wilson, the unavoidable Kyffin Williams, and the two predictable Ceri Richardses.

I'd prefer the two-faced kittens, Melog said, standing in front of an Augustus John. Let's go back to the monsters.

No thanks. I'm happy enough sitting here for a few minutes and looking at the Josef Herman and the Evan Walters. For some reason things like exhibitions and museums sap my strength.

Well talk about doubleheaded cats. Everything's double in this picture, Melog said.

That's the way Evan Walters painted.

Why? Did he have double vision? Took a drop too much?

Don't be such a Philistine, Melog. What's wrong with you? You're starting to sound like a real Welshman.

I don't like this room. It's too respectable. Too conventional. Come on.

What's the hurry, Melog? Sit down for a bit.

What's up? You've got tired all of a sudden. I hope you aren't going to have a heart attack.

I'm all right except for running after you like a lapdog all morning and listening to your endless prattle.

I'm a shy man of few words, Melog said. To tell you the truth, I'm actually taciturn so I try to hide it by talking all the time.

Then without warning, Melog froze, a wondering look in his eyes.

What's the matter now? The doctor asked.

I would like to do something.

Don't, Melog. What sort of thing?

Something to show that I've been here.

You can sign the Visitors' Book on the way out.

No chance I'll do anything as tame as that. Anyway, I want to do something to show I've been on this earth, not just in some quiet little out-of-the-way museum. I want to leave something behind, like those fossilised dinosaur footprints.

Right, Melog. Time we were leaving.

No, I've had an idea.

Now don't do anything foolhardy, Melog.

I'm going to write something on the wall with this marker.

That wouldn't be a fossil, Melog. That'd be vandalism.

Never mind, it'll do for now.

If anybody comes in, I don't know you, Dr Jones said.

You can go on out if you're frightened, Melog said, the marker in his right hand and its cap in his left.

But even before the doctor had a chance to shift his weary legs, Melog was writing in enormous red letters across part of the Richard Wilson, then the wall and then part of one of the Ceri Richards:

114

What does that mean? Dr Jones asked in spite of his urge to run away.

Don't you remember? Melog said in surprise.

Remember? Dr Jones said. I don't know what it is that I'm supposed to remember.

Don't know? Didn't the news get to this country?

What news?

The story of the three thousand? Well obviously not. Our little country doesn't merit any attention from anywhere outside its borders and the Sacrians aren't likely to go telling the rest of the world what they've been doing.

Melog grew serious. His face clouded and his blue gaze shifted to the floor. At the same time, while he spoke, he moved as if to leave the museum.

About twenty-five years ago, he said, there was a protest march from Laxaria into Sacria, to Estracôn Square in the capital city where there was a memorial column to Héla Skelmonn, one of the country's most important poets. He was born in Laxaria but the Sacrians claimed him as one of their own great writers. The protesters gathered round the memorial to talk about injustice and the oppression of Laxaria and the old Laxarian language.

Dr Jones and Melog were standing on the steps on their way out of the museum – fossils, darkened old paintings, animal pelts, stuffed birds – all of them listening with Dr Jones to the intensity in the voice of the whitehaired boy.

Our people stayed there doggedly. Our leaders made speeches, the crowd sang the traditional songs of our country. But nobody came from the Sacrian parliament to meet them, only the brutal police in their black uniforms to tell them to go away. But the Laxarians wouldn't move and they demanded to see government representatives. A whole day went by. Then two days. Then on the third day the Sacrian army came and shot every Laxarian in the square.

Three thousand people were killed in the massacre including students, intellectuals, writers, scientists, teachers, young men and children. The talents and hopes for the future of our country. Only the old and the weak and the sick and the apathetic were left in Laxaria. But it's from them – the sickly survivors – that our new generations are descended, myself among them. They pulled the statue of Héla Skelmonn down after the disaster and they removed his name from every book on literature and history. His books were burned in their thousands. The only copies that have survived are the ones hidden by the odd Laxarian booklover. So, Dr Jones, that's the meaning of the words 'Remember the Estracôn 3000'. But it's time for us to go.

Dr Jones was quite keen to slip out of the museum unnoticed but Melog stayed to speak to the man on the door and to sign the Visitors' Book.

What a stupid thing to do, Dr Jones said as soon as they were on the bus home and far from the museum. We're bound to get caught now.

Don't worry, Melog said. I put a false address in Sacria in the book.

Then the doctor noticed the plastic bag Melog had put on the floor between his feet. It contained something large and oblong.

What's that?

The white blackbird. Well, we couldn't just leave him there to get dusty, could we? Melog said.

INVENTION… There is a limit to the power of man's imagination. When the connexions are manifold, and necessary, and of the most extreme complexity, the mind has not the ability to contain them; and thus the synthetic imagination fails. For this reason man has never invented the mental image of a new creature…

The Encyclopædia

MR JOB

DR JONES! Where on earth have you been? It's quite a while since I saw you.

Melog!

He looked very weak, as though he were turning into his own shadow. He was smoking as usual when he called after Dr Jones that day in the grey rain in the brown street. The doctor had not seen him nor had word from him for several weeks.

Why don't you keep in touch? the doctor said, aggrieved. Say when you're moving, give me your new address? I've called at your old flat a few times but nobody there knew anything about you. You know where I live, you've got my phone number, why don't you leave a message for me?

I forgot, that's all. You know how I am. Untidy, forgetful. And I've been searching in earnest for the Imalic.

So, where are you living now?

Not far from here, as it happens. Just round the corner in fact. Would you like to come round for a cup of tea?

It was difficult for the doctor to refuse as he was wet through to the skin, though he was very angry with the boy for neglecting their friendship once more.

He had a room in another terraced house, the smallest room the doctor had ever seen, little larger than a substantial cupboard, and in it a single bed, a little chair and traditional Laxarian patterns – all Melog's own work – covering the walls. Next to one another on a small table stood the sculpture and the white blackbird.

The trouble with this place, Melog said, is I've got to share the kitchen and the bathroom with the owner of the house, the landlord. As a rule it's not a wise move to rent a place where the landlord lives in, but there wasn't a lot of choice. Anyway, the landlord here, Mr Job, is a nice enough old boy. He's happy enough for me to keep my cats here. But he's old and nearly blind and a bit deaf and full of aches and pains which make him a bit short tempered sometimes. Apart from that he's all right – a bit bonkers, maybe.

In what way?

Well for one thing he's living in the past and he mistakes me for his brother who's been dead for years. And for another, and this is what's quite interesting to me and the main reason I've taken the place, he's copying out some of the Welsh classics in their entirety, longhand. He's worked his way through *Culhwch and Olwen* (including all those lists of names), *The Dream of Rhonabwy*, *The Three Romances*, then *The Book of the Three Birds*, *The Visions of the Sleeping Bard*, *The Mirror of Main Ages* and all of the novels of Daniel Owen. Now he's working through some of the twentieth century texts. But he's got stuck on *The Littlest Dickhead* and he can't get any further.

After showing him his room, Melog took Dr Jones downstairs to have tea. When the doctor saw the room, he was not so keen on having anything to drink. The hearth was an old fireplace with a cast iron stove. Everything was blackened by a combination of dark paint, soot, and the dust of ages. In the sink was a precipice of ancient dirty dishes, stacked like the spoil heap of a slate quarry.

Don't worry, Melog said, we wash up once a month.

Quite deftly he withdrew two cups from the stack of dishes and swilled them under the single, cold tap. Then he had to try to boil a vast old pitchblack kettle on the ashen, dying fire.

Why is he copying all that material? Dr Jones asked.

That's what I wanted to know, because he's got print versions of all of the texts in his library in the parlour, which is pretty complete – he collects books as if he were a second Bob Owen. But he's said he's worried that the non-Welsh speakers will turn against the Welsh speakers sometime and ban us from speaking Welsh and take all the books and burn them. Well something pretty similar's happened to us in Laxaria so perhaps Mr Job isn't so bonkers after all.

Melog stirred the ashes with a poker and a little steam rose from the kettle as if to cheer the two friends.

And there's another reason, Melog said. Mr Job left school when he was fifteen and decided to educate himself. He hated school and he couldn't have cared less about colleges and universities. And yet literature is his only interest in the world. He thinks that there are enough books in the world already and that writers should give up writing from now on, and he thinks that the only way you can read a book properly is to write it yourself by copying it out word by word.

The water was not boiling, but it was warm at last and Melog poured a little from the black kettle into a teapot which was just as black – inside as well as out. And when the tea came out that was black too, like a distillation of beetles' wing cases.

At that moment a small thin man stumbled into the kitchen, his hands knotted with arthritis. He was bald and birdlike – a hairless Saunders Lewis.

Mr Job, Melog said, this is my friend Dr Jones.

Doctor! the old man said, alarmed. Are you ill, Robat? You're not ill again, are you?

No, I'm not ill, Melog said, and I'm not Robat, and Dr Jones isn't a medical doctor.

Not a doctor? So what right has he got to be treating you, Robat?

He's not a medical doctor, Mr Job, Melog said, as patiently as he could.

What are you then? Mr Job asked.

A sort of teacher, Dr Jones answered.

A teacher! Robat, I've told you and I've told you, no teachers in this house. Do you understand? No teachers.

But Dr Jones isn't a teacher now, Mr Job.

He's not a teacher, he's not a doctor. I don't understand. So what is he then? What are you? The old man scowled at Dr Jones from under his heavy grizzled eyebrows.

I'm an academic. I'm conducting a study of the Encyclopaedia.

A flash of interest showed in the decrepit old man's watery eyes.

Ah! The Encyclopaedia is it? Worth the study. Worth reading. I hope you're reading it properly. Word by word. Copying it word for word. That's the only way you can be certain you've read it properly. That is the only way that you can prove and prove beyond any doubt, mind, that you have read the text thoroughly. Robat, where are my copies?

I don't know, Mr Job.

No you don't, and a proper thing too, he said, laughing at his own joke, 'cause I've tucked 'em away in the house in places you don't know about, my dear little friend, or anybody else on earth either. But I'll go and fetch one or two for your friend here to see.

The old man darted from the kitchen like a weasel but before Melog had time to make him a cup of tepid tea he came back with two old manuscripts, the first clasped in the knotty fingers of his left hand and the second in the other misshapen, painracked fist.

Catch hold, he said to Dr Jones. This is *Visions of the Sleeping Bard* and this is *The Faith Unfeigning*.

Dr Jones looked at the two old manuscripts in amazement. It was incredible that anyone should take such pains to copy such intricate, convoluted texts with unsparing meticulousness in a small, neat, black hand.

And I've got a lot of other books too, Mr Job boasted. *The*

Mabinogi, Morgan Llwyd, both versions of Theophilus Evans's history, Daniel Owen. Now I'm working through the twentieth century: Saunders Lewis, John Gwilym Jones. But for the first time ever I've run into the sand. Stuck. Fast. Can't get out. The problem is with *The Littlest Dickhead*. It takes months, years with the long texts. Is it worth the effort? Somebody's got to do it, of course. There's nobody to help me and I'm getting to be too old. You wouldn't help me, would you Robat? What about you, Mr Morgan? Would you help me to read every word ever written in the Welsh language?

Well, Mr Job, I would like to help you but I don't have the time.

Don't have the time? But you aren't old. What do you do with yourself all day?

I study the Encyclopaedia.

Study? What's the point of study? After you're dead what does it matter what you've learnt? But my work as a reader will be there. I am the only true reader in the world. I'm saving our books for future generations. After the revolution that's coming, after the Antiwelsh rise up and attempt to sweep us away, it's possible that the language will die. Unless one last Welshman comes across the manuscripts hidden in this house. But if you aren't prepared to help... well that's that.

Mr Job snatched his manuscripts out of the doctor's hands and disappeared from the kitchen into the other dark rooms of the national library of his home.

Law is also the regulation of civil conduct. Here, the civil law is distinguished from the natural law and from revelation.

The Encyclopædia

POLICE

DR JONES was reading the papers. A heap of newspapers – his only self-indulgence – scattered across the floor of his small living-room. Papers local and national in Welsh and in English, magazines and community newspapers, all higgledy-piggledy. The doctor was combing the small print for any reference to Sacria, Laxaria, or Mocatria. There was nothing. Children being killed by the hundreds in a distant country. Plague and famine in another. Accidents. Bombs. Strikes and terrorists. The discovery of a fragment of bone many thousands of years old linking humankind with the animals. Dr Jones already knew that. Local news. A man ninety years of age who is going to walk from Llangofan in Dyfed to Ynys Gybi in Anglesey to raise money for charity. Two young men up before the judge for threatening motorists, James 'Zog' Evans, aged eighteen, and Arthur 'Buzz' Hughes, also aged eighteen, both from the Penywaun Estate. National news: a three year old child who has been missing for days, snatched from a shopping centre, his father in tears appealing for any information, the whole family very worried about him and desperate – naturally enough – to have him back and safe. Six cups of black tea per day help safeguard the body against cancer, a team of scientists in America have announced. Palermo: a man tries to commit suicide by gassing himself but lights a final cigarette; the explosion kills three people leaving ten injured, but Luciano Cargnino himself survives. New research into identical twins who were separated at birth or shortly afterwards changes old theories which maintained that the personality was

122

formed by nurture rather than nature, according to scientists at the University of Minnesota. The public foots the bill for homes for the aristocracy and relatives of the royal family. Taxpayers' money continues to support luxury homes where members of the King's court live rent-free. Vicar forced to pay fine of twenty pounds for stealing rare birds' eggs. A man has run amok with a gun in a country village, shooting eighteen people in a bloodbath before turning the gun on himself and shooting himself in the mouth. Why, the doctor thought, don't these lunatics shoot themselves first? Then there would be one suicide instead of all these deaths. Afterwards the police discover a note from the man explaining that he is going to kill everybody and then himself because the lottery is getting on his nerves.

Dr Jones looked around him. He looked at the papers on the floor. He looked at his notes for the Encyclopaedia on his desk in the corner. A desire came over him to give names to his possessions, like the philosopher Jeremy Bentham, who called his walking-stick Dapple and his teapot Dickey. Dr Jones considered giving a name to his fountain pen. He wondered what name. A literary one, naturally. He would have to mull it over and choose with care. Gwydion, because Gwydion was the best storyteller in the world. And what about calling his glasses Nisien and Efnisien? The one eye good and the other bad. And he could call his desk Bendigeidfran, because a desk is a sort of bridge. And what about his teapot? The doctor was every bit as fond of his teapot as was Jeremy Bentham or 'that hardened tea-drinker' Dr Johnson. So the teapot merited a good name; something better than Dickey, anyway. He could call his cutlery drawer Henry VIII and his biggest knife Anne of Cleavers. But Dr Johnson had a cat called Hodge, and Jeremy Bentham had a cat called The Reverend Doctor John Langborne. Great names for cats. But the doctor did not have a cat. He could have one of Melog's kittens and think of a good name for the creature then. Kafka, perhaps. Or Kafkat. The doctor laughed at his joke.

The doorbell rang and when the doctor went to answer there stood Melog. The doctor was going to ask him if he had a kitten straight away, but the young man was full of excitement.

Have you heard about the kid that's been snatched in the north of England?

Yes, the doctor said. I just read about it in the paper.

Well I've seen the child, Melog said.

Where? In this town?

Yes, in a manner of speaking.

What do you mean, 'in a manner of speaking'?

Well, Melog said, I've seen him in a dream, a vision. I'm psychic, see. And he's being held in a house in this town, and he's all right – I mean nobody's hurt him. I'd phone the police, but as you know I'm scared of speaking to them. So, would you phone them?

Me? Why? To say what exactly?

To say you've seen the baby in a dream and that you're psychic and that the child's safe and healthy somewhere in town.

No I won't. I won't do any such thing.

But you've got to. People are worrying about this kid, everybody's talking about him, he's on the news every hour. You've got to give this glimmer of hope to his family.

I'm not sure, the doctor said, stroking his beard, as if it were a cat.

Dr Jones, you don't doubt me, do you?

Why don't you phone them, Melog, and don't give them your name?

They wouldn't pay any attention to an anonymous phone call, they wouldn't take it seriously. Anyway, the police can trace any call and there's a danger I'd get caught and get sent back to Sacria against my will. No, you'll have to do it.

But what about the letter? Aren't you looking for the Imalic any more?

Of course I am, but take it easy, Dr Jones. I can think

about two things at the same time, I can walk and chew gum at the same time, read and listen to the radio.

In the end, Melog persuaded Dr Jones to phone the police and tell them the story of the dream. While the doctor was on the phone Melog stood at his elbow telling him exactly what to say.

An hour later, the police arrived at Dr Jones's house. They suspected him of abducting and concealing the missing child. By this time Melog had vanished from the doctor's home.

Dr Jones had considerable difficulty in persuading the cardboard constabulary that he knew nothing about the child. His house was searched. His garden was dug up. His floorboards were prised loose.

It was a dream that a friend of mine had, he said for the twentieth time. He made me phone you.

So where is this 'friend' now, sir? the hairywristed, apearmed cardboard policeman asked.

He's gone.

Gone where?

I'm really not sure. He moves house a lot.

And what's his name? another policeman asked. He had a bluish, steel-coloured chin, like Desperate Dan.

Melog.

Melog what?

I don't know.

To Dr Jones, the situation seemed hopeless. He could imagine himself putrifying in a cell and being mistreated by the other inmates although he was innocent, just like Stefan Kisko, and no one coming to his rescue, no one giving him any chance of justice. And hadn't something like it happened to him once before?

But the main policeman whispered something in the origami ear of one of his colleagues. Now they suspected that he was insane. But this was a blessing because the policemen went away without bothering to arrest him for wasting their time, their kindness arising from sympathy and compassion for someone who was clearly short of a few slates.

He isn't even a real doctor, one of them murmured, but Dr Jones heard him.

The main policeman spoke to him as if addressing a small, naughty child, warning him never on any account to waste police time again; they would not be so lenient in future.

Three days later, Dr Jones was reading the paper again. The child from the north of England was found fit and well (so that part of Melog's vision was correct) two miles from his home.

GRASS: moorland grass, or meadow grass; couch grass, which is to say grass which grows on dry soil; coarse grass, namely poor, rushy and worthless grass; malt-grass, namely the grass of wet uplands; and maram grass, which is to say the grass of coastal wetlands which are flooded by the sea.

The Encyclopædia

A COMPATRIOT

DR JONES was working on one his favourite sections of the Encyclopaedia, the article on the Inquisition, volume III, pages 210-14, with the picture (one of the Encyclopaedia's rare but delicious illustrations) of one of the appalling tortures on page 211; Ill. 220, a man suspended by his arms from a pulley, lead weights hanging from his feet, two men pulling on the rope, the Inquisitors sitting at a long table, two wearing mitres, one writing with a quill pen; on the table were two candles, a timing device (like an egg timer) and a hand-bell. 'This article must be viewed against the back-ground of Nonconformity and as propaganda against Catholicism,' Dr Jones wrote in an effort to be objective. He read again fragments from the article in the Encyclopaedia:

> Amid all the cruelties of the pagan world, there is nothing that can compete with the misdeeds of the inquisition; the which were carried out in cold blood, and all in the name of the blessed Saviour...

The author was incapable of finding fault with Christianity generally, only with Catholicism. Dr Jones preferred to read the entry (the only piece on the Inquisition in Welsh as far as he knew) as witness to the dangers of religious fanaticism, as a warning against the perils of Christianity as a whole, and as a reminder of its undeniably terrible past. He read on:

> The barking of the dogs of the inquisition was heard in the valleys of the Alps, before its name was known in England.

Here Dr Jones detected use of the famously ambiguous words – *Domini canes* – but the author had not drawn attention to it.

> Over 200 of these simple Christians were killed in a few months; the emissaries of this accursed court rested not until they were obliterated and excommunicated as hereticks, such that there were scarcely any left in either root or branch. But the numerousness of those killed is not fully indicative of the cruelty of these beasts in human form.

The descriptions of the torture were unexpectedly detailed. Then the article presented evidence from 'a section of Bonaparte's army' dated 1809:

> After opening the doors, I beheld scenes the like of which I would never wish to see again, the details of which are too horrifying to relate. In some of these holes, there were newly dead corpses, others in various stages of putrefaction, some where only the bones remained, and the chains still upon them... among the living prisoners, we found old men and women of three score and ten years, boys and lasses of fourteen and fifteen, and people in their middle years. Some of them had been there for so many years that they could not remember the number...

His work and his thoughts were interrupted by the sound of the door bell.

You look tired, Melog said when the doctor opened the door to him.

Well that's not surprising, Dr Jones said, after you caused me all that bother with the police.

I didn't cause you any trouble! Don't tell such lies. It was you who insisted on phoning them. You didn't listen when I told you it was only a dream.

There was no way of reasoning or arguing with Melog. He was right every time and would never take the blame or admit that he had done anything wrong.

I'm having trouble sleeping, the doctor said. I've tried everything; a pillow with herbs in it, camomile tea, counting sheep, clearing my mind and thinking of black velvet, tapes of whales and dolphins singing, tapes for self hypnosis. Still nothing works.

I've found the perfect answer when I have trouble getting to sleep, Melog said.

What is it? the doctor said eagerly.

I read a page from any prizewinning poem from the National Eisteddfod and then I get straight off to sleep. Mr Job's given up doing his copying and I've got plenty of volumes of *Compositions and Adjudications* from him.

Dr Jones made them a cup of coffee.

What are your plans for today? the doctor asked.

I'm going to visit a fellow Laxarian to see if he knows anything about Benig's visit to Wales and where the Imalic's hidden. Will you come with me?

Yes, Dr Jones said, even though he was unwilling to postpone his important work on the Encyclopaedia. Melog's words worked on him like a spell.

As it happens he lives not far from here, and believe it or not he speaks Welsh too.

Another one of that 'English' teacher's pupils, is he?

No, he belongs to another generation. It's just that he's quite a language nut.

Why haven't you contacted this person earlier? I'm sure that if I were living in a remote foreign country one of the first things I would do would be to contact some of my compatriots, especially if they could speak the country's language.

Why? Melog said. Just because you come from the same country as someone it doesn't follow that you're going to get on with them. I hate some of my compatriots. Do you love all Welsh people?

Not all of them, perhaps.

You aren't over-fond of that Professor Berwyn Boyle Hopkin, for instance, are you?

No, Dr Jones said, realising (as the professor's flushed face and cheery-conservative declamations conjured themselves before him) that the young man was exactly right once more.

And he's a cultured man who's interested in the same things and moves in the same circles you do, isn't he? And yet he gets on your nerves. And some of your countrymen are reactionary right-wing Tories, especially the Socialists. Some of them are stupid, some are hypocrites, especially the ones who pretend to be nationalists.

But in a small country with an oppressed language something binds you together doesn't it?

No it doesn't. Not at all. I've met Laxarians who are utter rats, and Laxaria is a smaller country than Wales, with a language that's more oppressed. I know more or less everybody who speaks Laxarian, there are probably only a few hundred of us left, and the Sacrians under the Socialists, so called, have turned against the language completely – no magazines, no radio, no television, no schools, no books. And even so, some of my best friends are Sacrians, individuals with no hatred of the language, and some of my biggest enemies are Laxarians who're murdering the language and prepared to betray other Laxarians for next to nothing, and sometimes for nothing at all. People are more complicated than factions, nations, genders and classes. Don't oversimplify things, Dr Jones. Having said that, I'm sure the old Laxy we're going to see this afternoon is a very nice person.

A long train journey, and Dr Jones was forced to sit next to a man with two odious, belltoothed sons called Tarquin and Crispin, the grey streets giving way to trees and green hills, and the green giving way to skyscrapers and factories and smoke. The two friends (used to the familiar, impersonal terraced streets of the small town) walked among the labyrinthine concrete blocks of the unfamiliar city – as labyrinthine as the traditional and overelaborated patterns of Laxaria – until (at last) they found the house where the Laxarian lived. He was an old man living in one room and was bed-ridden.

Dr Jones listened to Melog and the old fellow speaking for

a while in Laxarian. This was the first time he had heard the language used freely and fluently. It was full of clicks and something like a child imitating a car starting, the 's' sound often roughened with plenty of 'ch' and something similar to the French 'j'. The vowels were wet and guttural and deep and occasionally extremely nasal. The effect of the language was of some thick liquid, like treacle or honey, flowing over smoothed round stones. The two were obviously pleased with the opportunity to speak their own language again. Their tongues untied and slipped from the foreign leash, words came easily and the dam had burst.

While they chatted, the doctor looked around the room. Most of it was taken up by the bed. Spread over that was a large heavy quilt decorated with Laxarian patterns in gold and black and red. Framed and hanging on the walls were more of these patterns, some of them obviously very old. In fact the old man had created an island, a Laxarian sanctuary, in his poor room in the city. He had literally thousands of books obviously in Laxarian. They formed walls around his bed, volume stacked on volume on shelves, chairs, tables, under tables and chairs, on top of the wardrobe. Every gap was plugged with books. Dr Jones and Melog had had to squeeze their way through this ramshackle library to the old man's bedside, and Melog was actually sitting on the bed. From what Melog had said about the Sacrians burning Laxarian books and presses and then banning all literary output in the language, every one of these volumes was precious.

But an oddity of this bedcentric home was the pots on the shelves – or rather, that is, on top of the piles of books – and on the window-sill. The only thing growing in them was grass, plain, ordinary grass. The pots looked as though they had been neglected and left in place and the grass had over-grown them.

Dr Jones looked at the ancient refugee, tied by old age to his bed. His emaciatedness was different in nature from Melog's; time was to blame for his thinness. He was full of days and suffering and rotted with literature. How old was he? In his eighties at least, ninety, close to a hundred perhaps. He had lost almost all his hair. He was virtually blind. He cupped his right hand to his ear and leant forward on his cushions to hear Melog speak.

At last, Melog and the old man turned to Dr Jones.

Professor Lalula hasn't heard of Benig and he has no idea where the Imalic is, Melog said, unable to hide his disappointment.

I hev gat too ald and febble do geep in douch with all the exiles vrom Laxaria, the Professor said in his strange accent. Nod tad there are many, bud the wark has gat too mudge for me.

Despite the strange pronunciation, Dr Jones marvelled at the fastidious correctness of Melog's countryman's Welsh. At the same time the fastidiousness of the Professor's Welsh showed how completely Melog had been immersed in the language, as any trace of foreignness in his speech had almost disappeared.

At the end of the visit the Professor presented Melog with a volume of poetry in Laxarian, *The Poems of Héla Skelmonn*, and Dr Jones understood already the value of the poet's books for Laxarians.

On the train home Dr Jones asked what the reason had been for the pots of grass filling every space not taken by books.

An old Laxarian religious practice. Some Laxarians still believe that it's unpardonable to live without pasture land around you – really, within arm's length. You get thrown headlong into hell unless you've got grass within reach at all times.

But you don't believe this do you?

No I don't, Melog said. I've lost my faith.

LONDON... Taking them as a whole, the inhabitants of this great city are noteworthy for their adherence to order; even though there is there present extreme immorality, and there are committed within it the most villainous crimes, yet, when its populousness, and the temptations which it harbours to transgression of the law, are considered, then it is no worse than, even if it be so wicked as, many another place.

The Encyclopædia

A LETTER FROM LONDON

ONE NIGHT the doctor could not sleep. He ran his tongue across the ceiling of his mouth, feeling the weals and hard wet hollows of the little cave. Thinking, 'So this is what life is, is it? Feeling the roof of your mouth with your tongue.'

In an attempt to get to sleep, he tried to name ten famous Belgians. The artist Magritte was the most famous of them – *Ceci n'est pas un pipe*, and so on, the little man in the bowler hat. Paul de Man, the post-modern crapcritic – but he didn't really count because he wasn't famous enough and he had become an American citizen. Hergé the cartoonist, creator of Tin Tin and the dog Snowy – but wasn't it the pictures that were famous rather than the man? Who was Hergé, after all? But the pictures of Snowy were so wonderful that he deserved a place on the list. Georges Simenon, creator of Maigret, the unforgivably prolific author, so prolific that he wasn't taken seriously as an author. Jean Claude van Damme, The Muxelles from Bruscles; but did such a bad actor in such rubbishy films and vomitty videos deserve to be on the list? But that's five and after that it gets more difficult. Maurice Maeterlinck – a strange case; he was some kind of an earl and an author in two languages, a dramatist who eventually won the Nobel Prize – and who remembers his work now? Name one of his works, Dr Jones. *Pelléas et*

Melisande. All right, but you were thinking of the opera, not the play. That's six. Come on, Dr Jones, one more, one more name before you go to sleep. Spinoza? No. He was a Dutchman. And no, you may not include members of the royal family, only individuals who have won plaudits by the fruits of their own talents. One more? No? Ready to give in? The eyelids getting heavy, closing... Geulincx!

Geulincx? Yes, Arnold Geulincx, 1624-69 (pronounced 'goylinks'). Born in Antwerp, a pupil of Descartes. He said: *ubi nihil vales, ibi nihil velis*. I wonder if there's an entry about him in the Encyclopaedia. And as he was thinking that, Dr Jones's eyes closed and he went to sleep. Then his two alarms rang and he had to get up.

That morning Dr Jones received several letters; two about unpaid bills, one from the department of social security threatening to move him or cut his benefit, and one from Melog:

Dear Dr Jones,
    I am in London, and I must relate to you the tale of an adventure that befell me in the underground in this great and most antiquitous city.
    I was travelling on the train the other day reading the old volume of poems by Héla Skelmonn which I had from Professor Lalula, to keep the old language alive in my head, as it were, when someone came up and sat beside me. I felt uncomfortable immediately, as he came very close and pressed his body against me. Suddenly he held something under my nose and said (in English, of course, but I translate), 'There is gas in this phial and if I were to open it, the gas would kill you in seconds.'
    What, I wonder, would you have done in this situation, Dr Jones? My first thought was that the man was a maniac. But did the phial indeed contain poison gas, or simply hot air? You must understand that these considerations flashed through my mind all at once, as it were in the blinking of an eye. The problem was that either the idiot was idiotic because he was prepared to use poison gas, or he was mad because he believed

he was holding a phial containing poison but which was in fact empty. The first madman is extremely dangerous while the second is very innocent. But how was a man in my predicament to divine the difference? In these few seconds, I reasoned that the gas, if it were poisonous, would kill not only me but the madman too – but of course if he were truly insane, then perhaps his heedlessness of the danger to himself was a feature of his insanity. But even if the phial was empty and devoid of poison, I had in effect accepted and believed it to be a fact that it was poisonous, as I could scarcely move from fear. If a man insist that he is holding a poison-filled phial under your nose and threatens to open it, then you must take him at his word. To all intents and purposes there is poison in the bottle – poison or no, you are not in a position to negotiate or to try to test out his truthfulness.

What do you want? I asked him.

Money. All the money you've got.

I haven't got any money. (That was the problem – I had not a single bean, as the saying goes.)

All your money. Come on, quick.

It's the truth. I haven't got any money.

He moved his hand as if to open the phial. It was then I decided that killing someone and committing suicide à la Samson because a money-stealing-conspiracy had failed was stretching credulity too far. Perhaps a madman would be ready to kill and to kill himself, but I decided that I would take my chance. I rose abruptly and walked through the doors into the next carriage. The madman came after me. But there were more people in this carriage. Was the idiot going to threaten them all with his poison phial? He stared at me ferociously.

Do you see this man? I shouted to the other passengers. The phial in his hand contains poison gas and he's threatening to open it.

The Londoners scowled at me as if I had taken leave of my senses.

The man with the phial gave out a rabid snarl.

The train stopped at a station, the doors opened, I ran out and the man pursued me like a bloodhound. But my feet grew wings and I ran like the wind along the long and narrow corridors, taking an escalator five steps at a time, up into the street, out into the ünwholesome open air, and still I ran, ran like a greyhound, like a racehorse, never turning back, like a cheetah. Truly, I flew. And of course, I had left the madman far behind, I knew not where, because I did not know that I had lost him. As far as I was concerned, he chased me still like a hound running down a hare. He had frightened me, and the fear pursued me long after the madman had lost my scent. And for days afterwards I did not feel safe; at every corner I expected to come face to face with that fatal phial-keeper, behind every door, and needless to say, down every tube. I feared he would follow me to Wales, or even to Laxaria.

That is the way the mind operates. I still ponder this and ask where truly was the fear? Was it in the phial, or in the crazed man, or in my fleeing? And now, at last, the fear has receded. Receded without good reason, because the danger, the threat, is still there, and it is not impossible that I should meet the man again in this enormous city, or in Wales, or, indeed, in Laxaria.

I feel the better for sharing this (dreadful) experience with you.

Regards,
  Melog

P.S. In case you are surprised to hear from me in London, I have come here to visit some people and places that have connections with Laxaria which Professor Lalula mentioned. I will come back quite soon.

INVENTION… It should in addition be observed that invention, in the sense of imagination, can also present and display new forms, not only of objects in the natural world, but also of things in the world of the mind and the spirit.

The Encyclopædia

THE VISIT

DR JONES felt certain that the man with the phial knew something about Melog. Perhaps he was a Sacrian extremist and had noticed the young man reading a book in Laxarian. But having said that, the threats demanding money were consistent with the psychology of a man with his mind on one thing only, namely theft.

But Dr Jones was not sure. What did he know about Melog, after all? On one of the little index cards he used for his notes (three inches by five, a heavy blue line and nine lines of light grey in quarter inch feint) he wrote down what he knew about Melog:

1. Met him after he made a show of throwing himself off the Town Hall. Why? Don't know.
2. Incredible story about how he came to learn Welsh.
3. Took him to an exhibition. Boy stole a sculpture from it.
4. Stole a stuffed white blackbird from the museum in town.
5. He comes and goes like a ping pong ball.
6. Steals cars even though he can't drive.
7. He steals letters.
8. Claims he comes from Laxaria, small country oppressed by another, Sacria, but nobody's heard of either of them.
9. Goes off to Morocco and London without saying a word. Comes back and carries on as before.

Dr Jones tore the card into small pieces and threw them like confetti into the waste-paper basket (which was large and full of small pieces of paper) next to his desk. At that moment, an unpleasant question crossed Dr Jones's mind. Who was looking after all the cats? Perhaps he ought to go to his lodgings to see whether Melog had locked them in his room and forgotten about them. Although it was more than likely that Mr Job was taking care of them. But 'more than likely'! What if they had all starved to death in that little room?

Dr Jones went to Mr Job's house immediately. After all, Mr Job was confused and bewildered, wasn't he?

Come in, come in, the old copyist said. Now how can I help or be of assistance to you?

I'd like to know what arrangements Melog has made about the cats.

The old man looked at him like a blank blackboard. He had not heard a word.

But then Melog himself appeared. He came down the stairs looking thin and white as a ghost in the entrance of the dark house.

Don't worry, Mr Job. Dr Jones will come up and have a cup of tea with me now.

Perplexed, the doctor followed his friend (though he could not feel sure in his mind that this was his friend) to his one-room home.

There was no need for you to worry. I asked Mr Job to feed the cats. Mr Job is the greatest landlord in the world. For one thing he never takes a penny of rent off me, and he doesn't complain about the cats; in fact he's fond of them. He's learnt the names of every one of them, all ten.

Melog, I was under the impression that you were in London, Dr Jones said. He had accepted that this was Melog after all.

I have been in London. I've come back from London.

Did you meet any of your fellow countrymen?

Yes I did. Take a seat and I'll tell you the story. I'll make a cup of tea.

The doctor could scarcely find a place to sit in such a

small room so full of cats which monopolised every seat. He got scratched when he removed two ginger cats.

Yes, I found a man by the name of Gogo Lapula, Melog said, living in a room in Battersea. Have you noticed something? I and all my fellow exiles live in awful rooms. We never manage to get on in the world. Gogo's been moving round quite a bit, picking up odd jobs – cleaning, doing road mending, in shops and cafés, in garages. He's working in a shirt warehouse at the moment. Now Gogo's an odd one for you.

Does he speak Welsh too?

No, as it happens, and his English is pretty ropy. He didn't manage to master English properly and because of that he was persecuted mercilessly back in Laxaria and that's why he decided he'd better run away and come to this country, Britain, that is. It was too late for him to start learning English, he said. He's fifty-odd. To tell you the truth, I'm afraid his intellectual resources are a bit limited, otherwise he would have learnt more than 'Good morning' and 'My name is Gogo Lapula' and 'No English'. He can't understand why everybody laughs every time he says 'My name is Gogo Lapula'. Apart from the strange sound of his name to English people, of course, that's the answer he gives to any question he's asked. 'Have you got any money?' 'My name is Gogo Lapula.' 'What do you think of British democracy?' 'My name is Gogo Lapula.' Even in our own language you can tell he's weak. He thinks irony is what happens when you press your clothes. I stayed with him for an afternoon helping him to fill forms in and answering letters.

Don't talk to me about forms, Dr Jones said, I have enough trouble with the reams of them that come through the door every day, even the ones in Welsh.

The two friends sipped cups of strong dark tea. Melog sat on the bed and Dr Jones sat in one chair while cats sprawled and clawed on the other. Cats were lying on the narrow bed too, but there was enough room for Melog among them. The sculpture of otherworldly creatures which Melog had stolen from the exhibition stood on a small table and, still in its glass case, the white blackbird from the museum – but Melog had changed the background – in the corners there were Laxarian decorations and a landscape of small, rounded hills, a purple sky, tall, skeletal trees.

As though he was reading Dr Jones's mind, Melog moved his slender hand to the sculpture and started to stroke it as if it were another cat.

I love this, he said. If I do go back to Laxaria I'll take it with me, and the white blackbird too. I don't know how I'm going to carry them.

He's a criminal isn't he? Dr Jones thought. A law-breaker, a thief? And yet I don't feel angry with him. He's a free spirit. Nobody can pen him in, not even the Sacrian dictatorship. Is it because he's so white, so thin, so fragile looking, is that why I can't take his badness seriously?

SALT [L., sal, Ar., holem]: An extremely well-known substance and of the greatest import. It is contained, in greater or lesser amounts, in sea water everywhere. In Britain, and in other places, such as France, Hungary, Poland, Spain, & c., it forms enormous rocks in the earth. A great deal of it is also produced by salt springs; and the soil itself contains it in a large part of the desert lands of Africa and Asia.

The Encyclopædia

LAVCADIO

MELOG stood like an X-ray of a starved body next to the sculpture he had stolen from the exhibition, a cigarette in his right hand and a cloud of violet smoke turning around his head.

This afternoon, Dr Jones, I'd like to introduce you to my new friend.

What new friend?

You shall see. We're going to town to meet him in Jabez Ifans's potato tavern.

Even before he had met this unnamed person, the doctor felt envy hardening like a cancerous growth inside him. For some reason that was not clear to him he did not like the idea of Melog mixing with other people, let alone having friends.

Sitting at the only table in the café was a large black man. Melog went up to him immediately. The stranger stood when he saw the young man and a row of teeth as white as Melog's skin flashed in the dark face. The two embraced in warm friendship – nobody paid any attention as they clearly weren't British.

The black man was as tall as Melog, but he was as broad and muscular as Melog, beside him, was thin and weak (though Melog was thin and weak next to anybody). The other obvious contrast was the colour of their skin – one like paper and the other like ink.

This is Lavcadio, Melog said. Lavcadio, this is Dr Jones.

I'm pleased to meet you, Dr Jones, the giant said, grasping Dr Jones's hand and shaking it warmly enough almost to remove it from its socket. Melog talks about you all the time. 'Dr Jones this, Dr Jones that.' I'm happy to make your acquaintance at last.

He laughed energetically, revealing his glitterwhite teeth again.

Dr Jones was surprised to hear a stream of perfectly correct Welsh coming from such a foreign looking mouth – slab lips, pink tongue, alabaster teeth – in the accents of the capital city.

Thank you very much, Dr Jones said, without any idea of what else to say. After all, Melog had never mentioned this person before. Apart from which, Lavcadio's ebullience had rather thrown him.

The trio sat around the table and Dr Jones stared at the tablecloth and its greaseslicked pattern of yellow and orange flowers. Old Jabez came up to them.

Three coffees, and fish and chips three times, Melog said. This one's my treat.

Dr Jones watched the other two speaking, exchanging news – as it were, comparing notes. He realised yet again that he knew almost nothing about Melog and that he could not believe in the young man's life as an entity separate from his own. He was struck for the first time – or for the hundredth – by the horror of the fact that Melog was independent of him, free, and that he lived a full life through all the hours and the days when the doctor did not see him. To Dr Jones, that life was a mystery and an unreal fantasy, as alien and unreachable as Laxaria.

Suddenly the doctor realised that two pairs of eyes were staring at him, one pair skyblue as daylight and the other skydark as starlit night.

Dr Jones, Melog said, you're very quiet.

The cat's got his tongue, the giant said, laughing at his

own hilariousness, the muscles of his neck bulging and blue.

I'm sorry, the doctor said, I've got a sore throat. The doctor invented the excuse on the spot – the truth was that there was nothing physically wrong with him.

A sore throat? Don't worry, Dr Jones. I know the best thing for a sore throat.

Do you, Lavcadio? Melog said, glowing with admiration. I'm amazed how much you know sometimes.

Lavcadio took the spoon that lay on the edge of his saucer by his cup and took the salt cellar from the middle of the table. He poured a little heap of the white crystals into the hollow of the spoon.

Open your mouth, Dr Jones.

What are you going to do? the doctor asked, doubtfully.

Open your mouth wide, Lavcadio said, displaying again his own brilliant smile.

No I won't. Tell me what you intend to do, the doctor said anxiously.

Oh come on, Dr Jones. Open your mouth like Lavcadio's asking you to.

Hesitantly, the doctor opened his mouth. Lavcadio grasped his chin, pushed back his head, and poured the spoonful of salt into the back of his throat. Dr Jones gagged and coughed and thought he would suffocate. He gulped a mouthful of coffee. The coffee was hot.

Is your throat better now, Dr Jones? Lavcadio asked, smiling like a piano.

Yes, Dr Jones croaked.

There you are, Melog said. Lavcadio knows everything.

Always happy to be of assistance to anyone, Lavcadio said.

And that was the first time Dr Jones met Melog's bosom friend Lavcadio.

MEURYN AND MEURIG

IN THE TOWN AGAIN, on his own again, without Melog for company, Dr Jones walked, feeling himself on the one hand to be an outsider but on the other hand free once more. He always felt like this when he and Melog were apart; like a leg without a body, like that leg buried on its own in the graveyard at Strata Florida, like the knee in Morgenstern's poem, like the nose in the story by Gogol. He was in danger of starting to compose a story he was not able to finish. But Melog could be a strain on his nerves; he was a bother and a nuisance. How could he concentrate on his study of the Encyclopaedia with Melog complicating his life?

That morning it felt good to go to the social security office and be treated like a subnormal dog, to go to the post office and be ignored by his neighbours, to walk around Woolworth's, and to slip on a greasy bag of chipped potatoes that someone had thrown down on the pavement outside Jabez Ifans's – it felt good because these were concrete, material things; they were real.

Dr Jones went to the town library, overcome by a desire to read realist, naturalistic authors, the ones who could convince you of the world and what was in it by means of their descriptiveness and their conversational language. He looked for the works of Flaubert, the works of Graham Greene, Saul Bellow. He did not want any humour, nothing but the truth in every eloquent detail. He was looking for texts that were heavy and dense under forests of rich detail, and all of it leading to the realist effect.

He was coming out of the library with a copy of *Arthur's*

Nightmare under his arm when someone greeted him.

Good afternoon, Dr Jones.

Good afternoon, Dr Jones, f★★★ ★ff!

He knew them both instantly. The brothers Meuryn and Meurig ap Harri. Dr Jones had been at school with them. They were unignorable in their grey suits, their clean collars and their dead straight ties, standing side by side like toys; there was nothing for it but to go and talk to them. But talk about what? What subject should they treat of out of all that was in the world, under heaven, on the face of the earth? He had nothing in common with them apart from their childhood and the fact that they had been born and brought up in the same town and had lived there, the three of them, all their lives and still lived there, unlike their wiser or more successful or more ambitious contemporaries who had moved away to grassier pastures at the first chance. They had not the slightest interest in what interested him, his work on the Encyclopaedia, for instance, and Dr Jones had not the slightest interest in what interested them, which was the town's gossip. Everyone's horizons have their limits, and if the limits on yours are different from the limits on theirs, what can you talk about?

By this time, Dr Jones had crossed from the lobby of the library to where the twins were standing.

I haven't seen you in ages, Meuryn said smiling cheerily.

Haven't seen you in f★★★ing ages, ★uck o★★! Meurig said, smiling just as cheerily and happily.

No, Dr Jones said. This weather.

Been miserable, hasn't it? Meuryn said.

Nothing but rain rain f★★★ing rain, Meurig said, his smile as wide as a gate.

It makes me ill all this rain, Dr Jones said, and the wind.

The wind is cutting, Meuryn agreed.

It has been cutting, f###! his brother said.

That's all we get now is wind and rain. The winter's wet, there's no snow, and the summer's wet too.

And it's so cold for this time of year, Meuryn said.

Wind and rain, b*st*rd! Meurig said.

You never know what to wear, do you? Dr Jones said. I'm afraid to leave the house without wearing a mac and carrying an umbrella.

I always carry an umbrella, a little collapsible one just in case, don't I, Meurig?

Me too, always, a little collapsible one just in case it rains, *otherf***er!

And the garden gets sopping doesn't it? Dr Jones said, though he was no gardener.

Oh aye, the garden's sopping wet, isn' it, Meurig?

Aye, sopping bl**dy bl**dy wet, m*therf*ck*r!

And nothing gets a chance to dry out, Dr Jones said. Your shoes are wet all the time, your clothes are wet, your bones are wet.

Good afternoon, Meuryn said.

Good afternoon, f+++ o++! Meurig said.

They were not saying goodbye to Dr Jones but greeting Melog, who had come and stood beside his friend without his noticing.

You'll have to excuse my brother, Meuryn said to Melog. He suffers from something similar to Tourette's which causes him to swear all the time, completely involuntarily and against his wishes, of course.

I can fucking explain! You never give me a chance, do you? How do you expect people to learn about a thing such as Tourette's if the sufferer him bloody self doesn't get a chance to fucking explain! Fucker!

And Meurig turned to Melog with a gentle smile.

I'm sorry, I can't help it, I have no control over it. It's like a hick or a tic or a twitch. It's completely unintentional. You mustn't judge me, you must excuse me – MUTHAFUCKA!

By all means, Melog said.

And at that, the twins bade farewell to Dr Jones and Melog.

Good afternoon.

Good afternoon. Fucking shitbags!

What an unpleasant experience, Melog said when the twins were out of earshot.

You sound exactly like some old Welsh deacon.

What's that supposed to mean?

Judgmental, self-righteous, as if you expect the birds to cover their bottoms when they fly over you. He doesn't mean anything when he swears like that. The swear words mean nothing to him. Just as he said, it's a tic he's got no control over. The truth is it's rather a sad thing.

A pity he can't swear in Welsh, Melog said.

Then you'd accuse him of besmirching the language, just as an old chapel elder would. People like Meurig need our sympathy, and when you see him you should remember that to him the words are only sounds and unintentional exclamations completely without significance.

If you say so, Melog said, but I'm not so sure.

I can assure you that there's no harm in Meurig at all. I've known him and his brother, Meuryn, since they were children.

I wonder what he'd do for his 'unintentional exclamations' if he'd never learnt those Anglo Saxon words.

Some linguistic experts have traced the word f..., that word, to a Celtic root. It's actually an old Welsh word. But whatever the truth about that may be, what about you? Where have you been and what have you been doing?

LAVCADIO AND MELOG

THE OTHER DAY, Dr Jones was shopping in the town when he saw Melog and Lavcadio walking through the crowd. They were easy to spot; they were so tall and graceful, two towers above small, ordinary rooftops, two trees on the savannah, two mountains on the plains, both of them tall and beautiful.

The one so white and the other so black. So fair and shapely; an utter contrast with the squat grey and brown people around them – it was truly difficult to believe that they were members of the same species.

They walked so close together that the doctor could not be sure that they were not holding hands – was that possible? – their hands were out of sight; only their heads and shoulders floated, as it were, above the crowd. They were not conscious of him, had not seen him, and he could watch them moving slowly (everyone else was rushing) in an unaltering line away from him until they dissolved into the distance among the people and the cars and the shops and the streets. Two pretty ships sailing on a yellow river.

They were not aware of his existence. So young and so handsome they were, and, it seemed, so at peace with one another. Dr Jones had not seen Melog for weeks and then he caught a glimpse of him like this and an arrow went through his heart. He did not understand this pang. What did it signify? Melog was free wasn't he? A free spirit whom no one could snare or tame? He knew that well enough. And Lavcadio was sufficiently pleasant, always genial and kind, cheerful and obliging, courteous. The truth was, he was flawless.

Then Dr Jones saw Meuryn and Meurig coming towards him. There was no way of avoiding them but he did not want to speak to them because some fit of low spirits had suddenly taken hold of him and the necessity of feigning politeness and pretending that all was well was suddenly too much for him. His only hope was to greet them and then try to slip past. But when to greet? He was certain that the twins had seen him and it was obvious that he had seen them. If he greeted them too soon it would seem like a signal to stop and talk. If he left it too late, he would appear unwilling to acknowledge them. Why was something so simple and ordinary as saying 'Hello' or 'Good afternoon' so infernally awkward sometimes? It was all a matter of timing but there were no guidelines, no rules. Nobody knew the right time to greet.

Hello!

Good afternoon, Dr Jones.

Good afterf***ingnoon, Dr f___ _ff Jones.

Thank goodness, for some reason they did not stop to speak. All was well. Excellent. Both went by easily, without waiting to say anything, merely greeted him.

But had his unwillingness to stop and chat been evident? Had his feelings somehow been translated into his face or his eyes? Had they read his body language? Had his body itself betrayed him and his gestures said 'Don't you talk to me!'? Had they sensed his unsociable nature? Had his 'Hello' been too abrupt, too cold, unfriendly, high-handed? Now he was starting to worry that he had offended old friends without thinking, that he had hurt the feelings of his old neighbours with his selfishness and insensitivity. Too late now. They were gone, had taken umbrage, and he would get no word of Welsh from them again.

Dr Jones went in through the wide glass doors of Emrys Rees Evans's shop – indeed they were opened before him by invisible hands. This was the biggest shop in the town. It was empty apart from the assistants behind the counters. No one in the area could afford to look (not to mention buy) in

Emrys Evans's overpriced shop. Dr Jones gazed at the expensive aftershaves (small multi-coloured bottles, green, blue, yellow; bottles of every shape: aeroplanes, barrels, stars, pyramids, shoes, phials, flasks, diamonds, crowns, but every one of them made of glass and containing perfumed liquid – as Dr Jones went past a young man armed with a glass gun containing orange fluid sprayed him), he went to the umbrellas (most of them black, standing like exclamation marks, some opened like bats, some that you could fold like a handkerchief, some small, some huge so that they encompassed a man like wings – purple, red, yellow, orange – the odd one in three colours – yellow/blue/red or orange/green/mauve – some with stars on them, dogs, ducks, leaves, feathers, cups). He went to the leather goods department (cases, suitcases, wallets), through the light fittings department, and from there to the luxury foods, the chocolates – white and pink, with nuts, without nuts, dark brown, light brown, soft, hard, creamy, bitter – and resisted buying any because he was putting weight on and anyway they cost too much – then went to the fragile goods department, china and glass. The doctor felt nervous there, like the proverbial bull in a china shop. He remembered Jaco Saunders's collection. He worried that he would knock one of the horses or the shepherdesses or the brittle-looking swans to the floor and have to pay for it (in his mind's eye the doctor could see them falling and shattering now; the slender legs, the long neck, the thin long crook smashed to pieces on the hard floor). The best thing to do, he decided, was to leave the shop before his pocket suffered an expensive accident. After all, there was nothing he had to buy there.

But once again, the timing of his movements was all-important. If he were to move too quickly he would be accused of stealing something from the shop – and what if one of those little glass snails, by some diabolical happenstance, had fallen into his pocket? But if he were to move too slowly he would appear suspicious to the other occasional shoppers in the store, who were not shoppers at all but detectives waiting to trap an innocent such as himself and plant goods about his person in order to justify their jobs and their wages. Every time he went into a big store the doctor had this same horrific nightmare. He dared not put his hands in his pockets in case he looked suspicious. He crossed his arms, putting his left hand on his right shoulder and his right hand on his left shoulder to show the cameras which watched him and were recording his every move that he was not stealing anything. And locked in that unnatural and uncomfortable position, Dr Jones slipped out through the vast, wide doors of Emrys Rees Evans' (which were opened before him by invisible hands, as if to say 'God speed, and don't hurry back').

He had not travelled far through the busy streets of the town on his way home when he heard someone say:

Dr Jones, how are you? Long time no see.

The doctor turned to see the gaptoothed, malodorous mouth of the Saint smiling on him.

Well, well, and how are you? He counterfeited his delight.

The truth was that Dr Jones did not immediately recall Melog's old neighbour. The only thing that Dr Jones could see apart from that sickly jaw was a swollen, outsized, redrimmed yellowcentred pimple on the Saint's nose.

How are you? How is Melog? I haven't seen the fellow in a long time.

Neither have I, Dr Jones said.

I was rather fond of old Melog...

Dr Jones knew that the man was speaking; he knew because his mouth was opening and shutting and the tongue was moving and because words were falling from it higgledy piggledy, but the only thing he could see and the only thing he knew was the sore, ugly pimple, and that he, Dr Jones, was staring at it, was unable to tear his eyes from it, and that the speaker knew that Dr Jones was staring at his pimple. There was nothing for it but to look at the time and pretend that he was in a hurry.

Well, well, he said looking at his watch, there's the time. I must go. Excuse me.

Nice talking to you, Dr Jones. Remember me to that nice boy.

The trick worked – in spite of the fact that he was not wearing a watch – but as he turned and walked homewards he could not be quite certain whether or not he said something like 'Cheerio, Mr Bimple!' as he had left the Saint.

In his kitchen Dr Jones made a cup of tea. He looked around his home. All the possessions; the furniture and the pictures, the books and the compact discs, the electrical gadgets, the clothes, curtains, crockery, lamps, the cupboards and drawers full of odds and ends, not to mention his papers – the documents and the files and the envelopes and the notes and the notes on the notes and the footnotes on the notes on the notes. With all these things around him and his whole life grounded in them it was unsurprising that he was not free, as Melog was, to pack a bag on a whim and vanish and then reappear like a flash in the dark whenever he liked.

Have I misunderstood Melog? Dr Jones asked himself, looking at his anticlockwise clock. Yes, he said, answering his selfquestioning. Yes, I've misunderstood him, misinterpreted him, I haven't understood him at all, I thought I understood him but that was a mistake…

He looked at the clock again; it was a quarter past one, that is, a quarter to eleven. But Dr Jones was not sure what the time was; the trick clock confused him sometimes, and he knew that time did not run backwards in reality – that was self-deception – time flowed (metaphorically) forwards, as it would, inevitably, mercilessly, in spite of all the scientific-philosophical theories. The truth was that Dr Jones had grown older since he had met Melog but he understood him no better. He had misunderstood his hair, misunderstood his skin, misunderstood his eyes, misunderstood his lips, and the words that came from his lips. The gentle, comradely matiness was a deception – an intentionalunintentional deception.

Sometimes Dr Jones would meditate on his friend's planned suicide. Why had a young, healthy, able, handsome young man like Melog considered killing himself? He thought of his bluecold nakedness at the top of the high building that day and the disaster that was miraculously averted. The boy was surely serious about his intention at the time. This was not to be some half-hearted attempt, not some little scratch on the arms with a rusted razor, no handful of headache tablets and a call for the ambulance straight after but an act of terrible danger that would have made death a certainty. In his worst nightmares the doctor saw his beloved friend on the pavement at the feet of the cynical onlookers, at the base of the Town Hall, a heap of blood and bone – the fine long bones shattered, the porcelain skull in smithereens, teeth scattered, a leg here, fingers there, fragments of the crown like the shell of an egg, one blue eye in the gutter and the other hanging from a hole in the head like something out of Picasso, all of it in a stew of ruddled gore.

What, he wondered, had pushed him to such an extremity that he could think to annihilate himself like this, to throw himself away like a piece of rubbish? But the doctor understood the feeling – that was why he had not asked the young man about it. Hadn't he, Dr Jones, planned to do something similar using one of the, by comparison, far less painful and far more cowardly techniques? How often had he been ready to leap into the arms of death?

When Robby Beynon, the five year old child of one of his neighbours disappeared, the police had come straight to him and gone through his things and taken him to the cardboard police station and questioned him again and again.

Now then, 'Dr' Jones – he could hear the derision in their voices, could hear the quotation marks around the word 'doctor' – Now then, 'Dr' Jones, exactly where were you on the day Robby was abducted in the street? Where, 'Dr' Jones? What were you doing, 'Dr' Jones? Do you like little boys? How did you know where the lad's body was, 'doctor'?

I was in my house, on my own, working on the Encyclopaedia.

They did not believe him. He had no right to be in the house on his own. He could not prove that he was in the house all night. And afterwards he was released because there was no evidence against him. After all, he had done nothing to Robby Beynon. Only discovered his body in a bush one day when he was out for a walk on his own.

The press gathered round his house like birds of prey, and neighbours howled like dogs for his flesh. They – the crowd – had judged him and found him guilty. Even after the police had caught the true murderer – the child's own stepfather – even after the step-father's confession, some of the neighbours believed unshakably that he, 'Dr' Jones, was the guilty one (he looked like a dirty old man, a child molester; glasses, anorak, thinning greasy hair). And certainly nobody came to apologise – not one cardboard constable came and said 'We're sorry, Dr Jones', not one neighbour came and said 'We're sorry for what we said, Dr Jones', no apology was published in the newspapers which had suspected him and called for him to be hanged. In those times how easy, how pleasant it would have been, to fall asleep for ever.

When he became a school teacher for a brief period he could not keep control of the children; the work did not suit him, or rather he did not suit the work. The school became monstrous in his mind, the children demonic. He had to go into a mental hospital for 'treatment'. He could not think of that time. He had to wipe it from his memory.

And then, he had felt the same depression, that time of the disappointment about the doctorate.

Philosophers, writers, and poets have differed greatly in the characterisations and descriptions they have offered us of the capacities and actions of that sublime faculty called invention. It is frequently used of the ability to make objects present before the mind's eye in their absence.

The Encyclopædia

THE UNCLE

THERE IS NO SPRING IN THIS TOWN. The season does not spring, usually, but crawls, dressed in black. Sometimes when the weather is gentler than usual (that is, rainy), it staggers in in grey. But this year is exceptional, and so the season shambles in in shades of brown. The grey clouds roll back and a sun the colour of an old penny shows itself in a bronze sky. On the sootcoloured branches of blackened trees, leaves unfurl, but the leaves this year are the buffgreen of copper rust. And on these branches the small brown birds dart despite their lameness, their misshapen feet, their skewed wings, their blinded eyes – most of the birds are onelegged. This is the closest in living memory that anyone has come to hearing the sound of spring in the town – the chocolatey voices (their throats clogged with smoke and pollution) of the house sparrows. In the park, snowdrops, daffodils, foxgloves and crocuses prick through the brownsward – though only their leaves, because nothing blossoms in the town, even when it is shamble (rather than crawl). But leaves are better than nothing, the usual barren nothing.

There was a sheen to this brownness the town had. It was a new brown, a brown, that hinted it might become green. This brown shamble held intimations of true spring, before very long perhaps, but not yet, not this year. This year you had to welcome the shamble and take delight in that, or at least make something of it, the best you could.

Sitting on a bench in the park; a litter bin beside him; a buff envelope from the social security department torn into small pieces in the bin; looking across the yellowbrown lawn, watching a rust blackbird drawing a long, stubborn, elastic redbrown worm from the cococoloured earth, sat Dr Jones. It was a mild, sepia day in early shamble.

The doctor rose from his seat and walked down the slope towards the lake. He sat again on a bench at the edge of the brown, coffeelike, wrenbrown, shitcolour water.

And unexpectedly Melog came and sat beside him. He looked like a man who had just scratched his way out of his own coffin, grown so thin that you could count his teeth through the flesh of his cheek.

Do you remember the night we went across the lake to that little island, Dr Jones?

It's that night I was just thinking about, the doctor said. He could not believe that this was the same Melog, his friend, and not some illusion issued from his mind – but who else would know about their trip to the island?

That's an odd thing. I think about it often too, Melog said. It was fun, wasn't it?

A herd of small beastlike children charged past them, torturing a puppy. Another swarm stopped to pull faces and make fun of Melog before they ran off calling names.

But sometimes when I look across this lake, I think of Sacria.

I remember you saying.

No, not about my home Laxaria, about Sacria. There are ponds like this in the capital city. There's one like this one outside the huge office where an uncle of mine works.

You've got an uncle working in Sacria?

Yes. He's an important man, too. He's the Second Assistant Secretary to the Deputy Chief Inspector of the Sub-department in the Laxarian Office in Sacria. Needless to say, nobody in that office knows that he's a Laxarian or he wouldn't be working there. He changed the spelling of his name from Gelhamni to Gelhamnee to suit Sacrian orthography. His colleagues and neighbours all think he's a genuine Sacrian. He's immersed himself in Sacrian culture, language and literature, and he never lets a word of his first language get past his lips. He's done everything he can to get rid of his Laxarian accent and now he sounds more Sacrian than the Sacriest of them. Well, he'd be shot straight away if anyone heard him speaking Laxarian. Even so, I went to see him in his office once. He was all hot and bothered for fear it'd dawn on somebody that I was related to him.

'Come on,' I said to him, 'we'll go for a stroll round one of the lakes.'

But before we left his office I noticed a picture in a gilt frame on the wall; a fat man with a walrus moustache under his nose, quite amazingly like a cartoon character.

I asked my uncle, perfectly innocently, 'Who's that?'

'That is the Deputy Chief Inspector himself,' Uncle Gelhamni said. 'And I am his Second Assistant Secretary. He's my boss. A very pleasant man, extremely kind. I had a Christmas card from him once. A man of culture, too, as you would expect of somebody in his position.'

After Uncle Gelhamni put his hat and coat on and took his umbrella from the umbrella stand by the door of his room, he took his *nittalaag* – that is, his besteverydayubrella forawkwardautumnalshowerswhenwalkingintheparkat night, instead of his *nittatsug* – which would have been his besteverydayumbrellaforawkwardautumnalshowerswhen walkingintheparkwithafriend/relative, but I didn't take offence. We went out into the city. It wasn't raining. My uncle took my arm and dragged me, rather, away from the building where his office was.

'The Deputy Chief Inspector is a very important man,' my uncle said, 'and there are lots of calls on his time every day, but few people appreciate just how busy he is. That is my job, Malik. (He insisted on using the Sacrian form of my name despite my opposition.) I am responsible for putting the applications for interviews with the Deputy Chief Inspector into order. I have to discriminate between the ones which merit being put before him. Out of the thousands of applicants few get to see him personally. We have names that have been on our waiting lists for interviews for years – only to be rejected in the end. Some people come to see me rather than the Deputy Chief Inspector himself. That shows how important I am. The ones who can go above my head to see him are very rare.'

I asked him, 'What does he do exactly, Uncle Gelhamni?'

'Well,' he said (we were sitting on a bench like this looking across a lake not dissimilar to this one and the sun was glinting on the water, I'll never forget the moment), 'the Deputy Chief Inspector is responsible for choosing the names.'

'What names?'

'The Winners, the Fortunate Ones, of course.'

I can remember, Melog said, I can remember ducks on the water and the sound of a brass band in the distance, the sound of traffic and the busy-ness of the city when I asked him:

'And how exactly would he do that, Uncle Gelhamni?'

'A hat, my boy, he puts all the names in a hat, shakes it, and pulls some out. And those are the names of the Fortunate Ones.'

That, Melog said, was when I decided it was time to get out of Sacria and Laxaria.

What about your President? Dr Jones asked.

The last time I heard, Melog said, he'd been on a life support machine in a coma for eighteen months.

How can he run a country like that? He's useless isn't he?

Quite the opposite, the young man said. He's a very effective president, better than some members of the government.

But the government sounds appalling, Dr Jones said. I don't understand why the people put up with it. Why is there no opposition, no revolt?

There are protesters, Melog said, but they're a small

minority. The government is very popular.

Later, Dr Jones and Melog went to Melog's house.

Why are we drinking coffee from paper cups?

Because the dishes are all dirty, the young man answered.

So wash them then.

I don't know how to, Dr Jones.

Don't be so silly.

No, Dr Jones. I can't wash up and I can't count either. I suffer from dyscalculia, that is a form of dyslexia with numbers.

And you know what the clinical term is for somebody who can't wash the dishes, don't you? The skives. Lead-swinging. Laziness.

Don't make fun of me, Dr Jones.

The two were silent for a while, watching the cats climb over the furniture. Then Melog said:

Dr Jones, may I ask you a question?

What sort of a question?

A personal one.

What is it then?

What's your Christian name?

My first name? You won't laugh, will you?

Laugh? Me? Dr Jones, I hope you know me better than that by now.

You swear?

I swear.

… Marmaduke…

Melog laughed. He laughed until he cried, cried laughing, doubled up. He laughed until he became ill. In the end, all Dr Jones could do was to abandon the young man in his hilarious fever.

Dr Jones slammed behind him the door of the house where Melog was then living.

Lucky I didn't tell him my real name, he murmured as he walked down the street.

Our purpose in tarrying so long with these details is to demonstrate that it is no easy task to draw a line of distinction betwixt
that which is mythological and that which is genuinely and
authentically historical…

The Encyclopædia

A BIRTHDAY

LONG BEFORE HIS BIRTHDAY ARRIVED, Melog
dropped hints about it and canvassed for presents and cards
and said how he would miss all the fun of the traditional
Laxarian celebrations.

As a rule we make a great deal more of birthdays than of
Christmas or other holidays, which makes sense when you
think about it. Christmas only comes round once a year, after
all, whereas there's a birthday for somebody or other more or
less every day.

Quite right, Dr Jones said, whose hatred of Christmas was
Herodic – he hated buying birthday cards and presents too,
but at least he could ignore most people's birthdays.

We invite everybody, as many friends and family as we
can, and have a huge feast.

And these people whom you invite, they give presents to
who ever's having the birthday, do they?

You've got it, Dr Jones. But I don't know many people
here yet.

Everybody in town knows you, Melog. You speak to lots
of people, you make friends easily.

That's true. But I don't like everybody. You, Lavcadio and
Mr Job are my only real friends. And I haven't got any family
in this country. I'll have to make the best of it, that's all.

And what was Melog's age? He was twenty. And it went
without saying that twenty was the most important birthday
in Laxaria, rather than sixteen or eighteen or twenty-one.

Well just think about it, Melog said. Why sixteen rather than fifteen or seventeen? And what's so important about eighteen? What's the difference between seventeen and eighteen, or between eighteen and nineteen? Why twenty-one? Now twenty-five, a quarter of a century, would make much more sense. Your system in this country is totally arbitrary and impenetrable.

He would talk constantly about Laxarian traditions concerning the celebration of birthdays.

Needless to say, he said, the Laxarians have a great deal more style than the Sacrians when it comes to these things, and there's more sense in our way of looking at birthdays. What we celebrate is success at having survived. This time, for example, I'll be celebrating the fact that I've been on this earth for twenty years. The only alternative, after all, is being dead for eternity.

It therefore came as no surprise to his friends when they received cards, designed by Melog himself and duplicated on the photocopier in the town library, inviting them to a party in his room in Mr Job's house:

On December the first
at eight o'clock p.m.
you are cordially invited
to celebrate
the
BIRTHDAY
of
MELOG

Around the margins and in the corners one of his labyrinthine Laxarian patterns flourished – the lettering and embellishments in black on a blue ground. Artfully hidden among all the folds and curlicues was a picture of a man carrying a serpent in order to remind them all of his unusual star sign, not Sagittarius but Ophiucus.

With the guests, the cats, parcels of presents, and the

table heavily laden with eatables, there was scarcely space to move in Melog's room that night.

The centrepiece of the provender – apart from the sculpture Melog had stolen from the exhibition, which had candles in the mouths of its fantastical creatures ready to be lighted – the centrepiece was the cake. The base in blue, one of Melog's favourite colours – square and rather like a temple, with doorways and columns, small carved figures around the bottom standing in niches with a specklework of gold stars; on the second layer or the first floor, the cake was shaped like the courtyard of a castle surrounded with little ramparts made out of sweets, almonds, raisins, and orange segments; and finally on the uppermost layer, shaped like a green meadow with rocks, jelly ponds, nut boats, there was a statue of Melog himself in white icing with, of course, blue eyes. Although his friends asked him about it, Melog was unwilling to say who had made the curious cake or where he had got it. Surrounding the cake and the sculpture were triangular sandwiches containing eggs, meat, cheese, salmon and prawns; then pickled eggs, vol-au-vents, taramasalata, houmous, nuts, crisps, fruit, baby sausages, olives (green and black, some of them stuffed), biscuits, small cakes, red, yellow and orange jellies, blancmange, and chocolates. It was a feast for the eyes as well as for the stomach.

Dr Jones did not say a word, but he was trying to guess how Melog had paid for all this food and these dainties – in fact had he paid for them at all?

The doctor noticed that the white blackbird in its glass case was standing in a dark corner, a cat asleep on top of it.

Melog received the cards from his friends. There was a tasteful picture from Dr Jones, a print of a lithograph by M.C. Escher entitled 'Convex and Concave', and a simple message inside: 'A happy birthday and many of them'. Mr Job's card was rather an old-fashioned one, designed for a very young person; a picture of a river and a tree and on the river's bank a little sailing ship, a fishing rod, a ball, and a cricket bat – a senselessly jolly mixture – and inside, apart from the card's printed idiotic verse (My best wishes come your way,/My friend, upon your joyous day/To wish a birthday full and happy/To a lovely little chappy') a couplet by Mr Job himself: 'Most excellent tenant, behold, I send/Birthday greeting for Melog, my friend'. There was an extraordinarily colourful card from Lavcadio displaying three flying pigs, one blue, one yellow, and one purple, and in capital letters announcing in English: 'Pigs Might Fly' and inside: 'And You Might Tell The Truth About Your Age!' and Lavcadio had written in his florid hand, rolling hand: 'A million million best wishes – to Melog from your big friend, Lavcadio XXXXX!' Tudno's card was plain and red, with the words 'A Tranquil Birthday' in white letters and inside he had written (in red ink) – as if fulfilling the prophesy printed on the front – 'A tranquil birthday' and nothing else. The Saint's card was quite inappropriate, a Christmas card in fact, a sentimental picture of the baby Jesus and the Wise Men, a yellow star like a stupendous UFO above their heads, and gold letters proclaiming 'Season's Greetings'. The Saint's message was: 'A happy and a pleasant birthday, Melog; I will always remember you in my prayers'.

Some of the friends had also given him small presents: a cactus plant from Lavcadio, a tin of pineapple chunks from Mr Job, a Terry's Chocolate Orange from Dr Jones.

Thank you very much, all of you, Melog said, glowing with happiness.

Suddenly Lavcadio began to sing 'Happy birthday to you' and the others joined in, Mr Job's voice creaking like a rusty gate.

Right then, Melog said, how about some games? In Laxaria games are an essential ingredient of any party.

Some of the friends shrank back.

Not physical games, Melog said. There isn't enough room for us to move around. It'll have to be verbal games. Come on now, you've all got to join in the fun, all right?

One thing the Laxarian had forgotten was drinks, and no one had brought a bottle.

Now then, if I were a dog, Melog said, as if he had been inoculated against everyone else's infectious lack of enthusiasm, what sort of a dog would I be?

The companions stared at him.

Come on, it's a game. You've got to say what sort of a dog I'd be.

Well, it's too obvious, Lavcadio said. You'd be a thin white greyhound.

With red ears, like in the *Mabinogi*, Dr Jones said.

All right then, Melog said, what sort of a dog would Lavcadio be?

A boxer, Tudno offered.

A rottweiler, Dr Jones said, and the others, apart from Melog, agreed that that was the dog that Lavcadio would be.

Oh no, Melog said. Laffy's not fierce. He's too soppy. He's a big fat hairy gentle Newfoundland. But what sort of a dog would Dr Jones be?

A Chihuahua, Lavcadio said, laughing and displaying his rows of glittering, perfect teeth.

A Pekinese, Melfyn, the son of Jabez the Chips said. He had arrived late, without card, without present, and this was the first time he had spoken. He had been guided to the house by a kindly neighbour.

Let's change from dogs to trees then, Melog said. If I were a tree, what sort of a tree would I be?

You'd be a willow, Lavcadio said, who was the only one playing the game with any conviction.

And Mr Job would be an oak, Melog said, and Tudno would be an apple tree, and Dr Jones would be a bonsai pine tree.

But no one was playing and no one was having fun. They all sat in the little box of a room pressed against one another like sardines, cats occupying every lap. (Although the Saint did not like cats, he did not push away the one that had come and settled on his legs for fear of annoying Melog.) But a few of the cats were too shy or unsociable to come to people and they skulked, growling like small lions and tigers, in corners and on top of the wardrobe.

The air was, literally, blue since Melog, Lavcadio, the Saint, Tudno and Melfyn all smoked.

It was an uncomfortable moment, as no one was enjoying himself and yet no one could think of an excuse to withdraw from the deadened atmosphere of the party. No one wanted to offend Melog as he was determined to enjoy himself. As least the food was going down easily. People returned to the table time after time to load their paper plates with tasty morsels and sat to eat.

When the evening seemed to be coming to an end unreasonably prematurely – people taking biscuits and nuts and chocolates and coffee, the greedy cats finishing off the crumbs and licking any plate left unattended for a moment, attacking the taramasalata and one another – Melog said:

Anybody got a horror story?

The words closed on them like a snare, like a charm. Suddenly there was a reason to stay after all. But who would tell a story? They looked at one another; Melog at Mr Job, the Saint at Melfyn (who of course was blind and could not look at anyone), Dr Jones at Lavcadio, Lavcadio at Melog; everyone shy and waiting for someone else to be the storyteller. But in the end the tension was released by Lavcadio, who said:

Well, I haven't got a horror story, but I have heard about something terrible that's completely factual and pretty horrifying.

Excellent, Melog said, and he went to relight the candles which had gone out still standing in the mouths of the little monsters, the wax misshapen and the droplets hardened so that they looked as if they were vomiting foam or lava. Melog switched off the electric light so that the dancing flames threw long shadows that stretched alarmingly across the walls and ceiling.

In the gloom, the eyes of the little gathering of people and cats all turned to Lavcadio. The expectant silence was suddenly broken by his deep, velvet voice.

Judging by appearances, Reginald Stanhope was an extremely successful man. He lived in a palatial mock-Tudor house full of antiques, with a swimming pool, a tennis court, expanses of lawn all around it, a stable full of horses which were groomed daily till they shone, great dogs, hazel copses and woodlands surrounding the land. And in his garage were two cars: a powerful dark green Jaguar, and the Rolls Royce which he worshipped. All of his life, even as a small boy, he had dreamt of owning a Rolls Royce and now there he was. He had made his dream come true before he was fifty years old. The only problem was, that Reg Stanhope had not finished paying for the house, or the antiques or the horses or the cars. He had been gambling and had lost more often than he had won – and the sums involved were substantial. In addition to this, across this country, and in other countries too, a growing number of people wanted to get hold of him. These were his 'partners'. Individuals whom Reg had persuaded to invest many thousands of pounds in his various projects and businesses. But like Brigadoon, the business world of Reg Stanhope was an illusion, a lie without one jot or tittle of substance. He had debts of over one-and-a-half million pounds. He had lived in this way for years, convincing people by the force of his confident and spellbinding personality to trust in him completely. Innocents would hand their life savings over to him expecting hundredfold returns, and they would lose everything. Not that debt was anything new to Reg. In truth the burden of his debts had been a monkey on his back for longer than he cared to remember. His answer to his debts was to deceive someone else into paying them. But recently, events had caught up with him, and at last the net, inexorably, was closing about him. He had exhausted alias after alias like some talentless poet competing in the Eisteddfod year after year. A number of his creditors had succeeded in bringing actions against him. He was compelled to appear in court. And now he was awaiting the bailiffs. But he tossed off his sixth whisky in one and went to the garage. He looked at the Rolls Royce. He carressed the roof and the bonnet and the doors and the gleaming driver's-side doorhandle, opened the door, and sat behind the steering wheel. 'No one,' he said, 'is going to have this car.' And, believe it or believe it not, he kissed the wheel. 'I've worked hard to get this car, and I'm not letting anybody get it off me.' He started the engine and thrilled to its smooth quietness, like the purring of a cat – quieter, even. The great grey car slid out of the garage and down the drive, tall trees on either side, with the crunch of gravel beneath the wheels the only sound. Although he was drunk, and in fact he was still drinking from a whisky bottle on the passenger seat beside him, he drove with care. There was no rush. Through the countryside, the trees and hedges blending into curtains of green on either side of the car. At that moment he did not know where he was going, but he did know that he was leaving everything behind him; the large luxurious house, his debts, his persecutors, his enemies, all his problems, and for the moment he felt contented, driving his beloved Rolls towards some green, uncertain distance. He drove and he drove without worrying where, except that it should be very far away, very remote. The middle of nowhere. The very back of the backwoods. Drove and drove, far, far away. Drove until it grew dark. Drove until he reached the coast. Reg stopped the car close to a beach. He looked across the sea into the darkness, and there he saw a reflection of his future. There was no turning back. This was journey's end. The tablets were in his pocket; anti-depressant tablets, tranquilizing tablets, sleeping tablets, tablets for the saddened, hurt spirit. He poured a mix of them into his cupped left hand. Tablets like sweets – blue, white, pink, easy to swallow. He pushed a handful into his mouth and washed them down with a draught of whisky. He took another handful with another luxurious gulp from the bottle. Another handful and more whisky, and he would have taken more tablets except that the bottle was empty and he didn't like taking medicine without a drink. Then, before the night closed about him, he opened the door, hauled himself out, and stood. Then he forced himself to walk forwards as straight as a man in his condition was able to walk, towards the sea, into the very eye of darkness.

Lavcadio paused to sip his cold coffee and to chew on a salted nut, looking round at his listeners. Then he went on:

That same night, two youths from a nearby town had broken into a car, an old green Volkswagen, and driven it away, and had managed to push the speedometer up to eighty miles per hour. Too fast for the owner. Too fast for the police. Before anyone came after them, for the time being at least, they were on the loose in the countryside. Every so often they stopped to change places and take a turn at driving – neither had a driving license.

Dr Jones threw a glance at Melog. No one apart from the young man noticed.

They were both in a good mood; their spirits were high after drinking lager and sniffing glue. But they had something else, too, something to smoke. So the novelty of the car having palled, they parked at the edge of the sea, rolled their cigarettes, lit them, and relaxed in the car. Suddenly everything felt different, looked different – the sound of the waves, the moon, the wind, the dark. 'Want me to tell you a story, aye?' the one, Buzz, said to Zog, the other. 'Yeah,' he said, without much real interest. 'Remember the big snow last winter, aye?' 'Yeah.' 'Well,' Buzz said, 'these two queers went out in it one night and parked the car on top of a mountain and thought they'd have a bit of queer action, aye? So they have the action, right, in the back of the car, and then pull their pants up and try and start the car. But the car was buried, aye, under deep snow and anyway, it wasn't firing, you know, with the cold. No start. Well they had no idea how to get the car started because they're queers like, aye? So they cuddled up…' 'Ugh!' Zog said. 'Shut up, let me finish the story,' Buzz said. 'So they cuddle up to keep warm, aye, and wait till morning. "What are we going to do?" the one queer says to the other one. "Well, wait till morning, aye?" "Yeah, but what'll we do till morning, aye?" "Look, what about the radio?" "Radio won't work without the engine." "But look, there's a radio with batteries in the back." So they get this little radio to work. Only some local programme they could get because they were on top of the mountain. And the programme was boring, just playing stuff like Ffa Coffi Pawb and Catatonia and that. But any sound was better than listening to the wind howling, aye? All of a sudden, this voice interrupts the music. "We apologise for this interruption to the programme to announce that a dangerous man has broken out of Plasnewydd, the local Mental Hospital. The public are advised not to talk to this man on any account. We will return to this story later…" and then back to Gorky's again. Well these queers were shitting bricks in the car there and freezing cold in the snow like lollies in a freezer, aye? "What'll we do? Plasnewydd's just down the road," the one queer says to the other. "I'll go over to that farmhouse to phone the AA, aye," the bravest queer says. "I'm coming with you," the other one says. "No, aye. You'd better wait in the car, in case you catch cold," the other one says. So off goes the brave queer towards the light of the farmhouse in the distance.' 'I know the ending of this story,' Zog said. 'The one in the car hears a noise on the roof of the car and he hides in the back and then the police come and tell him him to come out of the car and not to turn round. And he comes out…' 'No, no,' Buzz said, 'this story's got a different ending…' 'I've heard it before, I'm telling you.' 'Zog!' 'I have heard it before, I'm telling you.' 'No, Zog, look, aye!' And Buzz was pointing through the window, pointing at something on the other side of a hillock. 'A car,' he said. 'A big car, aye? It looks like a Roller, honest.' 'What, a Rolls Royce? Pull the other one.' 'Come on.' And they both went in the dark along the beach, over the hillock, and there was the silver Rolls Royce. 'The door's open, aye,' Zog said. 'It's got the key in.' 'The boy who owns it isn't far away, then.' 'Who cares? It's ours now, aye? We'll never get another chance to drive a Roller. C'mon.' The two youths jumped into the huge and luxurious vehicle, scarcely believing their luck. 'Listen to that… It don't make any noise and we're doing sixty already!' The car sped through the darkness, the boys marvelling at its power – the electric windows rising and falling at the touch of a button – another button to open the sun roof, a cigarette lighter, a telephone – but best of all, there was the speed. One hundred and thirty miles per hour in the narrow, winding lanes of the Welsh countryside is insanity. And the next moment, the Rolls Royce was lying on its roof in a field. But by some strange miracle neither youth was seriously hurt; they were only briefly knocked unconscious. Zog was woken by Buzz's screaming. When Zog opened his eyes and looked properly, he saw his friend lying under the body of a big fat man, blood on his head, seaweed and salt water in his clothes, and blood and vomit covering Buzz's face.

Is that it? the Saint asked.

So far as I know, Lavcadio said.

I feel sick, Melfyn said.

Me too, and I've got to walk home now, Tudno said.

I'll come with you part of the way, Dr Jones said.

I'm tired, I'm sorry. I'm going to bed, Mr Job said.

On the way downstairs as he accompanied his friends to the door, Melog said:

But I don't understand the end, Lavcadio. What was Reginald Stanhope's body doing in the car?

He'd intended drowning himself but when he got to the water he threw up all the tablets and the drink and the cold sea made him come to. Then he went back to the car and went to lie down on the back seat and fell asleep. When the boys drove away they didn't know that they had another passenger in the back.

It wasn't a horror story, and it wasn't a ghost story either, but it was a horrible story.

But Reg met his end in the end, Melog said.

Yes he did, Lavcadio said.

Good night, Melog said to Melfyn and Tudno and the Saint and Dr Jones.

BEANS. The earliest extant historical reference to these podded seeds can be seen in the Holy Scripture, wherein it is said that beans, among other items, were taken by Shobi, the son of Nashash, Machir, the son of Ammiel, and Barzillai the Gileadite, as a gift "for David, and the people that were with him, to eat," when they had fled in fear from the hosts of Absalom…

The Encyclopædia

A DINNER

MELOG had not phoned. In any case, Dr Jones's phone had been cut off because he had not paid his bills. Then Melog sent the doctor a message on a card:

> Dear Dr Jones,
> You are cordially invited to join us for a meal tomorrow night
> [and then there was a joint signature]… Melog and Laffy

Lavcadio had his own flat in a terraced house in the town which had a number of bell buttons (each with its own label and name) on its front door, mounted one above the other like the buttons on a shirt. The doctor depressed the one labelled 'Lavcadio Heaming' in flowery, extrovert handwriting.

The door was quickly opened – and filling it, arms spread and teeth radiating welcome, was Lavcadio.

Dr Jones, Dr Jones! You're very punctual. Come on in. Let me take your anorak. And what's this? Oh! A bottle of red wine! You're far too kind, thank you very very much. Come on up.

Dr Jones followed Melog's friend up a number of stairs and through a yellow door. There Melog was standing to receive him, like a lath, and white as a druid's robe on an Eisteddfod Monday, the inevitable cigarette in his right hand as usual.

Lavcadio's apartment was a jumble of colours and bright

patterns; carpets and rugs striped red, blue, purple, orange; chairs in tomato red; a table cloth in blue with yellow and orange stars; frames of mirrors in extraordinary pink; curtains diamond-patterned in (sea) blue and (lawn) green and (butter) yellow; throws draping two armchairs and a sofa like the three arches of a scattered trinity. Everywhere, in every nook and cranny, as they say, in every window, on every shelf, on top of the television, on several small tables and several stools, and standing on the floor, green plants flourished; rubber plants, yuccas, ferns, cacti, ivy, and palms stretching their windmill leaves and transforming every shady corner into a patch of green midsummer. The little bathroom (sky blue and ocean green), with all its glossy-leaved plants was like a tangled tropical grove.

On every wall there were framed pictures – tigers, parrots, peacocks, fishes, birds of paradise – and some of Melog's Laxarian labyrinth patterns. Lavcadio had created an atmosphere that was bright, sunlit and exotic in a narrow attic.

The three went to sit at a round table in the centre of which stood Melog's stolen sculpture (Lavcadio had borrowed it for the evening), candles burning in the mouths of the creatures of which it was composed.

May I ask a question? Melog asked.

That depends, the doctor said.

On what?

On whether the question is of a personal nature or not.

And what would you do if it were a personal question?

If it was personal I'd kill.

Melog realised that in his own laborious way, the doctor was in a jocular mood. Lavcadio darted between the kitchen (which was actually no more than a cupboard) and the table, serving delicacies for his guests.

It's obvious that you're an academic, Melog said, but I don't understand why you haven't got a job. Why can't you get work? Now in Sacria...

Yes, well we aren't living in Sacria are we? This is Britain.

You're lucky, Dr Jones, Melog said. You've lived all your life in a peaceful country without ever knowing the shock of war. The experience of getting to your age – whatever your age is – without experiencing war must be quite unusual. For most of the world, and for every age in the past, war was something that was unavoidable. But for you and some of your compatriots, war's a thing that happens to other countries, far off or in the past.

But, Dr Jones said, I sympathise a great deal with people in countries where wars are going on. Every war affects me.

Affect? Sympathise? What about Sacria and Laxaria? You didn't know anything about them till I came here and taught you. Therefore it's not true that every war affects you. You don't know what it's like to live in a country where it's commonplace for bodies to be left in the streets; you don't know what it's like to wake up in the morning and see a hole in the road where your friends' and neighbours' house used to be; what it's like to have to vary your movements every day for fear somebody's watching you, for fear the enemy might attack, for fear you'll get bombed. That's what it's been like all my life in my country. And know what? I never got used to it. Every day the fear runs through me like new.

Friends, Lavcadio said, don't be all sad and serious tonight, please. Help yourselves. Enjoy the food!

The food does look great, Laffy. A feast for the eyes and for the stomach, I'm sure.

Yes indeed, Dr Jones said. It looks excellent.

Melog searched through his rice carefully and thoroughly. He examined a round green pea spiked on a tine of his fork.

Do you know, he said, that the pea is a vegetable that dates back eight thousand years? They ate peas in ancient Syria. Peas came to Britain with the Romans.

Very interesting, Dr Jones said, in a not very interested way.

The significance of that, of course, is that the peas we're

eating here tonight are the direct descendants of plants our ancestors were eating in the distant past.

In some Roman takeaway, was it? Dr Jones said.

Peas-U-Like, Lavcadio said.

Oh, ha ha, very funny, Melog said.

No peas for the wicked, Dr Jones said and he and Lavcadio laughed.

Oh yes, it's easy for you to laugh, but I had to live on peas, more or less, during the last war with Mocatria. My family couldn't get anything but peas for months, nothing else at all, and we were grateful for the peas. I'm already starting to sound like the old folks, remembering the hardships in the war. You know how old people always go on about the past: 'During the war we didn't have any food, or clothes, or chairs'.

No chairs? Dr Jones and Lavcadio exclaimed together.

The President brought in a tax on chairs during the last war.

Why chairs? the doctor asked.

War is war, Melog said, and a tyrant is a tyrant. As I understand it there was a time when there was a tax on windows in Britain. And Mao declared a ban on grass and sparrows.

But we aren't going to talk about wars and oppression tonight, Lavcadio said. We're going to be happy and celebrate and we're going to have fun and forget the problems of the world.

Lavcadio poured wine into three glasses (none of them was a proper wineglass – they were all elongated tumblers and each of them came from a different set). The wine was thick and dark and oily.

Mmm, Lavcadio said. A well-rounded liquid, nicely balanced and with plenty of fruitiness, mature, yet still lively, aged sensibly in the wood. The tannin is soft and kind and gentle.

I was concerned, Dr Jones said, that it would taste a little green or that it might seem a little baked.

You're too modest, Doctor. It's a good choice. I'm happy enough, anyway. Let's all forget our problems for tonight.

The three raised their glasses in agreement.

But I can't be happy, Melog said. Not with you leaving, Laffy.

Going, Lavcadio? Where to? Dr Jones asked.

To America. Tomorrow. That's the reason for the dinner. To celebrate. Personally I'm looking forward to going.

Laffy's going to work in a huge expensive restaurant in New York. He's a professional chef.

It's no wonder that this is such a special meal, then, Dr Jones said.

But I'm not happy, Melog said. I'm losing a friend.

Then a terrifying idea came into Dr Jones's mind, and he had to ask the question straight away and try to seem as if it were of no consequence.

Have you considered going to America with him, Melog?

Yes I have, but I don't like America, and I've got to stay here to try to solve the mystery of the letter, though I'd almost forgotten about it, and find the Imalic, of course.

The tension went out of Dr Jones and he tried to hide his sigh of relief by stuffing a slice of cheese into his mouth.

Anyway, Melog added, I don't like this restaurant where Laffy's going to work. It's immoral. They sell meat from rare animals. Believe it or not, Dr Jones, the place is called Endangered Species – just think how immoral that is, Dr Jones. Millionaires paying fortunes for panda steaks, or rhinoceros, or gorilla.

Ych-a-fi, Dr Jones said.

But don't worry, Lavcadio said, there wasn't any meat at all in tonight's meal.

The young are, at first, quite playful and amusing; yet it is but little time before they begin to show signs of the cruelty that is their nature. They launch merciless attacks upon any creature that is smaller than they or that they can overpower. In this way, the presence of the cat is destructive in the extreme of birds, mice, the mole, and divers other small creatures.

The Encyclopædia

CATS

MELOG AND DR JONES went to Melog's room. On their way upstairs Dr Jones noticed the smell of cooking oil – potatoes frying.

That's Mr Job in his kitchen cooking his supper, Melog said. He has chips every night but since he lets me stay here for nothing now I'm not really in a position to complain to him.

Goodness, Dr Jones said as he went into the room. There are more cats here now than the last time I was here!

Yes I know, Melog said, pulling a young cat from Dr Jones's shoulder. I found two more – they were in the street, lost in the rain. And one of the others has littered since you were last here.

How many have you got living here now, then?

Seventeen, if you count the five newborns in the corner, but they'll be going to good homes in a few weeks.

But this place is too small for so many animals, Melog, and they make the place stink.

Stink, Dr Jones? Do you have to be so horrible? Perhaps I've got a right to keep the odd pet for company during my exile and, now that Lavcadio's gone, my dreadful loneliness – even if you don't like cats.

To tell you the truth, Melog, I was thinking of getting a cat myself. I was going to ask you for one, but you went off to London or Morocco or somewhere – or was that after you came back? Oh, I can't remember. But I'd only want the one, mind. One or two, perhaps three are plenty – but seventeen!

The doctor was grateful for the smell from Mr Job's kitchen which masked the unlovely vapours that drifted from the cats' shitbox in the corner.

Oh no, Dr Jones, a cat wouldn't suit you at all.

Why do you say that?

No, a cat wouldn't be right for you.

But why, Melog?

The cat has a cunning mind and a spirit and nature full of nuance and variation; they're mesmeric and keen-eyed and profound.

So why am I not qualified to have one? Dr Jones said, offended and beginning a childish sulk.

Lovers and snobbish old academics alike are fond of cats. Loving and cruel cats – they take possession of people's homes – they're prickly like lovers and comfort-loving like professors.

But you aren't answering the question, Melog.

They're intellectuals, and they love quiet corners and the terrifying dark. If it had ever occurred to cats to work for a living, they would have been generals in hell, that is if the devils could only get the cats to listen.

Are you trying to say that I'm not good enough to have one of your cats? That's what you're trying to say, is it? That I don't even know how to look after a cat?

When they sleep, have you noticed how all cats look like sphinxes stretched out in the wilderness, dreaming endless prophecies. Their backs and their legs charged with electricity and golden sparks, like fine sand glinting in the deep mystery of their eyes.

What are you on about?

So, you want a cat? There's five small ones in the corner if you'd care to choose.

Aren't they rather young?

178

Yes. But you can choose one now and have her when she's independent enough to leave her mother.

I'm not sure, Melog.

There you go. You aren't a cat person or you would've gone straight to the basket and chosen one, maybe two, and nothing and nobody would have been able to stop you, if you were a real cat person.

Hurt, the doctor tried to swallow his pride along with the fullstrength and rather hairy coffee Melog had made for him. He sat in sulky silence for half an hour then thanked his friend and got up to leave.

As he was going down the stairs a cloud of smoke ballooned from Mr Job's kitchen, a whiff of fat clinging in the sickly haze. Mr Job was enjoying his supper.

The doctor walked along the rows of houses, through the shadows and the drizzle, which was orange in the globe of light around each streetlamp. He hurried through the dark avoiding the menacing gangs of youths – Dr Jones was scared of seeing Buzz and Zog again – but they were in prison, weren't they? – well, their sort anyway.

It was a cold, unpleasant evening. The darkness lay like a heavy quilt thrown over the town. Yes, he was feeling poetic; he always felt poetic when he had to leave Melog's company, especially after a little uncomfortable tension had developed between them, as it had that night, like the hand of a giant holding them apart. His loneliness always brought on these poeticising spasms. But he knew that he could not be a poet.

The chasm between his own home and Melog's home – what did it amount to? Just a matter of a few streets – but in Dr Jones's heart it felt like the distance between Laxaria and Wales, or rather in his head it felt like that, because the doctor knew that the heart could not think – or at least his heart did not think, otherwise he would be a poet.

The house was dark and cold and welcomeless, without even a cat waiting for him. Too late to work on the Encyclopaedia. He fills a kettle with water to make himself a cup of hot chocolate and to fill a hot water bottle. He observes himself doing this. He studies himself, sees his slow, measured movements. The way in which he fills the kettle, reaches a cup down from the hook, the way in which he cuts open with a scissors the packet of chocolate, cutting it not any old how, but straight. Who is this man? A stranger. He sees his thin, grizzled hair, his monkish bare crown, his narrow, rounded shoulders, his thin arms; a man who has spent his life – these are the marks of half a century – bent over his books; he is myopic, despite the thick lenses of his spectacles. But he realizes that the small man he observes, as it were, from far off, is himself, getting ready to go to his bed, his unwarm bed, with his hot water bottle.

In his bed, he lies on his left side, nursing the hot water bottle as if it were a kitten. He cuddles the yielding bottle. He lies hunched, as one does. But sleep will not knit up the ravelled sleeve and so on. He cannot let consciousness slip away. Melog has stirred his mind too much, with his opinions, his personality, his looks.

In his desire for sleep, in his eagerness to throw himself, as they say, into the arms of Morpheus, his mind whirling with the things that Melog has said and the things that Melog has done, he does not notice how tense his own body has become. His fingers grip the hot water bottle like claws; his arms and his legs are locked like vices. And yet he sees this as if he were flying above the bed, and senses his own tension as if it were someone else's. But inside him he knows nothing of it, in spite of the storm screaming in his brain.

Tranquillity. Contentment. Quietude, Dr Jones said in his mind. Tranquillity. Contentment. Quietude. Tranquillity. Contentment. Quietude…

He repeated the words over and over, trying to quieten his nerves. He had heard that the words could soothe a troubled spirit, that the blend of sound and meaning could compel you to relax and become calm. It was impossible to say any of them quickly – Traaaaangng-quiuiuiuiui-liityyyyy,

Cooooooonn-teeeeeen-tmeeeeentt, Quiuiuiuiui-eeet-uuuuud-dde. Long, intertwining, deliberate words. Nobody could say them quickly without doing violence to them, biting them. Swallowing them or grating them. They worked like a spell, there was some magic in reciting the words over and over, some enchantment. Who was it who had noticed this conjunction? The meaning, the words, the spelling and the spell – who ever it was they were nothing less than a genius.

The doctor intoned the words quietly as protection against losing patience with Melog. He was a tax on his forbearance, a strain on his friendship – he got on his nerves.

Melog called early the next day, at six o'clock in the morning in fact, and woke the doctor by ringing the doorbell continuously and when the doctor had opened it the young man had come into the house in complete panic.

François is gone! He's left me!

Who on earth is François? Dr Jones asked, beginning to worry about his friend's condition; his anxiety was terrible to see – the shaking, the sweating, the pallor – yes, Melog was more bluewhite than ever, unfeasibly white.

François, Melog said again as he rolled a cigarette and filled the kettle (he was quite at home in his friend's house), François is my favourite tomcat. He got his name from a novel by Zola, and he turns up again in one of the novels of Saunders Lewis.

A cat? Dr Jones said, surprised that he had managed to stop himself saying 'a bloody cat?'

François was no ordinary cat, Melog said. He was my favourite cat, my friend. He talked to me, answered me, had long conversations with me, in his own way. He'd come with me for a walk in the park. When I threw a ball or a bit of paper for him he'd bring it back to me in his mouth like a dog. But he was more intelligent than a dog and more intelligent than any other cat too.

Well, Dr Jones said, trying to sound sagacious, tomcats do have a tendency to wander. That, Melog, is in their nature. A university in America spent millions of dollars on a detailed scientific study of the habits of tomcats, and the conclusion of their researches was that tomcats have a tendency to wander.

He was castrated when he was a kitten, Dr Jones.

Describe François to me, Dr Jones said. He had not looked at Melog's cats closely enough to recognise them or to distinguish them one from another.

François is the thin ginger tom with orange and yellow stripes on the tail, shaped like a Siamese cat. Long head, orange eyes, intelligent, slender graceful body.

The young man's eyes filled with tears again.

We'll go and look for him together, Dr Jones said.

That was in the morning. Until three o'clock in the afternoon of that wet, windy, cold day they searched continuously, calling his name, asking neighbours and people on the street, without success. Passers-by stood in the street and stared after Melog, marvelling at his pale frailty.

Tranquillity. Contentment. Quietude. Tranquillity. Contentment. Quietude. Under his breath, through clenched teeth, Dr Jones recounted the verbal trinity. They had walked around the park – one of François' favourite haunts, Melog had said – at least seven times, had looked in every bush, every shelter, every litter bin (in case François had fallen into one of them). Dr Jones had borrowed a map from the library and they had systematically gone through every street and left a card in every corner shop: 'Lost – one cat...' and a description of François, and Mr Job's phone number, '...Answers to the names François, Fra-fra, Fraffs, and Fraffzy...' and the offer of a reward of £20, Melog's life-savings. They looked in literally hundreds of gardens, combed every patch of open ground, and they walked the railway lines and the children's playgrounds. Melog caused a commotion wherever he went.

No hide. No hair.

Melog wanted to climb to the top of the Town Hall, from

which vantage point, he said, he could survey the whole area. But Dr Jones persuaded him not to pursue this course.

After all, he argued, you aren't going to spot a kitten, not even an orange one, from such high spot over such a big, scattered area, are you?

This time the boy listened to his older friend.

Then they sat together in Jabez Ifans's potato tavern, Melog saying François, François, where are you? What's happened to you? again and again, Dr Jones saying (quietly) Tranquillity. Contentment. Quietude.

Suddenly, the Saint appeared as if from nowhere and joined them and asked what was wrong with his former co-tenant. (The Saint still lived in the same old lodgings.) Then, after listening to the history of the tomcat's departure, he said:

Don't worry about it too much, Mr Melog, Dr Jones – pets have the ability to get back home and find their owners in spite of the most incredible obstacles.

The Saint settled himself at their table with a plate of chips and bread and margarine (although Jabez Ifans's blackboard quite clearly announced 'bread & butter', his customers were not taken in.)

For example, the Saint said as he loaded a slice of the thin white bread with fat and greasy chips, an experiment was conducted in Germany with a sheepdog called Maxi. They took the dog up hill and down dale, so to speak, until he was about six miles from his master's home. The next morning they set the dog loose. He went and wandered aimlessly for an hour or so, then suddenly off he went like a flash, and within another hour he had got home and his master was glad to see him again.

He paused to ram the doorstep sandwich between his blackened teeth and while he chewed he continued to expound examples:

A dog by the name of Spook walked from Vancouver to California in May 1877, following his master who had gone there in March. Another dog by the name of Barri walked from Italy to southern Germany in October 1974, believe it or not, but it's a famous case. And perhaps you heard about the terrier by the name of Micky who walked fifteen miles to his old home – he was fifteen years old and deaf, that's what was strange about it – but he managed to find his master, and die at his feet straight after.

You're forgetting one thing, Melog said making no attempt to hide the impatience in his voice when the Saint fell silent for a moment to make another sandwich. You're forgetting one small but very important thing. They were all dogs. François is a cat.

Don't be angry, Mr Melog, I was just coming to the cats. There are numerous examples.

Tranquillity. Contentment. Quietude.

The Saint squeezed lardy chipped potatoes and limp bread and margarine into his face. In spite of his distended cheeks, he managed to say:

Sooty, a cat from Durham, walked to the county of Surrey in June 1967; another cat by the name of Smokey walked from Oklahoma to Tennessee in the seventies; a cat by the name of Gypsy went on a walking tour that lasted for two years before returning to her home in Chicago where her owner had given up hope of ever seeing her again; in fact she fainted when she saw Gypsy, thinking that she was a ghost. And of course in 1600, Henry Wriothesley Earl of Southampton, to whom Shakespeare dedicated 'Venus and Adonis' and 'The Rape of Lucrece', was imprisoned in the Tower of London for his part in the Essex Plot. And what did his faithful old cat do? Well, she searched for him and climbed down the chimney to get to him in his cell!

There was no stopping the Saint, but Melog got to his feet and walked out of the café and the doctor had to follow him.

He was starting to get on my nerves, Melog said.

The two walked, quiet and disheartened, back to Melog's

lodgings. People stared and pointed at Melog shamelessly. Because of his appearance Melog always became a one man parade.

I've lost him. I know it in my heart. He's been knocked down by a car or he's been tortured to death by hooligans.

His voice cracked. And Dr Jones could not think of any words to comfort him.

But when he opened the door to his room, his cats and kittens came to him in one many-coloured pride, and one of them, an orange cat, jumped on his shoulder.

François! Melog shouted. François, my darling!

Then the young man looked at Dr Jones with rather an awkward, sheepish look.

Now I remember, he said. He went to sleep in the bottom of the wardrobe last night. I must have shut the wardrobe door this morning without realising it. But that shows you how clever he is because he's opened the door all on his own. You're a clever one aren't you, Faff-faffs, you are, you're a clever old Fraffzy. You've been playing naughty old bibbly-bobblies with us, haven't you?

Tranquillity. Contentment. Quietude, Dr Jones said under his breath. Tranquillity. Contentment. Quietude.

And at last Dr Jones fell asleep.

If two substances are brought into contact with one another with unusual force, then heat is generated to such a degree that they will become incandescent.

The Encyclopædia

A FIRE

HAMMERING ON THE DOOR. Doorbell ringing and ringing assaulting the morning and splitting open his sleep, him. What's going on in the dead of night? Throws on his dressing gown. Runs downstairs barefoot. Opens the door. Except it is not Melog.

Are you Dr Jones? Do you know Melog? Do you know a Mr Job?

Let me take your questions in order, Dr Jones said, angrily. Yes. Yes. And yes. That is, yes I'm Dr Jones; yes I do know Melog; yes, I also know a Mr Job. But who, if I may be so bold as t…

There's no time. The house is on fire!

For a moment Dr Jones let the words sieve down through his brain and repeated them once in his head: 'The house is on fire'. Then he leapt back upstairs and threw on his clothes – sweater over his head, something on his legs, something on his feet. Afterwards he jumped downstairs again and ran with the stranger to the house.

High, straight flames were spewing from the door and every window of Mr Job's home, including Melog's window in the roof. The fire brigade were already there, spraying the building with water from the long clumsy eels of their hoses. But nothing worked. The home was ablaze.

A circle of people stood in the road staring at the bonfire. No one dared get too close, the fire was too hot, the long flames lashing and stretching as if to grab people like demon limbs out of a hellsmouth.

Dr Jones himself stood thunderstruck by the appalling scene, mesmerised, struck dumb, like the others around him, by the awfulness of what he saw. Looking at the hoses, Dr Jones thought of his hot water bottle and the comfort of his bed in place of this paradoxical mix of the cold of the morning and the heat of the blaze. The watergush thundered in his ears like a cataract. Hot colours danced on its surface – orange, red, yellow, white. He heard the sound of the water pumping. Heard the gnawing of the flames, the sound of the frame of the house cracking. He felt the heat. Felt the smells. His nostrils filled with smoke and the smell of things burning – wood, plastic and paper – the doctor thought about Mr Job's work – and the smell of something else. What was it? Not meat. Flesh.

Hours later, the blaze was subdued and had been kept from spreading to the houses on either side and other buildings nearby.

The intense heat had singed Dr Jones's eyebrows and his clothes had been splashed with water. He was both wet and brittle-dry, hot and cold all at once. The doctor did not know how long he had been standing motionless watching the struggle to snuff out this huge lantern.

Where was Melog? Needless to say, the question had been dinning through his consciousness the whole time. But he was struck speechless and helpless by the disaster and the swiftness of it before his eyes. Now with the fire-fighters getting the upper hand and the audience beginning to move away, he allowed himself to consider the question. He ventured towards two of the fire-fighters (about whom there was something rather machine-like):

Was anybody in the house?

Yes, one of them said robotically. He's in hospital.

The other (mechanically) told him the name of the hospital and the name of the ward. Dr Jones jumped into a taxi. When he arrived at the hospital he asked for Melog.

There's nobody of that name come in today, the scrawny man on reception told him.

Are you sure?

He looked over the list again with painful slowness.

Nobody of that name, he said listlessly. What's his address?

When Dr Jones gave that, a little light glimmered in his eyes.

A man with that address has come in. His name's Mr Job.

Mr Job! Has he been burned?

I don't think so... No, he's not in the burns unit. He's suffering from shock I'd say.

By being persistent, Mr Jones got permission to visit the old man. He was sitting in an Arctic bed, looking weak and confused, his crumpled face almost as white as Melog's.

How are you, Mr Job? Do you recognise me?

He scarcely did at first, but gradually his mind cleared.

You're Melog's friend... thanks... thanks for coming to see me.

You've had a terrible shock, Mr Job, Dr Jones said.

Yes.

You've been quite shaken up. How do you feel now?

How what?

How do you feel now, Mr Job?

To tell you the truth, I feel like crying my eyes out.

You will get over this in time, Dr Jones said, listening to the stupidity of his own clichéd words. It will take time, he added.

Get over this you say? No, I won't get over this. My entire life's been burnt in that fire. All my papers and my books. All my readings. And I who was aiming to save our literature by copying it all out.

You never know. Perhaps some things have been saved.

But his old eyes filled with tears. He had not even heard these (pathetic) words of comfort.

That's all I wanted was to be a perfect reader. Read, read, read.

Mr Job, Dr Jones ventured, do you know what happened to Melog? Mr Job? Melog?

Read, read... Who?

That afternoon Dr Jones phoned the police. No, they had not discovered any human remains in the aftermath of the fire. The only corpses were those of some fifteen cats.

> The feeling at work in the nation at the time was such that the invention of such characters would not be possible...
>
> *The Encyclopædia*

NEWS

EVERY DAY, twice a day, Dr Jones would telephone the police hoping for news of his friend. He gave them a detailed description of Melog – it was not difficult – he went over the long, thin body, the angular, porcelain bones, ran his hand through the purewhite hair, and looked again into the depths of the glitterblue eyes, in his mind, in his description. And he felt that anyone who had seen him would be able to recognise him straightaway from the word-picture, the boy was so unusual. But no word came to ease Dr Jones's grief.

Every second day, Dr Jones would visit Mr Job in hospital. He did not seem to be recovering. His face turned from white to sickly yellow.

The police are saying it was me burned the house down. It started when I was cooking supper. I'd taken my work into the kitchen with me. I was copying a piece out of *One Moonlit Night* and having a fair bit of trouble with the dialect and I kept having to go back over the same piece. It was an accident. There were so many bits of paper round even in the kitchen. But it was an accident. I wouldn't burn my own house down, would I? I wouldn't burn my papers, my books, my work, not on purpose, would I?

No, you wouldn't, Dr Jones said. This time he could think of no words of comfort. The old man was homeless and so very naturally depressed. The whole reason for his life had been destroyed in a night.

Then one day Dr Jones was sitting at his desk working through the closely printed pages of the Encyclopaedia when the doorbell rang. The doctor felt that there was something

190

familiar in the quality of the ring. A picture of Melog flashed before his eyes and he rushed to the door. But when he opened it, it was not Melog whom he found standing there. Even so, the visitor was familiar. A little, short man, his prominent front teeth sticking out over his lower lip, his eyes magnified by thick round spectacles, no chin. He resembled a perplexed mole. Although this individual's appearance was so strikingly cartoonish, the doctor could not for the life of him call to mind where he had seen him before.

Dr Jones, forgive me for callin like this.

The voice was also familiar. And Dr Jones did know him after all.

It was me oo called ere the night o the fire, he said, echoing and confirming Dr Jones thoughts.

Come in, the doctor said, leading him into the house. And thank you for coming that night. I've been thinking about you, but you'll have to forgive me, in all the commotion that ni…

I know, the little gummyeyed man said, you didn notice me. I can ardly blame you, in the circumstances.

May I offer you a…

Cup o tea? Lovely. Thank you very much. Tea like concrete, please. Lot o milk an five sugars.

I'm sorry, but…

My name? My name is Ambrose Bing. I do reside in the abode which is the next door save one to Mr Job's residence. The conflagration did not touch my dwellinplace, thanks be to Providence. I'm a Seventh Day Adventist, you know.

Dr Jones could not see the connection between the fire and Ambrose Bing's religion.

I'm sure you must be wonderin wy I've called ere today, aren't you?

Yes and no. I'm glad to see you anyway.

Well wen I saw the fire there I was thinkin about you straight. I've seen you and tha Mr Job's lodger comin back and fore often. I got a bay window. Double glazin.

The visitor's train of thought was sometimes difficult to follow, not to mention his strange mix of dialect, English words and some surprising and unusual Welsh words. The doctor found it hard to concentrate on his confused prattling. Apart from that, he was not sure that he liked the man. Had he been watching Melog and the doctor from behind the lace curtains in the bay window of his abode?

A general interest in people it is, thass all, Ambrose Bing said. We're not so neighbourly these days, are we, Dr Jones? But I do still believe in bein neighbourly, anyway. Iss no odds about America. I do remember the last war. Everybody's door wide open all day. Everybody droppin in an out o one another's ouses. But there we are, the old days ave gone an iss no point us sittin ere come over with iraeth for em is it?

No, quite. More tea, Mr Bing?

No thanks, Dr Jones. This cup was rather weak, like cricket's piss, if you don mind me sayin. Too much water, not enough milk. A truly lamentable cuppa, with all due respects, o course.

Little by little, this character was driving up Dr Jones's blood pressure. Why on earth had he called in?

It's a fortnight since the fire, Dr Jones started again. But once more, Ambrose Bing interrupted.

I know, and you aven seen a siw or a miw of your andsome young friend, ave you?

No, I haven't. Do you know anything of his history since then?

Oh, istory is it? Is story. Now then, let's see. I don know where e is. I could tell you that much now, Dr Jones. Well, I got an artificial ip so I got to be carcus. But before the fire tha night, I can remember lookin out through the lace curtains in the bay window and seein your beautiful friend leavin the ouse with an orrible ornament under is right arm an a box tucked into is sinister oxter.

The sculpture and the white blackbird. Where was Melog going with the glass case in a box and the sculpture?

I do wonder where was e go-yin, your comely comrade? Ambrose Bing said, meditatively. I do wonder, in all truth, where e ave gone. Back ome, I suppose, more than likely, isn it? E came from some foreign country, didn e, Dr Jones?

Dr Jones felt a deep need to throw some hard, weighty object with unyielding spiky corners at the head of Ambrose Bing.

Well, I thought that you'd be glad of that information, Ambrose Bing said. At least you know now that e ave excaped from the bonfire in one piece, and that e ave took that sculpture and that box with im. But I'm a pensioneer, Dr Jones, an I'm not able to work.

Was this old crawler fishing for a reward of money?

I'm unemployed too, Mr Bing.

Well, Ambrose Bing said finally, I can't be sittin ere all day drinkin tea.

No, Dr Jones said. No you can't.

Although we here set down the strictest canons of judgment as they are to be discovered in the most renowned and most recent authors, yet it is certain and beyond doubt that tradition plays its part in the transmitting of facts from age to age.

The Encyclopædia

MORE NEWS

IN THE LIBRARY, Dr Jones met the twins Meuryn and Meurig.

Where's your friend today, Dr Jones?

Yes, the thin one with the hair white as f___!

Don't know. He's disappeared and I haven't seen him for weeks. But he has disappeared periodically in the past and come back again. But this time I'm afraid that he might have gone for good.

You never f***ing know, Meurig said.

No. Perhaps he'll come back again. I hope so.

But time passed and Dr Jones heard nothing. On one occasion, he saw Professor Berwyn Boyle Hopkin.

I'm putting together a monograph for one of the series from the Centre for Higher Pan Celtic Studies on vanished handwriting of the eighth century, he said. I'm getting the footnotes into order at the moment, sixty of them this time. Not a record breaker, I know. What are you working on? Where's your friend? The strange one with the odd look. White hair. What was his name? How are you?

The Encyclopaedia, still. I don't know. Melog. I'm all right, thank you very much.

But though everything was all right in Toy Town, everything was not all right with the doctor, by a long way. He worked doggedly at the Encyclopaedia in order to prevent himself from dwelling too much on other matters.

CUCUMBER... The original word in its singular form of *cisha*, so Kitto tells us, is so like the Arabic word *cissa* that it is very likely that they signify the same object. Celsius gives *ceta*, *cati*, and *cusaia* as the various renditions of the same word in the oriental languages. This does not prove that the names invariably signify the same varieties, as it may be that they are applied in the different countries to those varieties that are most common, or perhaps, those that are the most lauded in particular places. In Ejypt, it appears that the word *cati* is applied to the variety which is named *cucumis chate* by the botanists, and which is named "the queen of cucumbers" by Hasselquist; the which is portrayed as the most celebrated of all those cultivated in Ejypt. In India the name *cissa* is applied by the Mohammetans to the *cucumis utilissimus*, or the common *kukree* of the natives; while it is highly likely that the name is only applied to the common cucumber (*cucumis sativus*) in Persia and Syria, since the other two sorts are not well known in those countries.

But one day a letter came to the house:

Dear Dr Jones,

I'm truly sorry that I haven't contacted you sooner than this, my old friend. I've been on the trail of the mysterious Imalic, and that's led me here, to Edinburgh. I hadn't intended to be here so long but a set of gangsters – what else can I call them? – have been after me for a fortnight, hunting me in rings round the city like a fox. In the end they caught me and tied me in a chair and threatened to slit my throat from ear to ear unless I told them where Harry was. I had terrible trouble convincing them that I didn't have the faintest idea who this Harry was. But they believed me in the end and set me loose healthy and in one piece, to my great surprise. And how on earth did I get them to do that? Believe it or not, by claiming that I could put a curse on them so that each one of them would come to a tragic, bloody end. I believe that wicked people everywhere have a fear of that.

When they untied me, I asked them if they knew somebody by the name of Benig. I've spoken to a number of criminals since then, and met other exiles from Laxaria, Sacria, and even Mocatria in this country, but without the tiniest hint of success. Therefore, the purpose of this letter is to advise you that I shall be coming back to "Wales" in the near future.

Yours truly,
Melog
P.S. I hope Mr Job is still looking after the cats.

Within an hour a knock came at the door and Dr Jones knew instinctively that it was Melog this time. The letter had a second class stamp and had been posted on the day he had started his journey back from Scotland, probably, and here he was arriving almost at the same time as his message.

Except that it was not Melog at the door, but a pair of blank, circular spectacles staring up at him from the nose of Ambrose Bing.

Good afternoon, Dr Jones.

Hello.

I've seen your friend in town. Just got off the bus e ave.

Melog! Dr Jones said, not attempting to hide his delight. Where is he now?

Go to Mr Job's ouse. Praps I shoud say wass left of is ouse.

I'd like to get there before him to tell him the story…

Oh, don worry, Dr Jones. E ave seen the mess an I ave already told im war appened.

Dr Jones quivered, suppressing the urge to punch the little man on his beaky nose.

Do you kn…

Know where e is now, Dr Jones? Is tha wha you were about to ask? O course I do know.

But Ambrose Bing did not say another word, only stared up at the doctor's face, waiting for the inevitable next question, which he would answer before the doctor had finished asking it.

I would like to know, Mr Bing…

Look ere, Dr Jones, if you do want to know where e is, why don you ask? I ould be ony too glad to lead you to im, artificial ip or no.

Mr Bing, please tell me where he is at this moment, that is if you know, and I'll go to him on my own.

Melog is waitin in my ouse, Dr Jones.

It is considered that especial benefit is consequent upon the blessing of the father; but his curse falls most heavily and with injurious effect...

The Encyclopædia

FATHER AND SON

FROM THE OUTSIDE, the house of Ambrose Bing was an attempt to imitate number ten Downing Street in plastic, while inside it was luxurious without being tasteful. The lounge floor was covered with a deep, orange shagpile carpet. In the middle of the carpet was an enormous red sofa. Sitting in the middle of this, bolt upright, his hands on his knees like a nervous child before the headmaster, as terrifyingly thin as ever and white as an apparition, was Melog. His skin was as if drawn taut across the nose and the sharpened cheek-bones. There were no cheeks, only grey hollows. The skull under the face was clearly visible. The blue eyes stared out of this background of deathly white.

Dr Jones ached with the need to comfort him and ask what had happened to him and where he had been – but he had had time to reconsider. The azure eyes aroused compassion, but the doctor thought, it is a stupid thing to be fooled by the colour of someone's eyes. He did not understand those people who fell in love with someone because of their eye colour; after all, it was not something over which they had any control. And anyway, hadn't Melog left – again – without saying a word, and been away for ages without making contact? Why in the world should he take pity on him?

Dr Jones, you must be very angry with me.

Not at all, Dr Jones said. Liar. He was furious.

You have every right to be.

Not at all.

I'm afraid I've been very neglectful of our friendship, once again.

May I make a cup o tea? Ambrose Bing asked – Dr Jones had forgotten about his being in the room, but there he was, at his elbow, staring up at him with the question, his eyes dull behind the cloudy lenses.

You may, Dr Jones said, as if addressing a junior servant.

And for me, Melog said.

Ow do you like you tea, Dr Jones? Like tha terrible ych-a-fi dishwater stuff I ad in your ouse is it?

No, the usual. Ordinary tea.

Milk an sugar?

Yes. One.

And you, Mr Melog?

I like black tea, weak and watery so I can see the bottom of the cup through it. No milk. Three sugars.

I'll fetch the sugar bowl for you, you can pu your own sugars in then.

The little man vanished into the kitchen and Dr Jones gave thanks under his breath. All this stuff about tea, tea. All the small talk when he wanted to speak with his friend. But for some reason a great wall of taciturnity had risen between them. Had Melog changed? Was this a different Melog, or, the doctor thought, had his attitude towards Melog changed? They sat opposite one another in the soft, comfortable lounge in an awkward silence.

Then Ambrose Bing was back before there was a chance even to test the ice, let alone break it.

Wass a marrer? he said. Nor a word between you? I'm surprised, an you two nor avin seen one another for such a long time too.

Mr Job's house…

I ave told im all about the fire, Dr Jones. You don ave to mention tha. It was a bit of a shock for im. Ave you tea.

Mr Job is in hosp…

I've told im about tha too. You two will aff to go an pay im a visit some time, I'm sure.

Did you hear about the ca…

Yes, e ave eard about the sad story o the cats, Dr Jones, don upset im again.

Yeah, don't talk about the cats. It breaks my heart to think about them burning to death in that room. If only I'd been here, perhaps I could have saved their lives – and Mr Job's papers, or some of them, anyway.

Or, Ambrose Bing said like a Job's comforter, praps you would ave burned to death with em.

I only just escaped getting burned in a fire in Scotland, Melog said. I was staying in an hotel – well, a bed and break-fast to be accurate – and I'd been smoking that night as usual…

E do not smoke in this ouse, as you've noticed, I ope, Dr Jones.

Well, I'd been smoking and I'd lain on the bed and I must have dropped off to sleep. Next thing, I'm awake and the room's full of this hellish black smoke…

Dangerous thing, smokin, en it, Dr Jones? Apart from the fact that iss bad for your ealth.

Thank goodness there was a smoke alarm in the room, and that was screaming like a mouse in a frying pan and water shaped like an umbrella was spraying from the ceiling. Then the hotel manager came to the door. There was nothing on fire but the cigarette had fallen from my fingers onto the bed and the clothes were smouldering and gone black. In fact there was a layer of black over everything in the room, a mantle of this sooty stuff. The whole room was black.

You was lucky, wasn e, Dr Jones? Iss the smoke usually, not the fire do kill you.

Anyway, I had to leave the hotel that night.

What do you intend to do tonight? the doctor asked.

E's stayin ere tonight with us, en you, Mr Melog?

Dr Jones could not believe the way in which Ambrose Bing knew exactly what you were going to say before you said it.

An I do know wha Mr Melog is go-yin to say too, Bing

said, as if he had indeed read the doctor's mind. E is go-yin to say, 'Yes I'm going to stay with Mr Bing tonight'. En you, Melog?

Yes, Melog said.

There, see. I told you didn I? I do know wha people are go-yin to say before they do say it. Well, iss easy to do. We do all read God's scripts in the sky, we do all pronounce the words of Esperanto from the Great Author in Eaven.

At that, suddenly and unexpectedly, a man appeared in the door of the lounge. Although he was considerably older, he was otherwise exactly the same in appearance as Ambrose Bing. The same thick spectacles with three-colour frames, the same oozy eyes, the short stature, the protruding, rabbit-like front teeth. The only difference was the signs of age. He moved more slowly than Ambrose Bing, his hair was white and his fingers were knotted with arthritis.

Well, ello, Ambrose Bing said to his reflection. May I introduce you? This is my father, Ambrose Bing; Daddy, this is Dr Jones – the friend of our guest, Mr Melog.

Ello, Ambrose Bing the elder said, and went to sit next to his son. The cartoonish similarity was astonishing as they were wearing the same clothes.

E ave noticed that we're dressed the same, the old Ambrose Bing said.

Yes, Daddy, an now e ave got completely confused. E's go-yin to get up.

An e's go-yin to make an excuse to leave, en e?

Yes, Daddy.

Dr Jones got up. He felt that there was no point in his saying anything as father and son knew exactly what was in his mind. An unpleasant feeling which sent a shudder through him.

E do wan to say goodnight to you, Melog, Ambrose Bing the younger said.

E do wan to arrange to meet you tomorrow, Ambrose Bing the elder said.

But you're go-yin to phone im, en you, Melog? the son said.

Yes e is, the father said, and they both laughed. They both laughed until tears ran down their cheeks behind their milky spectacles.

Dr Jones cast one glance at his friend and saw him sitting uncomfortably on the vast sofa; he had not moved a sinew.

Good night, said the father.

Good night, said the son.

Good night, said Melog.

Dr Jones left without saying a word – in case he should scream, Good night, Zebedee, Good night, Johnboy!

The authentic is that object in which all of the elements which that object may contain inhere in it; and the contrary to the authentic is that which does not contain those elements, save to an imperfect degree.

The Encyclopædia

DEATH

THE VOICE on the phone said, *Mea culpa, mea maxima culpa.*

?

I'm very sorry I didn't get in touch with you, Dr Jones.

I didn't know you spoke Latin. To tell you the truth I didn't recognise your voice after all this time, Dr Jones said, with a touch of sarcasm.

It was impossible to talk last night, wasn't it?

Yes, with Tweedledum and Tweedledee present.

Can we meet in town to talk?

Yes, Dr Jones said, though his entire soul was screaming at him to say 'no, never again', yes of course we can meet and talk.

And they arranged a time and a place. On his way through the back streets – dog mess, stinging nettles, the discharges from cars – Dr Jones felt angry with himself. Why have I given in to him again so easily? He disappears for weeks and comes back and expects us to carry on as friends as if nothing has happened. I let him off too lightly. He's got some power, some hold on me that I can't understand. I know that I ought to ignore him but I can't. It doesn't matter what dreadful things he does; I can't resist him. He's cast a spell on me, some magic.

By the time he got to the café where he was to meet Melog his anger had evaporated completely, and the doctor was inwardly calmer and looking forward to seeing his friend. But he was not expecting him to be there already waiting for him at the appointed time because being late was in his nature. Yet there he was, like a skeleton at one of the tables, his sapphire eyes gazing at the cup of tea going cold in front of him, unconscious of all the attention he was drawing from the people around him, who stared at him like brown house sparrows amazed by the colours of a kingfisher, mere people struck dumb before an angel. But that was how it usually was; wherever he went he turned heads, though this had no effect on him at all. The doctor sat opposite him.

Good morning, Dr Jones, Melog said. There were dark circles round the blue eyes.

The doctor ordered a cup of coffee and looked around at the café which once, recently, had been brand new and modern and shiny, but now everything in it looked a little worn. The curtains and the tablecloths had lost some of their colour (green and yellow); the furniture had dated (seventies); some pieces of crockery were cracked and there was a small chip on the edge of the saucer on which his cup of coffee was served up by the sour young waiter. It had degenerated from a café to a caff. The tired, automatic busy-ness of the restaurant staff as they set about another routine day was visible in their listless movements, their dulled eyes. Dr Jones felt strangely conscious of these small details and everything else around him. The other customers, with their burdens of shopping at their feet under the tables, smoked and ate chips, committing leisurely, delayed, but workman-like and determined suicide. What would these people be talking about, he wondered. He didn't know. The lighting in the café was weak and the doctor felt that he would hear the conversations more clearly if it were stronger, just as he felt that he had to turn the volume up when he watched television without his glasses. Their voices mixed in the smoke of the cigarettes above their heads and blended in one garbled conversation, the words, like the items in their bags, making no sense to him. If that is 'reality' Dr Jones thought, give me chocolate, give me sherry, give me Prozac. Not that he was a snob, but he was not part of that world and anyway would find no place there.

What's the matter, Dr Jones? Are you all right?

Yes. Everything's all right. My mind's wandering, that's all.

Thinking about the Encyclopaedia, ey?

That's it.

Dr Jones looked at his friend (though he could not be sure that this was Melog, the same Melog) and watched him speak, drink tea, smoke. He was talking about his time in Scotland, but Dr Jones did not believe him. Gangsters? He hadn't been captured by gangsters. Surely he'd been to see a gangster film.

What do other people talk about? Dr Jones still thought. The people sitting at the other tables, the tired, irritated waiters, the people in the street? Melog (or the Pseudo-Melog perhaps) was talking about the Imalic. Other people talked about the weather, the family, their work, their colleagues, football, the government, television, money, health, lack of money, the lottery, the royal family, sex, romantic problems. But Melog hadn't traced the Imalic; he'd come close, touch and go, but missed it in the end. Dr Jones was guessing about other people's talk; he had no clue, no idea on earth what they actually talked about. Melog was alternately happy and sad. Happy to be back in Wales with his friend, Dr Jones, and sad that he'd failed to solve the mystery of the Imalic. He'd had a letter from Lavcadio in America saying he was fine, so Melog was happy. But because Lavcadio was in far away America, Melog was sad. His eyes glittered like rockpools in the sun with these polarised emotions – sadness, delight, sadness, delight, sadness, delight – he was waving his slender hand, the ciga-rette between his long shapely fingers, a big black ring on the middle finger, iddle inger, farreach, Long Harris, John Bowman, Tom the Barber, Will Bibby, longfinger, dinnereater.

What's the matter, Dr Jones? Are you listening? Are you sure you're all right?

Of course I am, Melog.

Well, what am I going to do now? I can't live with the Ambrose Bings can I? And I've lost my cats. Even my beloved François. And what am I going to do about the Imalic?

I truly don't know, Melog.

How about if we order two huge chunks of chocolate cake?

Good idea.

They ordered the cakes. Dr Jones knew it was he would pay for the treat, out of the remains of his giro.

Why did you go and stay with them? Why didn't you come to me?

A long story, but to cut it short: I met Ambrose Bing, the son, in the station after I came back from Scotland and he came up to me and he told me about the disaster of the fire and the death of the cats. I didn't know him, but I started crying there and then when I heard about my cats and Mr Bing kindly gave me his shoulder and he was kind enough to lead me to his home and offer to let me stay there because I was pretty well homeless. I accepted before I realised there's a sinister side to him and his father. I'm moving out the first chance I get.

Dr Jones did not attempt to persuade him to come and live with him. He knew that that would not work.

What about going to see old Mr Job this afternoon? What's going to happen to him now, I wonder? He's homeless too, poor dab.

And depressed, I'm afraid. But that's natural of course. Yes, another good idea. We'll go and see him this afternoon. He'll be delighted to see you, Melog.

But when Dr Jones went to the hospital later that day Melog was not there to meet him as they had arranged. But that was Melog for you. Promising one thing and doing something else. He could not be depended on. But afterwards, when the doctor went to the ward where Mr Job had been staying, he was not there either. Dr Jones was shocked to see that the bed was empty and neatly remade. And he leapt to the obvious conclusion, but the shiftless man on reception told him that Mr Job had been moved to an old people's home a long way away the previous night.

As he walked home from the hospital through town, he saw Ambrose Bing jnr and Ambrose Bing snr. His first reaction was to avoid them, and he believed that that would be easy because of their defective eyesight, but they came straight to him, calling:

Dr Jones! Dr Jones!

What is it? Dr Jones asked, irritated.

Me an Daddy ave been looking for you everywhere, aven we, Daddy?

We ave. Been to your ouse. No answer. Been to the library. No sign. Been to Jabez Ifans's chip shop. No siw, no miw.

An ere we are wanderin the town in the feeble ope o seein you somewhere.

But lucky to ger olt of you in the end. You ave been to see Mr Job but Mr Job ave been moved…

We could ave told you about tha.

Stop jabberin, Ambrose Bing, we ave got something much more important to tell Dr Jones, aven we?

We ave. Something bad we've got, Dr Jones.

Bad? What about?

About your friend, Melog.

What's happened to him?

A number of scenes flashed through the doctor's mind. Melog stealing a car and crashing it; Melog mauled by ferocious dogs; Melog in a fire; Melog captured by gangsters; Melog going to Morocco; Melog climbing onto the roof of the Town Hall. But Melog came through it all in one piece, of course.

E's dead, Dr Jones, said Ambrose Bing the elder.

Dead? Dr Jones laughed in their molish faces. But I was

talking to him just a while ago, at lunchtime. We went to a café in town and had chocolate cake together.

Lunch time? Ambrose Bing the younger said. Oh! I don think you ave seen Mr Melog today, Dr Jones.

No, Ambrose Bing the elder said. E was pronounced dead in the town this morning an e's lying in the spare room where e slept last night, down our ouse.

Stone dead. His son's voice was hard and cruel, matter-of-factly underlining the point.

But Dr Jones did not believe them. He could not comprehend their words, or why they should tell such untruths. It was obvious to him that they were lying; hadn't he sat and drank and eaten and spoken with Melog a little earlier? Hadn't he seen the boy quite clearly? True, he looked like a picture of a corpse in a medical encyclopaedia, but he was there, present, in the flesh, before his eyes. He had paid for his cake, everybody around him had noticed him; there was no shortage of eavesdroppers and eye witnesses to their meeting.

May I see him? Dr Jones asked.

By all means. Come to our ouse where e is lyin in bed all cold an stiff, one of the Bings said.

Come sharpish mind, the other Ambrose Bing said, before they do come an collect im for the post mortem.

Things moved quickly that day, and shortly the doctor was standing in the tasteless luxury home of the Bings. The spare room was entirely decorated in light blue. Skyblue curtains, skyblue carpet, skyblue armchairs, skyblue cushions, skyblue wallpaper, skyblue paintwork, skyblue bedspread, skyblue bolster, and between the bedspread and the bolster, his eyes closed, his skin white, lay Melog. Dead. Stone dead. No breath. No motion. Quietude.

You wan to know ow e died, don you? Ambrose Bing jnr. asked.

Right again, Dr Jones answered.

Committed suicide e did, the father said.

You wan to know ow, don you? the son asked.

Yes.

E threw isself off the top o the Town All, the old man said.

When?

This morning, Ambrose Bing the younger said. E wen out, climbed up, an jumped down. There was a crowd o people there watchin im but nobody could stop im.

But there's not a mark on him, Dr Jones said.

Obvious you en a medical doctor. There en a mark on is face, thass true, but lift the bedclose up an you'll see the bruises on is back, an the back of is ead too. Ave a look, Dr Jones.

No, thanks. But I don't understand how he got to this bed.

The ambulance brought im ere. Daddy appened to be passin the Town All jest after Mr Melog it the pavement, an e was able to tell the police that e do live with us. Lucky en it, or e would ave ad to lie in some cold old mortuary all day.

And was this Melog? The real Melog, or some counter-feit-Melog? An idiotic question. With skin and hair like hoar-frost, the long fingers and the fragile bones who could it be but Melog? There was no one like him. But there he lay, lifeless, unbreathing in his corpse. The free spirit, the wild animal, the creature that could not be tied or tamed. Cold and limp. He who had been all energy and life and vibrancy, the mocking adventurer full of tricksiness. Dead.

Why?

God said to im to do it, the old Ambrose Bing said.

What god?

The God, said the son.

The *Livin* God, said the father.

Mr God, said the son.

The *Lord* thy God, said the father.

God is *love*, said the son.

God God, said the father.

Dr Jones bent at the side of the bed and pressed his fore-head against the back of the boy's right hand. And at last the tears poured from his eyes.

A CONFESSION

TO TELL YOU THE TRUTH, Melog said, I'm glad to get
away from the two Ambrose Bings and their home. They
were bonkers the both of them. Bananas.

I'm not talking to you, Dr Jones said. I haven't forgiven
you for playing such a mean trick on me.

Oh come now, Dr Jones. It was their idea.

A sick idea, Dr Jones said. He had still not managed to
convince himself that he was not talking to an artificial
Melog, a clone.

Fun, they said.

Perverted fun I'd say, Dr Jones said. And there was no
need for you to go along with it.

But they forced me to, when I went back to their house
after I saw you in the café.

The two had arrived at the old people's home where Mr
Job was now living; there was a garden surrounding it like a
public park and a row of pinetrees around the garden. A
brass plaque above the doorbell said: PINE TREES
NURSING HOME FOR DISTRESSED GENTLEFOLK.
Melog rang the bell. Suddenly a greyish, grizzlehaired, grey-
clothed young man opened the door to them.

And you're Mr Job's visitors, I take it. We've been expecting you. Dr Jones and…?

Melog, Melog said, shaking the greyster's hand.

I'm Nigel, he said. Come in. Your friend is sitting in the
parlour.

And there was Mr Job, looking terrifyingly old, sitting in

a comfortable chair, held upright by multicoloured cushions.

The two looked around the parlour; paisley carpet and furniture, William Morrisish wallpaper, several aspidistras in china pots with chinoiserie patterning.

Apart from Mr Job, the only other person in the room was an utterly bald little old man who sat in front of the television nursing in his arms three teddy bears.

That's Mr Owen, Nigel said. Mr Owen! Visitors for Mr Job! Nigel shouted. Mr Owen took no notice.

I'll leave you for the time being, Nigel said, but if you need anything – tea, biscuits, tablets, oxygen – let me know. I'll be in my office.

Nigel slipped away like a thief. Dr Jones and Melog sat in front of Mr Job.

Mr Job, how are you? Melog and I have come to see you.

Ah yes, of course. I recognise you both, Mr Job said. Wil and Sionyn, Sionyn and Wil, you were procreated at exactly the same time, and in the same place, by the same lover, and the same passion.

What's he talking about? Melog asked.

I'm not sure. He's confused, I think, been dozing maybe. Do you remember us, Mr Job? Melog and Dr Jones.

Of course, of course. Here's Wil, Mr Job said grasping Melog's hand, who's kind and open-hearted but day by day the consciousness grows in me that he is not a good boy. He talks without due consideration for the detailed rules of the seiat; and it is only rarely that he address anyone by their given name. And you, he said, grasping Dr Jones's hand, you are 'that learned Supralapsarian'. I have always enjoyed reading about you: how it was that you furnished your house with books, and books alone; how you would travel in France and Holland 'seeking comely editions of the Fathers'...

No, no. I'm sorry to interrupt you, Dr Jones said, but this is Melog – he lodged with you at your house, Mr Job.

Yes, that's it, I am sorry, I recognised you straight away, Mr Job said. The child is father to the man, the proverb says.

And doubtless there never was a truer word, if there be means to grasp it fully. Although at ease enow with many sorts of people, yet, in my heart of hearts, I was ever the man for small company. There can I come closer to my true self.

Is he trying to tell us to go? Melog asked. Perhaps he's not feeling very well.

Oh, I'm sure he's all right, Dr Jones said. He seems pleased to see us. He's taking a while to come to himself. I am Dr Jones, and this is Melog. Mel-og.

Oh yes, I remember him properly now. Everybody calls him Mike. A small group call him Mihangel, and the elite are allowed to call him Mihang. You enjoyed that terrifically for a while, didn't you, until one night somebody a bit wilder than the rest made up a song: 'Mihang mihink the bonkers Chink', and then you sulked, didn't you?

I don't know what he's talking about, Melog said.

We've got to be patient, Dr Jones said. Speak normally with him, that's the secret. How do you like this place, Mr Job? Nice isn't it? Here in Pine Trees.

It's all right, Mr Job said, but there is a funereal air about the place, an impression which is strengthened by the parallel-sided mounds which mark the limits of the irrigation trenches, mounds resembling the graves of thin giants. Plants grow in rich disorder in the reddish clay, flowers grow where God wills, and the myrtle brakes seem as if they were here to obstruct rather than to make easy the path.

We're getting a bit more sense from him now, Dr Jones said. Ask him a question, Melog.

What about your health, Mr Job? How are you feeling now?

I am afraid that I remain extremely old-fashioned – and sensitive, and the quiet minutes continue to oppress me... But tears – tears of sadness and compassion, tears of delight and laughter, and, too, mingling with these, the tears aroused by moving and attractive expression – have been a part of my spiritual heritage, whatever the biologists' explanation may be for all this. And I do not feel the least shame for them, whether that is a weakness or no.

Strewth, he can't half talk poetically, Melog said.

Melog's saying that you're talking po-et-ic-all-y, Mr Job!

To the relics of the Normans, Mr Job said, I will set my harp where streamlets meander to the centre of the holy wafer in the forests of Cwm Cynon, my one man... my one man... I'm sorry, he said, my memory's starting to go.

Don't worry, Mr Job. Would you like me to ask for a cup of tea?

Zit by ze table, Mr Job said, a glazz to each of zem who would have bread and a loaf to each of zem and meat and applez of ze earth, zem let zem take!

Well, it sounds as though he would like some tea doesn't it? I'll go and look for Nigel, Melog said.

No, don't, Dr Jones said. Let's talk with him for a little longer.

About what, for instance?

Well what about talking about the cats...

Cats! Mr Job said. Yes, cats. Don't look so idiotic when I ask a question like that. One can learn a great deal about village life from the study of cats, just as one can learn a great deal about town life from the study of dogs.

Say something to him about the neighbours, Dr Jones said.

What neighbours...?

Our neighboures are indignant with us that we make boast of Arthur. And there is on times some palterer who would attempt to hold that there never was suchlike man as he in all the worlde. But let the Reader know this, and let him believe it as a truthe beyond disappointment, that that same man hath no more ground for saying such, than if a man were to contend that the Sun had never risen for the reason that the Sun was set when he made observation of it.

Hey, Melog said in admiration, now that is excellent Welsh!

There are plenty of us who are Welsh by birth and by language, Mr Job said, suddenly switching to a northern accent, who can be our own selves without feeling the prick of conscience. But you can't bear to think – can't bear to consider the possibility even for a second – that life could be completely meaningless. You have to keep a straight face – turn the language into the meaning and see yourselves as the defenders of the last bastion of civilization or something like that… it's so good to live a meaningless life… but the best thing is getting rid of meaning. Everything is interesting instead of being significant. If people were to renounce their too certain beliefs, this world would be a better place to live in.

He's starting to ramble now, Dr Jones said.

For the vigils of the night are long and even in my solitude I will not cheat the ravings of the moon, Mr Job went on, now in a quiet monotone. Her laughter drags at my darkened lids and her mocking pierces to the depths of my captivity, yet hope is not ended…

Melog and Dr Jones rose quietly.

For none can doubt the government of the sun, and none turn back the dawn's fair sallying…

The two slipped away, past the colour television and Mr Owen and his little bears, past Nigel's office and out of Pine Trees.

What a sad experience, Melog said, the memory going like that.

Soon the friends were walking through the town park towards Dr Jones's home.

I don't want to see those Bing people again, the doctor said.

If I were only to see them once more before the end of eternity it'd be too soon for me too, Melog said.

You're only saying that to appease me, Dr Jones said.

No, really, Dr Jones, I didn't like them at all. They wound me up; there was something unpleasant about them wasn't there? Comic but malign. Odd how the funny and the tragic are so closely related, isn't it?

In Dr Jones's house the sculpture which Melog had stolen from the exhibition stood on the same table as Dr Jones's notes – in fact Melog had put it on top of some of his latest writings on the Encyclopaedia.

I'm going to have a bath, Melog announced, and then I'm going to write a letter to Lavcadio in America. I miss him very much.

The young man ran upstairs to the bathroom. Dr Jones heard the water running and Melog energetically singing Laxarian songs.

He appeared a quarter of an hour later, a green towel wrapped loosely round his waist, his wet hair as it were vanished, transparent with wetness; his shoulders, his back, and his chest like marble running with water and glistening. Dr Jones remembered the first time he met his friend in the hands of the police. Really, this moment was similar to that time when Melog came and stayed overnight at his house at the beginning of their friendship.

The young man took up a pen and a sheet of paper, sat at the table near the fantastical sculpture, and started to write.

Melog, Dr Jones said, you're welcome to stay here. Not just tonight, but you can stay here. You don't have to look for other lodgings.

Thanks, Melog said, drawing on the inevitable cigarette, not turning his head, not saying more.

Melog, Dr Jones said again, I've got to tell you something. I wouldn't tell this to everybody. I've thought about telling you before now, but I never had the opportunity. Now's the time. Are you listening?

Yes. The boy continued writing.

You won't criticise me will you? You won't think any the less of me, will you?

Well I can't promise because I don't know what you're going to say yet.

Well, Dr Jones began, a long time ago after I'd graduated,

in Welsh of course, I started my research work. I wasn't a full-time student because I didn't have a scholarship to follow my studies. After an unsuccessful attempt at being a school-teacher I worked in a book-shop during the day and worked on my thesis by night. Not in this town, you understand. I went away to college, to the nearest city. Well, I was working closely on the research thesis for eight years, adding notes, piling up the words, turning out the pages, till in the end the thesis was quite a fat volume. The time came for me to present my study. Professor Berwyn Boyle Hopkin was the external examiner.

Oh yeah. I remember him in the exhibition, Melog said, stopping work on his letter. Face like a furnace, thought about nothing apart from footnotes. Not a creative bone in his body.

The Professor refused to give me the degree. My thesis wasn't worthy of any sort of degree he said. Not worth a potato, he said.

But he called you Dr Jones that night of the exhibition.

He was taking pity. And taking a rise out of me. I'm a laughing-stock. The butt of the academic world's jokes.

What did you do then?

Can you imagine the disappointment, the shame, after working towards that goal, after working on that one thing and living with that one thing for almost a decade? I decided to kill myself. I couldn't see any point in living. Even in my own opinion I was a complete failure. And the first thing I did was to take every copy of the thesis and every draft and every note and burn the lot. I put the entire work of eight years of my life into a rubbish bin and burned it to ashes.

But you didn't kill yourself.

I came back to this town, to this house. I came to my senses on the bus home. No, I wasn't going to end my life for such a stupid reason. You don't need a doctorate to live. We're all born without qualifications aren't we? And you certainly don't need qualifications to go to the grave.

Everybody calls you doctor anyway.

Everybody in this town took it for granted that I'd got the degree, and to my shame I did nothing to correct them. I'm Dr Jones to everybody in the area. But as far as the cardboard constabulary are concerned, recently I've become 'Dr' Jones. They've got some new information from somewhere. Then about three or four years ago I set myself the task of restoring the text of my thesis, chapter for chapter, page for page, word for word. The problem is that I've got an appalling memory and the truth is that I'm writing a completely new thesis on the Encyclopaedia.

The doctor hesitated. He looked at his friend.

So what do you think of me now, Melog?

I'm going to finish this letter to Lavcadio. How about some cheese on toast, Dr Jones?

It would seem that the compositional facility of invention comprises various elements: – Firstly the facility of reduction: having perceived a human person, I can imagine a man as small as the Lilliputians of Dean Swift. Secondly, the facility of exaggeration: – having perceived a man, I can imagine a giant, and take pleasure in the portrayal of his manly accomplishments.

The Encyclopædia

A CARNIVAL

I WANT TO GIVE IT ONE MORE GO, make one last attempt to find the Imalic, Melog said to Dr Jones over breakfast (half a grapefruit each, no sugar, black coffee). I'm not going to give my life up to a wild goose chase, I don't even like detective stories and I'm no Hercule Poirot.

Don't you like whodunnits? Dr Jones asked.

No thanks, Melog said. I hate suspense novels. I can't cope with the rules of the game. A long time before I'm half way through the book I'll say 'Who cares who killed him?' and look at the last page and chuck the book in the bin. I lose patience with all the manufactured, artificial situations and stereotypical characters and smart detectives.

Myself, I tend to suspect the detectives, Dr Jones said.

And me. And the whole thing's a sort of trick. The writer piles suspicion on Mr Blubberguts, but the most suspicious character is never ever the murderer! It's Mr Nice. And it all gets 'explained' in the last chapter.

Melog said the word 'explained' with such scorn that Dr Jones laughed.

I hate things that get 'explained', Melog said. I prefer mysteries. Who wants to look at a crossword after somebody's solved it? I prefer things like the Mary Celeste, Jack the Ripper, The Man in the Iron Mask – mysteries without solutions. The red herrings, the wild geese, are the only things I like in a detective novel.

217

So, why are you pursuing this business of the Imalic?

To tell you the truth, I'm starting to get tired of it. My interest has faded recently. I'm not sure I believe in it – the Imalic.

Really? You don't believe in your national treasure?

I'm afraid that the manuscript has disappeared, but, as you well know, Dr Jones, I've been through fire and rain. Through too much trouble, really, to give up without one more shot at it. But unless, Melog said rolling one of his flimsy cigarettes, unless I can get some sort of solution to the mystery this time, I'm going to forget about the Imalic for good.

After breakfast they went into the living-room. They cleared all of Dr Jones's notes and files and papers from the table and pushed the curious sculpture safely to one side against the wall.

So, Melog began, what do we know about this? The name Benig, the poem, the letter. It's not in London, not with Professor Lalula, not in Scotland. In other words, nothing, nought, nothing can come of nothing. A collection of loose ends, that's all. One thing's obvious – I'm no Sherlock Holmes and you aren't Dr Watson.

So what will you do? What'll we do?

I can't think about what to do here. How about going to the park? Clear the head, look for inspiration. Perhaps the answer will come in a moment of revelation.

But Melog, Dr Jones said, the park will be heaving. Today's the carnival.

The blue sky – as blue as Melog's eyes – had caught some infection, a measled, comic, multicoloured plague of pimply balloons that had appeared across its face – red, white, blue, orange, green, yellow, pink, purple, even – as colourful as Lavcadio's room.

Melog and Dr Jones were standing in the high street so that they could watch the parade slowly streaming past. The sky's sickness was infectious. There were so many clowns, monsters, vampires, witches and cartoons come to life, incarnations of the magical – the Flintstones, Deputy Dawg, Top Cat and his friends (Melog thought of François), Huckleberry Hound, Pixie and Dixie and Jinx, Zebedee and Dougal, Super Ted, Fireman Sam, the Smurfs – these were all adults. Some walked – the old man who gurned, he was in the parade every year (how on earth did he manage to get his lower lip up over his nose like that, like Gwefl ap Gwastad in the legend of Culhwch and Olwen?) – others were composed in tableaux on floats. Rumpelstiltskin the Dwarf; Tweedledum and Tweedledee; the Werewolf; Quasimodo with the hunched back and bells. People on unicycles; jugglers throwing one, two, three, four, five balls in the air (red, yellow, blue, green, orange) where they spun and spun in the happy wounded sky – and the dextrous jugglers catching them all, not letting one fall to the ground, although they walked the whole time in the flow of the parade. An amazingly tall man on stilts, his head in the sickblithe air. Another man licking a flame like a lollipop. A man dressed as a skeleton and another as Death. Another float and on it Dr Jekyll and Mr Hyde. Walking past was Dic Aberdaron with his dictionaries and his cats – how could he lead all those cats? Only to remind Melog once more of all his late cats, poor things.

This was an exceptionally cultured carnival; however, a little lack of taste was essential, otherwise it could not fairly be called a carnival at all. And there were the brass bands and the inevitable jazz bands with the inescapable, silly kazoos like swarms of maddened bees – this was after all a carnival in the Valleys of the South.

Suddenly the happy-idiotic procession came to an end and the onlookers followed the show through the gates and into the park.

There, Dr Jones and Melog saw the marquees and stands that had mushroomed everywhere overnight. It seemed that the entire population of the town was in the park that day.

The smell of hot dogs, Welsh cakes, toffee apples, candy

floss, hot chestnuts and crisps, cockles in vinegar, fish and chips, whirled in the air and around their nostrils. And meat, the smell of meat cooking. There were Death and the skeleton eating beefburgers.

An enormous slide had been erected on one of the lawns. People – mainly boys – climbed the steep metallic staircase, high like a ladder, and would stand hesitating on the brink of the chute – whether to turn back before it was too late or to let go and fall into danger and elation. The refusers were few. But everyone who got up the nerve and launched down the slippy path let out an involuntary scream. The dinning of the screams was almost unbearable. Pain and elation in one sound.

The first marquee was the plant and flower show. Dr Jones and Melog saw row after row of geraniums and fuchsias, orchids and roses – red, purple and white, and pink like babies' cheeks. There was a whiff of tension among the competitors, envy and malice, enmity in the air.

That bastard Reynolds have won again, one competitor said to another. It's him wins every year with his bloody pelargoniums.

He's the judge's nephew, see, the other said.

In the next marquee the cookery competitions were on display. The judges were licking at spoonfuls of crimson jam and amber honey, others were pondering over slabs of creamy cakes. The two friends saw three slices of bara brith side by side on plates; the red card for first prize on one, a blue second prize card on another, and a yellow third prize card on the last. What was the difference? To Dr Jones's great shame, Melog snatched the winner and the runner-up when no one was looking and ran out of the marquee to the dog show.

Among the competitors was Jaco Saunders with Fang and Satan. Everyone kept a safe distance between themselves and the dogs' teeth and red, slavering flews. But they wagged their cropped tails happily when they recognised from afar their old friend Melog and he had no choice but to divide the second prize bara brith between Fang and Satan. Melog had gormandised the first prize before he had even got to the dogs, and had not offered a crumb of it to Dr Jones.

There were other dogs there too, of course; snappy corgis, terriers bearded and eyebrowed like old men, patient sheepdogs, hunting dogs and greyhounds quaking as if it were winter, pom-pommed poodles, and rare dogs like the pulik in its dreadlocks, keeshonden, chihuahuas. Melog searched for owners who looked like their dogs, and although he found resemblances in the occasional pair (one man and his bulldog and another with his Afghan) he could not find a likeness to please him.

The two went on, weaving through the crowd. In the carnival, Melog did not attract attention in the usual way. For one day at least he was part of the crowd. They went past a Guess the Weight stall and a Test Your Strength pillar (Dr Jones thought of Daniel Jones in *The Squire of Havilah*, one of his favourite stories) on to the tent of Tudno the Fortune-teller, who according to the sign outside (in sweeping red letters) could read the stars, tealeaves, palms, the crystal ball, the runes, and the tarot cards, in English or in Welsh.

I've got to go and see him again, Melog said. Perhaps he can guide me to the Imalic.

Don't waste your money, Melog.

I've got to give it a try. This is the final attempt and then I'll give all this stuff about the Imalic up. But I can't think of anything else to do.

It's your decision, Melog.

Will you come with me, Dr Jones?

Don't be silly. What are you? A child?

Come on in with me, just to hear what he's got to say.

Oh, very well then, the doctor said irritably, but secretly he was just as curious as his friend.

They had to wait in a long queue before seeing the psychic. Dr Jones recognised the big hairy sourfaced man in a big hairy, bearlike coat, the thin young man with thin hair and a limp moustache and a scrawny little boy holding his hand; he had seen them in the social security office. With the sun behind him, the child was trying to step into the middle of his own shadow on the ground and trap it under his foot. Every time he moved towards it the shadow moved too. Dad, why is it doing that, Dad? the little boy asked. Fuck off, the father said.

On the other side, the paunchy, baldheaded man tonguing a cloud of candy floss was a stranger.

Skeleton ran past closely pursued by Death the Leveller – his cloak across his dark face, a scythe in his hand.

Our turn next, Melog said. To tell you the truth, I feel quite nervous.

Dr Jones lifted the flap in the wall of the tent and they both stepped through. When their eyes had become accustomed to the gloom and the smoke of incense, they saw Tudno (short, emaciated, feeble-looking) sitting behind a small round table on which was a crystal ball. He wore a cherry red shirt, a red tie like a slit throat, and a tomato red sweater.

May I help you? the shaman asked (pretending he did not recognise the doctor and Melog).

Melog sat on a rickety chair before the wizard, who stretched his hand out to Melog who placed two fifty pence pieces on the open palm.

I'm searching for something, Melog said, and I'm afraid that something dreadful has happened.

Let me look into the crystal ball, Tudno said. At the moment I see nothing, nothing but mist, mist upon mist, a great mist that masks the mystery, but it is there that that after which you seek is lurking. But prithee! The mist begins to clear and I see some sort of long tunnel, or a funnel, or some long path, I see the sea and clouds and water lashing and wind churning and blowing, I see foam and smoke and stew and fog, and I see the sky at night without stars; what is this now? Leaves, wings, feathers, flakes, flakes of snow? I see a sound,

I taste a smell, I hear a feeling, a soft feeling, like a sponge, like clay, like goo, like dirt, like earth, and in the earth there are little fragments, little stones, gravel, grains, granules, like something smashed to pieces, ground down and then dispersed, scattered about, blowing away in a puff of wind, breeze, breath, blowing away like dust, like chaff, like steam melting into air and vanishing; I see shapes, shadows, figures, colours, patches of colour, white patches, black patches, slabs of blackness, grey slabs, some wan, some brown, some yellow, breaking and reuniting, shifting shape again and again, flying, hovering, coalescing and scattering again, turning and turning, swirling and falling, falling, falling, and ascending once more, ascending to the firmament, ascending to the zenith, upwards and upwards once more, higher and higher, closer to the sun; I see a blazing light, rays, fire, flames, sparks, red, orange, yellow, explosions, flashes, detonation and quietude, a fog of gas, quietude, contentment, tranquillity, and nothing, nothing but darkness…

That's it? Melog asked.

That, Tudno said, is it. That is the end of the crystal ball's revelation. What about a tarot reading? Your palm? Tea leaves? I could run you up an astrological chart in a trice. What's your birthday? Ophiucus, isn't it? Where were you born – the location is important. It's important to be very exact. No? What about your friend? The runes then? Don't go yet. Come back!

Out in the fresh air again, the daylight hurting their eyes for the moment, they saw the skeleton and the Grim Reaper waiting their turn to consult Tudno.

A waste of time and money, Melog told them.

Where shall we go now? Dr Jones asked.

I don't care, Melog said. I was so disappointed with that stupid performance. Anyway, that's an end to looking for the Imalic.

The two walked on through the crowd. Melog was morose and paid no attention to the celebrations, the sound of hurdy-gurdies, the balloons, the fancy dress, the dinosaurs, gorillas, sasquatch.

Look, Dr Jones said, look at the lake!

Floating on the lake were hundreds, perhaps thousands, of little yellow plastic ducks.

A duck race. What about having one?

On our lake, Melog said, around our island.

Dr Jones stood still for a moment. Against his expectations, Melog had remembered that night on the island. He thought of it as 'our island'. The phrase settled deep in the coffers of Dr Jones's mind, for him to treasure as long as he lived, or until his memory failed him. After that, he thought of the island as a bridge connecting a piece of Wales with a piece of Laxaria.

How about going to the hall of mirrors? Melog suggested, revitalised and charged with enthusiasm.

In the hall of mirrors marquee, the two friends watched one another change shape in the glass. Dr Jones long and thin – Melog-shaped. Melog short and small – Dr Jones-shaped. Melog swollen huge like a snowman. Dr Jones with a hollow in his stomach. Melog all waves like a human river, no bones in his body. The two side by side, blending into one another – Dr Jones's arm coming out of Melog's shoulder; Melog's legs part of Dr Jones's side, their cheeks (Melog's left, Dr Jones's right) become one, one head, four eyes, two of them brown and bespectacled, the other two blue brilliants under the same forehead (Melog had to stoop to do this). They both laughed like boys mitching off school. And then other people came into the marquee. The skeleton again and Death Triumphant. Suddenly there were six skeletons and eight Deaths.

Can we go to the freak show? Dr Jones asked like a little boy. There's a gang of circus people there. You've got to pay to see them.

The friends looked at the smallest man in the world. His name was Arthur and he was smaller than the children who came to see the show. His smallness was accentuated by the huge aspidistra on a high table positioned next to the dwarf's chair. They watched a threelegged man kicking a football. The thin man was thinner than Melog but not by much. The Siamese twins read one book. Playing chess against one another were a man with three arms and a man with seven fingers on his right hand and nine on his left.

But the figure whom the friends liked the best, who truly made them gasp, was the fat man, the fattest in the world according to the sign at the foot of the bed where this creature lounged – a claim which they had no difficulty in believing. The man more resembled a sea of flesh than a mountain as every part of him was soft and flaccid (he was naked except for a broad nappy covering his shame) and every time he moved he would wobble like blancmange. His corpus covered every part of the bed, in fact avalanches of flesh slid over its edges. Each of his legs was the size of a fat person; one of his arms would have made three Dr Joneses. And all the time, ignoring the stream of staring, slackjawed visitors, he ate cake after sumptuous, creamy cake, whole gateaux, one after the other, washing down his food with frequent swigs of cola.

Melog was transfixed. He stood there staring at this behemoth of a man. Others would pass by saying things like 'ych-a-fi' or 'poor dab' and leave quickly. Dr Jones wanted to do likewise – the fat man oppressed him – and had said 'come on, Melog' several times without response.

In the end the lardyman could ignore him no longer; after all, wasn't Melog striking enough himself?

What do you want? the fat man said, his mouth and his voice full of cream.

Who're you? Melog asked.

I'm Bryn Tirion, but believe it or not they call me Tintin Tirion. No idea why.

Melog did not move. Dr Jones had seen his friend staring like this twice before; when he had seen the sculpture in the exhibition and when he had seen the white blackbird in the museum.

Well, clear off out of it, Tintin said. If you want to work here go and see my brother. It's him who runs the show.

Work here? Why would I think of doing that? Melog asked.

Well you're enough of a freak yourself aren't you?

He laughed and stuffed another gateau in his mouth to try to stop the shudder that spread across the slabby pancake of his belly.

Another cake for the flies that'll feast on me, Tintin said.

Come on, Dr Jones said. I've had enough here.

Melog gave in to him, but on the way out they saw a sort of kiosk with the word MANAGER on the door in square black letters. Melog knocked, in spite of Dr Jones's protests. The door opened and a fat man appeared who was obviously Tintin's brother, though he was only a quarter of his size.

Mr Tirion?

That's me, Harry Tirion, but everybody calls me Rintintin Tirion for some reason.

He laughed at something funny (in his own estimation) in something he had said.

I enjoyed your show, Melog said, but I'd like to know something of your brother's story.

Why? Rintintin asked.

Philosophical inquisitiveness, Melog answered.

Don't worry, Rintintin said. The thin man, our friend in the show, Richard Teifi his name is, but he's Ricky Ticky Teifi to his friends, is writing our biography at the moment – Rintintin and Tintin Tirion!

As he said this he traced the names in the air with his arm and swelled with pride.

You don't want a job in the show here, do you? Rintintin asked. I'm sure I could find a niche for you.

Come on, Melog, Dr Jones said taking his arm and guiding him away, out of the freaks' tent, past the hall of mirrors' marquee and the duckcrammed lake and the other marquees and exhibitions. Apart from the skeleton and Death, Dr Jones and Melog were the last to leave the carnival.

We've had a special day today, Dr Jones said to Melog in the kitchen as he made a cup of coffee.

A special day, Melog said sadly, and we still didn't find the Imalic.

Don't worry, Dr Jones said, you can try again tomorrow.

I'm never going to try again, ever, Melog said.

THREE LETTERS

DR JONES cut the grapefruit into equal halves – a little of the juice squirted over his fingers – and put one half on Melog's plate and the other half on his own plate. He boiled the kettle ready for the coffee. Usually, Melog would come downstairs when he heard the sound of the water boiling. Dr Jones glanced at the anticlockwise clock; it was five minutes to three, or five minutes past nine.

He waited for a little and listened. Not a breath, not a sigh, not the slightest sound from Melog's room. He was tired after yesterday's carnival, the doctor thought. He boiled the kettle again. No movement.

Then the post arrived and Dr Jones went to the door to collect the letters. A letter for him and one for Melog. He saw that Melog's was from the United States and on the back of the envelope in the American manner, was the sender's name and address: L. Heaming. So Melog had an answer from Lavcadio. He would be delighted.

Slowly and hesitantly – because he had learnt to expect nothing but bad news and trouble – Dr Jones opened his own letter, a brown envelope from the social security department. As he read the letter parts of it fell in his mind like an axeblade – 'Dear Dr Jones', chop, '…you have not succeeded in demonstrating…', chop, '…we are sorry, therefore…', chop, '…your benefit will come to an end from…', chop, chop, chop. He looked around the kitchen trying to comprehend the inescapable fact that soon he would lose his home and lose everything; that was the burden of the letter. He felt as though an elephant had kicked him in the stomach. He had feared this; he had had several warnings. They had heard, too, that he had taken a lodger without informing the office.

On thinking of Melog, Dr Jones decided to take a cup of coffee and the other letter up to his room. As he climbed the stairs, he noticed Lavcadio's beautiful handwriting on the back of the envelope.

He knocked on the door. No answer.

He opened the door, and of course, there was no one in the bed, no one in the room. What else was to be expected? Hadn't he learnt his lesson yet? Didn't he know Melog by now?

There on the hollowed pillow where Melog had briefly laid his head, he saw the envelope. He opened it feeling almost too afraid to read it. The message was much more terrible than the official one:

Dear Dr Jones,

I've decided to accept the offer of Rintintin and Tintin Tirion and go and work (and travel) with the show. Perhaps we'll meet again. Who knows? Thanks for everything.

Regards,

Melog

P.S. By the way, on my way through town to join the show I stopped to browse in the second hand book shop, and there, under a stack of old Welsh magazines, was the manuscript of the Imalic, in good condition, too, considering it dates from the tenth century, and who knows where it's been since it was first written down? I got it for twenty pence. The book seller didn't realise how valuable it was. To that old ignoramus it was just a pile of papers covered with meaningless scribbles.

Dr Jones took the note, and the letter putting an official end to his benefit, and Lavcadio's letter, and he took his notes and his files and his papers and the entirety of his work on the Encyclopaedia, and that morning he burned all of them on a bonfire in the garden.

The only items Melog had left behind were the sculpture and the white blackbird. Dr Jones smashed these with all the energy he had and buried the fragments in the soil, in the dirt.

...I was made in secret,

And curiously wrought in the lowest part of the earth

Psalm CXXXIX

DR JONES

BEFORE he leaves his old home forever and for an uncertain future, he opens his eyes. Something of an achievement. He turns his head and looks at his wristwatch, which lies on its side on the small bedside table. Enough light comes through the drawn curtains for him to make out the time. But as with the kitchen clock, the position of the numbers does not make sense. It looks like half past six. He sits up and looks at the two alarm clocks – the one on the chair, the other on top of the wardrobe (placed strategically thus in order to force him to get up when they ring). A quarter to nine. He stays in bed for a little longer. Stretches his legs, his arms. The only sound is the humming of mechanical things – the heater, the refrigerator. He scratches his ear. Farts. He sits up. Sunday. Town closed. A day of relaxing and doing nothing until the last minute. He gets out of bed, puts socks on his cold feet, puts on his dressing gown over his pyjamas. Goes immediately to the toilet. Pisses. Long and noisy and warm. Oh, the healthy folk shit in the mornings, but not Dr Jones; he merely farts. He is not yet ready to look in the mirror. Too early.

He opens the curtains. The living-room curtains. There is the back garden, but without his glasses he cannot see it clearly. At least it is not raining. It is windy, because the trees are moving and the slightest breath brings withered leaves down from the branches – it's raining Cornflakes!

To begin, what about something to eat? Takes one cod liver oil capsule. The bottle has a red cap. The capsule is elliptical, amber and transparent. He places the capsule on the back of his tongue and swallows it with orange juice. It slips easily down his throat. The juice is cold and wakes him up a little. It is good to be awake again; what is sleep's annihilation, after all, but a wouldbedeath? And having said that, what is Sunday but deathsregent, or zombeing?

He goes into the bathroom. Combs his greasy hair. He is a pathetic spectacle. More hair falls out every day. His hair thins as the time remaining shortens – a hair fewer, a day gone. The water is warm upon his face. He will not take breakfast after all. Cleans his teeth. Good teeth, for his age. Looks after them.

He dresses. He takes off his dressing gown and his pyjamas. Stands in cold nudity for a minute or two while he arranges his clothes. Sees himself in the mirror. It is not a very pleasurable sight. Sees his thin arms and legs. A bundle of bones. Sees the swell of his belly, the muscles hanging slackly on his frame, a garment of flesh.

The same old clothes. Grey corduroy trousers. Dark blue socks. A vest that has turned yellow. A brown shirt. Brown shoelaces.

He puts on his coat. Ensures that the keys are in his pocket – he is master of the house for a few hours more. The air is cold, but not so cold as was expected. It is windy, but the house is colder without a fire. There is little distance between his house – or rather *the* house – and the shop on the corner, and nothing of moment to see, only houses and cars. Cars parked on both sides of the street. A car outside every house. What is going to happen? Is the world going to fill with these metal things that pollute the air and knock people down and kill many thousands every year? Everybody depends on cars, even Dr Jones, who has no car. And cars are status symbols and there is no hope of changing people's attitudes to symbols of power and wealth – therefore, yes, the world is going to be filled with these metal things until the air is poisoned and there is no space for the damned things to move anyway, only to park, because there will be so many of them.

Dr Jones has arrived at the shop. He opens the door. Bell rings. He chooses the newspaper with the shiniest, most interesting magazine. So interesting, it is sealed in a little plastic bag. There is a picture of a celebrity with good dentistry and a bad reputation. Dr Jones pays for the newspaper and Mr Huws behind the counter says:

Worse for me not to listen to the radio instead of talking to myself.

What? Dr Jones asks. He was not listening and does not understand the northerner's dialect.

Worse for me not to listen to the radio instead of talking to myself.

The shop keeper turns up the volume and there is the chattering of well-informed voices.

On the way back he walks through the withered leaves in the gutter, kicking them as if he were a small boy. But dog dirt is sticking to his heel, his left shoe.

In the house, he boils water in the plastic electric kettle. The coal is already laid in the fireplace. He lights a match under the firewood and screens the chimneymouth with the business pages. He has to strike match after match until the fire takes.

He sits and reads the papers.

Five die in fog-bound train-crash. A child of ten steals five thousand pounds, his friend, twelve, pretends to be ill and the owner of the shop goes to him to help and the other boy steals the money. The police say that the boys have planned the job carefully beforehand. Scientists are able to estimate the lifespan of the sun after discovering another sun which has burnt out. After thousands and thousands of years our own sun will burn to nothing and the earth will die. Everybody will be homeless then. Sixty members of a religious sect commit suicide. Innumerable advertisements for cars on almost every other page.

Then, an inch of news among the small items; a young man was discovered near Frankfurt-an-der-Oder in Germany, wandering the streets naked, not knowing how he got there. He died later in hospital. He said that he came from Laxaria in Sakria, but – according to the reporter – these places do not exist.

TRANSLATOR'S AFTERWORD

Umberto Eco's description of the act of translation in his book *Mouse or Rat?* as a 'negotiation' between 'the encyclopaedias of two cultures' is peculiarly appropriate when it comes to translating Mihangel Morgan's *Melog*. The Encyclopaedia to which Morgan's protagonist, Dr Jones, devotes so many hours of apparently pointless study and which provides epigraphs to all but one of the novel's chapters is a real book.

The Welsh Encyclopaedia, *Y Gwyddoniadur Cymreig*, was first published in ten volumes between 1854 and 1879, edited by John Parry and later by Thomas Gee. It was, at about nine thousand closely printed pages, as Dr Jones tells us, the most ambitious publishing project in the language. Given the wholly fictitious book of myths, The Imalic, for which Melog searches, and given the numerous other goose chases of varying degrees of wildness in the novel, a reader without a background in the culture could be forgiven for mistakenly crediting the Encyclopaedia to Morgan's imagination too.

This isn't the place to pursue the ways in which the author's playfulness with the borders between the real and the imagined seeps into every aspect of the novel. But for the translator, some of those bits of the real *Gwyddoniadur* present special problems. For instance, some of the entries Morgan quotes are in effect dictionary definitions. In a couple of cases where etymology is important I have included the original Welsh word in my translation of an epigraph. These are 'Mêl' together with 'Og' on page 16, and 'Ffuglith' on page 27. My instinct was to include footnotes at these

234

points, but given the treatment reserved for academics and footnotes in the character of Professor Berwyn Boyle Hopkin, I've decided to save discussion of these for this Afterword.

The first, 'Mêl' and 'Og', deals, of course, with the name of Dr Jones's beloved visitant. As the *Gwyddoniadur* tells us, 'mêl' is the Welsh for 'honey'. But 'og', in addition to being the name of an obscure Biblical king, can in fact be an adjectival suffix. So 'Melog' can be translated as 'honied', or 'honey' understood as an adjective.

The second, 'ffuglith', is an archaic word, not even listed as an archaism in modern dictionaries. A modern Welsh reader might guess its meaning as something like 'pretend-lecture' from its components. The author of the *Gwyddoniadur* entry defines it as having roughly the same multiple meanings as Latin 'legenda' and English 'legend', but the compound elements of the Welsh word, important to the explanation and to the weave of the story, come together in no useful equivalent in English. So it resists attempts to domesticate it into some Anglo-Saxon version, which, given the novel's (albeit playful) concern with cultural difference, is quite appropriate. It's worth noting the similarity between 'ffuglith' and the modern Welsh 'ffuglen' – 'fiction'.

Elsewhere I've attempted to negotiate between those figurative encyclopaedias less obtrusively and English has been more accommodating, for instance in allowing me to coin 'readerhood' (p. 78) for the curious *Gwyddoniadur* word, 'darllenyddiaeth'. But the frequently quoted entry on 'Invention' is the most intriguing one to me here. The *Gwyddoniadur* entry is titled 'Dychymyg', which in modern Welsh would almost invariably be translated as 'imagination'. To the contemporary Welsh reader it is mildly surprising to read the multiplicity of meanings attributed to 'dychymyg' and this, I suppose, is where some of Dr Jones's pleasure in linguistic shifts derives. That multiplicity would have made no sense to a reader of the English version had I used 'imagination'; on the other hand it's not so surprising of the word 'invention'. I console myself that the sense is preserved, and Jones's bookish pleasure is contained instead in the fact that 'invention' as used to mean 'imagination' has become an archaism in English.

The Encyclopaedia apart, *Melog* contains a great many other cultural references, literary allusions and intertextualisations, some of which may be obscure even to Welsh readers. I've added notes on some of these, keyed by page number. There are no marks in the text itself to show when these notes apply. This is not primarily so as to avoid the Boyle Hopkin effect, but so that those readers who already know the references or who don't care about them can read the novel untroubled.

CHRISTOPHER MEREDITH

NOTES

Page 25: '…weeds and thorns, where there had never been greatness…': Dr Jones is thinking ironically of a famous line of poetry by Ieuan Brydydd Hir (Evan Evans) 1731-1788, describing the ruins of the court of a medieval prince – '*mieri lle bu mawredd*' – 'thorns where once was greatness'.

Page 45: 'Ysgolan': This obscure figure is the subject of at least one medieval poem and is alluded to in several others. As well as having the power of invisibility he seems to have been notorious for burning books.

Pages 78-80: All the texts mentioned here, except for *Tiorry Tilng Puttag*, are real. Perhaps the most significant are *A Week in Future Wales* – *Wythnos yng Nghymru Fydd* (1957) by Islwyn Ffowc Elis, and *The Squire of Havilah* – *Sgweiar Hafila* (1941) by T. Hughes Jones. The former is a propagandistic novel in which the protagonist travels to two alternative futures, one in which Wales survives as an independent country, and another in which it's been absorbed and redesignated 'Western England'. *Sgweiar Hafila* is a striking short story set in west Wales whose protagonist loses his mind after buying non-existent land in the Biblical country of Havilah from a charlatan at a fairground.

Page 98: 'One brief thrill twixt two long nights': 'Un ias fer rhwng dwy nos faith' – a line of cynghanedd from *Caniadau* by T. Gwynn Jones (1871-1949).

Page 107: 'In the home there is a country': 'Yn y tŷ mae gwlad' from *Yn y Tŷ* by Waldo Williams (1904-1971).

Pages 118-121: The numerous texts and authors mentioned in these pages cover a huge range of Welsh prose from the middle ages to the twentieth century.

Page 119: '...as if he were a second Bob Owen.': Bob Owen Croesor (1885-1962), a largely self-educated antiquarian, popular lecturer and bibliophile.

Page 123: '...Gwydion... Nisien and Efnisien... Bendigeid-fran': These are all characters from the early medieval tales, *The Mabinogi*. There, the magician Gwydion is described as 'the best storyteller in the world'. Nisien and Efnisien are good and bad brothers in the Second Branch of the Mabinogi. Efnisien, by a random act of violence, helped precipitate a war, and one strand of the tale shows how he exculpated himself. He must be one of the earliest examples in European literature of an anti-hero. Bendigeidfran was his giant half brother, and the king, who used his own body as a bridge for his men to walk across, saying, 'He who would lead, let him be a bridge'.

Page 129: 'Compositions and Adjudications': *Cyfansoddi-adau a Beirniadaethau* is a book of winning work and judges' assessments of it published annually amid great excitement on the field of the National Eisteddfod.

Pages 144-145: 'Arthur's Nightmare': *Hunllef Arthur* (1986) by Bobi Jones, is a booklength and not in the least realistic poem.

Page 190: 'One Moonlit Night': *Un Nos Ola Leuad* (1961) by Caradog Prichard (1904-1980). The best-known modernist novel in Welsh.

Pages 210-213: In these pages Mr Job's speeches are a collage of pieces from many sources from the seventeenth to the late twentieth century and include fragments of poetry as well as prose, as well as at least one fragment translated from Italian.

Page 220: 'Dic Aberdaron': Dic Aberdaron (Richard Robert Jones, 1780-1843) was the son of a carpenter, a linguistic prodigy who taught himself Latin at the age of twelve and who went on to teach himself many other languages. A tramp-like figure, he wandered the country with his cats and books becoming well-known simply for his strangeness and seemed unable to put his gifts to any use.

THE AUTHOR

MIHANGEL MORGAN was born in Aberdare, south Wales. He has published six novels, five books of short stories, two books of adult verse, a book of verse for children, and a short novel for Welsh learners. His novel *Dirgel Ddyn* won the prose medal at the National Eisteddfod. He lives near Aberystwyth, where he lectures in Modern Welsh Literature.

THE TRANSLATOR

CHRISTOPHER MEREDITH was born in Tredegar, lives in Brecon, and lectures at the University of Glamorgan. His first novel, *Shifts*, won the Arts Council of Wales Fiction Prize, and his second, the historical novel *Griffri*, was short-listed for the Book of the Year Award. His most recent book is his third collection of poems, *The Meaning of Flight*.